GORGEOUS PRINCE

USA TODAY & WALL STREET JOURNAL BESTSELLING AUTHOR

CHARITY FERRELL

DEDICATION

For Jill and Brooke,
Thank you for reading the many versions of this book, for your
support, and believing in my writing when I struggled to.

A NOTE FROM THE AUTHOR

Hi reader,

Gorgeous Prince is darker than my usual stories. This story contains graphic violence that could be triggering to some.

PROLOGUE

NEOMI

Ten Years Old

Before today, I've never heard of the term *arranged marriage*. And from the way my cousin, Carla, is crying about it at her wedding, it sounds like a bad thing.

"Please don't make me do this," Carla whimpers. "I'm in love with someone else." Tears slip down her cheeks and smear her mascara.

Rumor has it, Carla went off to college and fell in love.

He comes from a long line of law enforcement.

Marrying such a man would put shame on our family.

We're gathered in the bridal suite to prepare for her special day. The maid of honor is in the corner, chugging champagne. My mother kneels at my feet and fluffs my flower girl dress to perfection while my sister Bria whines about wearing pink.

My aunt scoffs. "Love is for idiots, my dear daughter."

Carla's sobs grow louder.

"I don't love Aldo." Carla says her fiancé's name with a sneer.

My mother pauses her fluffing to swat at Carla's ankles and glowers at her. "Your heart belongs to you and *only you*, my beautiful girl." She captures Carla's hand and gently squeezes it. "We never give something so valuable of ourselves to anyone."

Carla cries harder.

"Arranged marriages are our families' way," my mother adds, dropping Carla's hand and returning to my dress. "It's what keeps us strong. You have to keep your heart out of it."

"Prepare yourself, sweet cousin," Carla says, glancing at me with sad brown eyes. "Arranged marriages are all we get from this life." Her face twists, as if she envisions a grim fate for us both. "And whatever you do, don't fall in love with your husband. He'll rip your heart into pieces." She peers over her shoulder to my aunt. "It's what my father did to my mother."

Carla gasps when my aunt roughly tugs her back.

"Skip the fairy tales, Nee-Nee," Carla continues, using my nickname, her crestfallen gaze pinned on me. "True love isn't meant for girls like us. Read true crime to understand your future."

"Enough," my mother warns Carla. "Don't fill her head with such nonsense."

Eighteen Years Old

It isn't until I turn eighteen that I realize Carla's warning was true. My father has contracted me to marry Benito "Benny" Marchetti—heir to the most feared Mafia family in New York.

The Marchettis are criminals.

Ruthless and cunning.

Benny's father, Cristian, is known as Monster Marchetti.

A monster only creates monsters.

When my father breaks the news, I sob and swear I'm fleeing the country when the day comes.

I live my life with the dark cloud of marriage looming over me and pray it never does.

CHAPTER ONE

NEOMI

Twenty-Five Years Old
Three Years Before the Wedding

S tabbing him was a bad idea.

But it's not like I'd planned to choose violence when I walked into Seven Seconds nightclub tonight.

"Stupid bitch," he hisses, clutching his hand over the wound on his stomach.

I roll my eyes. You'd think he was auditioning for a movie role with his dramatics. I've seen people lose limbs and act less theatrical. It's his fault he's in this pain.

Earlier, he offered to buy me a drink. I declined, as I always do. When I had turned twenty-one, my father had handed me a credit card and instructed me never to allow anyone but him to buy me alcohol.

An hour later, the man cornered me on my walk to the restroom. His breath reeked of liquor, and he slurred his words while offering a drink for a second time. He attempted to push a glass into my hand, insisting I take it, but I refused again.

In response, he grabbed my ass and shoved me into a secluded corner against the wall. My heartbeat raged as I snatched the drink from him, smashed the glass, and stabbed him with a sliver of it.

"You grabbed my ass. I made you bleed." I shrug and sarcastically smile. "Consider us even."

When I attempt to step around him, he blocks me.

"I have a better idea to call it even." He licks his chapped lips.

I wrinkle my nose and go to push him away, but someone beats me to it. He cries out in agony, and his feet scrape against the floor when two guards drag him backward. The guards restrain the man as someone steps in front of them.

My spine stiffens, and the small piece of glass I've kept, just in case the man didn't back off, drops from my fingers.

Benny Marchetti looms in our view.

The nightclub's lighting isn't the best, so I can't make out many details, but I know who *he* is. Nearly everyone in this city does.

That's further proven by the man screaming, his knees buckling, when he sees Benny. His cries attract clubgoers, so two more guards appear, blocking them off.

"I have a better idea."

I hold my breath, and everyone turns silent when Benny speaks.

"I gut you and watch you bleed to death like the pig you are," he says, his voice taunting.

I keep my mouth shut, wishing I could disappear into the wall.

"No! No! No!" the man repeats.

Benny rears his fist back and punches the man in the face. He cries out in pain, and blood pours from his nose.

Benny tips his chin toward the men holding the guy back. "Take him to the utility room. I'll be there shortly."

The man continues to plead with Benny as he gets hauled away. My ears ring as I scan my surroundings for an escape plan.

I find a small opening between two guards and dash in that direction.

I don't make it far.

My chest caves as I gasp when Benny wraps his hand around my arm and jerks me back into his chest.

The smell of cedar, black cherry, and danger wafts into my space.

Alarm shoots through me when he lowers his mouth to my ear.

"You're not supposed to be here," he hisses. His deep voice is filled with warning.

"I was just leaving." I'm proud of how clear my voice is.

I attempt to release myself and walk away, but he doesn't allow it. All he does is tighten his grip on me.

"I'll show you out then."

"Sounds good to me."

"But first, let's have a little chat."

"Hard pass."

"Hard *I don't give a fuck.*"

I grunt when Benny yanks me backward and lowers his hold on my elbow. I swat at his arm, cursing him, as he drags me through a back door and down a long, empty hallway.

A man is waiting at a door, and he opens it when we reach him. Benny shoves me inside and then slams the door shut behind us. I catch my balance right before I face-plant into a massive desk in the middle of the room.

I turn around to face the second-most feared man in the city.

Mob prince.

Killer.

My fiancé.

He stands tall, shoving his hands into his pockets, and his dark eyes burn into mine. His presence takes over the office … takes over my thoughts. He has my full attention.

He's wearing all black—from his unbuttoned blazer to his

button-up shirt and Italian leather shoes. His oil-black hair is thick and pushed back.

Benny Marchetti is gorgeous.

But not your typical gorgeous.

He doesn't belong on the cover of *Vogue* or on a runway.

He is the gorgeous villain you shouldn't want in your story.

A face chiseled with perfection and fury.

Dark scruff scattered along his cheeks and jawline.

There's a small scar above his right eye—an imperfection, a warning he's dangerous.

Coming to Seven Seconds was a mistake, but my friend Sienna had begged me to celebrate her birthday here. Joke's on me because Sienna ditched me thirty minutes ago and left with some guy.

Time stands still when Benny advances toward me. "What the fuck are you doing in my club, Neomi?"

I don't take a step back.

As scary as Benny is, I know he can't kill me.

He raises his voice. "Not only are you here, but you also stabbed a man *in my club*."

I roll my eyes. *We get it. It's your club.*

"He grabbed my ass," I explain. "It's not like I did any serious damage." I cross my arms. "If anything, I should be angry with you for allowing ass-grabbers in *your* club. I'll be giving this place a negative review on Yelp."

"I'll punish the man who touched you." His Adam's apple bobs. "Just like you'll be sent the bill for the broken glass you smashed to get your little weapon."

"That bill will go straight into the trash."

He couldn't care less about the glass.

It's more about his disdain toward little ole me.

I scrunch my face. "And by punishing, you mean?"

It's pointless to ask the question since I already know the answer.

"After I'm finished dealing with you, I'll put a bullet between his eyes." He smirks as if it's a reward.

Typical man in my world.

Has an attitude toward me for stabbing a man, yet no problem murdering that same man.

I slap my thigh—the dramatics as big as the creep from earlier. "It appears I'm done here, then."

I struggle while walking toward the door. Even though I'd prefer to keep my distance from him, I have to pass him to leave. He doesn't make my exit easy.

Shocker.

As I inch past him, he grabs a handful of my hair and tugs me backward.

I grind my teeth at the sudden twinge of pain.

"We're not done until I say we're done." Turning his hand, he tightens his grip. "And we're not finished until you promise to get the fuck out and never come back."

I smack at his hand. He releases me, as if I were suddenly tainted, and I glare at him.

"I promise not to stab anyone else, my dear fiancé." I spit out the last word like it's poisonous.

He works his strong jaw. "I'd much rather put a bullet between my eyes than consider you my fiancé"

"I can do that for you, if you'd like?" The words come out before my brain processes what a bad idea they are.

He raises a brow. "Oh, really?"

"Really." I gulp.

I threatened to kill Benny Marchetti.

My mother has always said my mouth will be the death of me.

She also says it's why my father drinks heavily.

Benny laughs—it's calculating and biting—and strolls to the desk.

This would be the perfect opportunity to escape, but I don't try.

Shoot, I don't even glance at the doorway.

Instead, I stupidly stare at Benny as he opens a drawer and pulls out a gun.

My pulse races.

Benny turns off the safety, points the gun in my direction, and makes a *tsk* sound while his finger plays with the trigger.

And this is opportunity number two when I should dash for the door.

In my defense, it's smarter to watch the man holding a gun and not have your back to him.

He twirls the gun around a single finger, as if it were a toy, and walks toward me. "Do it then."

I wince. "Do what?"

"Shoot me." There's no humor in his voice or face as he holds out the gun.

I force a laugh. "Your family would murder me and everyone I know if I so much as laid a hand on you."

"Who says they'd know it was you?"

"I walked into this room *with you.*" *More like shoved in, but whatever.* "You end up dead, all fingers will point straight to yours truly."

He snatches my hand, shoves the gun into it, and strolls toward the bar cart in the corner. He has no concern about being the person with their back to a weapon.

I stay still, the gun in my palm, as if on a platter, while he pours himself a drink.

When he turns around, the glass hanging from two of his fingers, I shake my head.

"I'm out of here." I force myself to move to the door.

But Benny is faster than me.

These damn heels.

He blocks the doorway and rubs his chin. "Looks like I called your bluff."

I straighten my shoulders. "I'm leaving."

He slowly shakes his head. "You leaving now suddenly sounds so boring."

"I enjoy boring."

He scoffs. "Neomi Cavallaro, you do not enjoy boring."

We're so close that his glass brushes my face when he takes a drink. It's a teasing drink—one only enjoyable because he slowly sips on it to fuck with me.

He tips it toward me. "They call you Wild Cavallaro."

"And they call you Psycho Marchetti."

"Watch your mouth, or I'll prove I live up to that name."

"What are you going to do? *Kill me?*" I smirk. "You can't. There are only a few people off-limits to murder in this world, and one of them is me."

"Wrong. It'd cause me a few headaches, having to off your father and brother as well, but I don't have a conscience. It wouldn't be too bad of an idea, considering I don't want to marry you anyway."

I shudder and tighten my grip on the gun.

"I can't marry someone who's dead," he continues, as if further convincing himself killing me isn't such a bad idea.

"Are you forgetting *I'm* the one holding the gun?"

He sprawls out his arms. "Take your best shot then."

My fingers sweat as I raise the gun and aim it at him.

He coldly chuckles and tips his glass toward me. "You won't do it, you fucking coward. Just like your family, who had to blackmail my father so I'd marry you."

My heart smashes into my chest.

It's one thing to insult me, but insulting my family is crossing the line.

I graze the trigger.

Benny doesn't move.

Cockiness burns on his face.

The room grows silent.

I'm not sure how much time passes until there's a loud bang on the door.

I jump, causing my finger to jerk and brush the trigger. The gun firing almost knocks me on my ass.

My mouth falls open, and I scramble backward as the bullet buzzes by Benny's head, nearly missing him.

Oh my God.

I am so dead.

Benny doesn't wince at the gunshot.

Nor does he freak out when a drop of blood falls onto the carpet next to his shoe. Another one of his cruel laughs leaves him when he presses his palm to his ear, holds it up, and shows me the blood.

I don't get the chance to reply.

Three men shuffle into the room and take in the scene. The same ones who took the man from earlier grab my arms.

"Let her go," Benny demands, waving them off. "She won't hurt anyone. Her aim is pathetic."

I glare at him. "I missed on purpose."

He levels his gaze on me. "Don't step foot in my club again."

CHAPTER TWO

BENNY

"Benny! She was crazy! I didn't even do anything!"

I rub my temples and stare at the ugly motherfucker Neomi stabbed. Kurt is tied to a chair in our *utility closet*—AKA the soundproof room where we torture idiots. His hands are bound in front of him, and blood drips down his chin. My men must've already started the fun.

My turn.

Kurt isn't a stranger.

He was banned from the club after groping one of our bartenders. I warned him there'd be serious consequences if he returned.

You don't fuck with my employees, and you don't harass women in my club.

Period.

Kurt is in his late twenties, a post–frat boy who hasn't accepted that his glory days are over. I'd guess his favorite pharmaceutical is the date-rape kind.

I punch him in the jaw. "Did I say you could speak?"

Kurt bows his head and whimpers.

"Pick up your fucking chin," I yell.

When he doesn't, Diego, one of my men, pulls Kurt's head back so he has no choice but to look at me.

"That's more like it." I circle him. "Now, Kurt, didn't I tell you to stay away from my club?"

"Benny"—my name comes out in stutters—"please. I won't come back. I promise."

"Kurt, do you think touching women without permission is okay?"

"I … I didn't … I didn't touch her."

"Are you calling my security team liars?" I nod toward Raul, the head of my security team. "He's calling you a liar."

Raul steps forward, ready to have some fun.

"No, no, no," Kurt cries out. Spit flies from his mouth, and saliva drips down his chin. "I … I didn't. You're … not a liar."

I break Kurt's hand bones first.

He sobs, pleads, and apologizes.

It gives me a goddamn headache.

Raul smacks a piece of tape over his mouth.

Then, I relax against the wall and watch the free show.

Raul and Diego saw off Kurt's hands.

It takes them a good forty minutes to complete the job.

I need to have them practice more.

Kurt slumps, half dead, in the chair when they finish.

I untie him and drop to one knee. "How're you feelin', Kurt?"

He gurgles in response.

"Ah, man. I'm sorry." I pat his back. "You want me to let you go?"

He nods and gurgles more.

"If you can fight off my men, throw some handless punches before bleeding out, then, of course, you can go free."

He slouches further, my words not motivating him.

I hate ungrateful pricks.

Here I am, throwing him a bone, and he denies me.

Luca, my cousin, laughs beside me. "I love Marchetti games, man."

Raul steps forward. "Come on, Kurt. Box with me." He fake boxes the air and laughs.

Kurt collapses on the floor.

I don't check if he's still breathing.

Even if he is, it won't be for long.

Blood pools around him.

I draw my gun from my pocket. Kurt's body doesn't move at the impact.

I grab a towel and toss it at Diego. "Clean this up. Take the body to Viktor at the funeral home and have him fry it. Then, flush his remains down the toilet."

Diego nods.

Raul salutes me. "Got it, boss."

I peer up from my computer when Raul steps into my office.

"Job is done, boss."

"Thank you." I open a drawer, remove the stacks of cash I took from the safe earlier, and place them on the desk. "Payday for you and Diego."

He grins. "Thank you. Tomorrow is my girl's birthday."

"Buy her something nice."

He takes the cash and shoves it into his pocket. Diego is his brother, and they always collect each other's money.

Raul bounces on his toes. "That's your future wife, huh?"

I rub the tension at the back of my neck. "That's her."

"She's cute."

"She's fucking crazy."

"Cute, though." He fishes a cigarette from his pocket and sticks it into his mouth. He won't dare light it in my office though. "When do you think you'll tie the knot?"

"Unfortunately, I have no say when our day comes." I jerk

my head toward the door. "Take tomorrow night off and treat your girl to a nice dinner at L'ultima Cena. I'll tell them to add the bill to my tab."

When he leaves my office, I kick my feet onto the desk and relax against my leather chair.

There are many reasons I don't want to marry Neomi Cavallaro.

Years ago, my father went to Severino, her father, after the Morozovs—a rival family who disappeared from the city after we were done with them—murdered my mother. He asked Severino to connect him with his weapons suppliers, cease any sales with the Morozovs, and have his back if they went to war. Since the Marchettis and Cavallaros had been allies for decades, Severino could've simply said yes.

But he didn't. He gave my father a stipulation.

He'd agree to his requests if I married his eldest daughter.

My father came to me before signing the contract and explained the situation. I wanted vengeance for my mother and agreed. He told me we wouldn't have to marry immediately, but when the time was right. So far, that time hasn't come.

If tonight has told me anything, it's that marrying Neomi Cavallaro will send my world into a tailspin. My life is stressful enough. I'll take a hard pass on the out-of-control wife. Her behavior at the club gave me an idea of who I'll have to marry.

My men didn't know who Neomi was when they called me into the security room. They only wanted me to be aware Kurt had returned to the club and was causing trouble. When I stared at the screen, my heart rate doubled. I hadn't seen Neomi in years, but her face isn't one you forget.

Just as I was about to charge out of the room, I heard, "Boss, she just stabbed the motherfucker," and then the room erupted in laughter.

My cock jerks when I think about her stabbing him and how she challenged me in my office. I shut my eyes and wish I weren't replaying how intoxicating it was when I gripped her hair.

God, how I wanted to fuck that back-talking mouth until she could no longer speak.

There's one certainty I have: our marriage will create chaos.

CHAPTER THREE

NEOMI

Twenty-Six Years Old
Two Years Before the Wedding

"My father will kill me if he finds out I'm here," I tell Sienna.

I follow her into a home in serious need of TLC and realize *what type* of home she brought me to. Music blares through the house so loud that it shakes the walls.

I pass three people snorting lines of coke.

A man with half-lidded eyes mutters, "What's up, ladies?"

"Relax," Sienna says, drawing out the word. "Logan is my boyfriend. He won't let anything happen to us."

I lower my voice. "Pretty sure you left out the part where he's a drug dealer."

She flicks her brown hair over her shoulder. "Drug dealers need love too."

"Then, let someone who *does drugs* date the drug dealers."

When she asked me to go out for drinks and meet her new boyfriend, I pictured martinis and a fancy restaurant. Not a filthy home in a sketchy neighborhood. Hell, I could probably go to jail by just being here.

"Did you forget the business our family is in?" she asks. "Thou shall not judge others."

"Thou shall also not be agreeable when their friends are going through a *dating drug dealers* phase."

I wrinkle my nose when we walk into the kitchen. A half-naked couple is making out on the counter. Empty food boxes, trash, and alcohol bottles litter the rest of the space. The couple pays us a quick glance before returning to their business.

Sienna opens a cabinet and grabs a glass. "Stay with me for thirty minutes, and then we can leave." She pouts. "*Please.*"

"Fine." I shake my head when she offers me a glass. "Thirty minutes, and *no* ditching me."

She taps her fingers along the array of bottles, selects a cheap vodka, and pours herself a drink. When a skinny man stumbles into the kitchen, she squeals and jumps into his arms. Her vodka spills onto his ripped shirt.

"This is Logan," she says, smacking a sloppy kiss onto his mouth.

He stops her when she attempts to pull away and slides his tongue into her mouth. They become couple number two making out in the kitchen. Sienna separates from him when I start to leave the kitchen and finishes her introduction.

Logan is a thirty-year-old guy with bloodshot eyes, a sluggish voice, and a teardrop tattoo underneath his right eye. I glare at him when he suggests I'd be the perfect woman for them to have a threesome with. It doesn't take long until Sienna and Logan wander into a bedroom, and I make a dash for the bathroom.

A bathroom where I refuse to touch anything in fear of getting hepatitis.

"This is the nastiest bathroom I've ever—" I announce as I walk out, but I stop midsentence when the front door is kicked in.

Commotion thunders around the house—shouting, fighting, and shit breaking. On instinct, I spin on my heel and run through the kitchen toward the back door.

"Oh no, you don't," a man says, shoving me into the living room.

The men who were snorting coke are zip-tied on the couch. One man escorts Sienna and Logan out of the bedroom and instructs them to sit next to them. Three other men—the ones I suspect kicked in the door—stand in front of them.

My heart thrashes in my chest when I spot Benny in the middle.

He motions toward Sienna and Logan with disgust. "Tie them up too."

I backtrack a few steps to hide in the corner, but the man who grabbed me pushes me forward.

"Found this one trying to run off," he shouts, catching Benny's attention.

Benny's gaze flicks to me. The room turns quiet as he holds it there.

He stares, contemplating how to handle me, and revulsion smears along his features. No doubt because I'm in this hellhole.

"Raul," Benny says, glowering while pointing at me, "take her to your car and don't let her out of your sight."

The man to his right nods and approaches me.

"Can I go with her?" Sienna perks up on the couch. "We came together. We're best friends."

Benny's eyes don't leave mine. "No."

"But—"

"No," Benny repeats, his voice almost roaring now.

I attempt to flee, but the man who stopped me before pushes me back. I flip him the bird at the same time Raul captures me from behind. I'm surprised at how strong Raul is as he hauls me out of the house to a black sedan.

Raul opens the passenger door. "Watch your head." He shoves me inside.

"Go get my friend," I demand. "We have nothing to do with those guys."

"I take orders from Benny. Not you." He rubs his mustache before slamming the door in my face.

I open the door, but he shoves it closed with one hand. Like he knows I'm not a quitter, he leans back against the door to stop me from trying again. I don't know if he's guarding me from leaving or from anyone getting me.

I rifle through my crossbody purse for my phone and slump in the seat when I realize it's dead.

Whatever is happening in there, I want no part of it. But I do need to rescue Sienna. Her bad taste in men shouldn't be her death sentence.

When I turn on the overhead car light, Raul opens the door.

"Oh, don't mind me." I lower the visor mirror and wave him away. "Just checking my makeup."

He rolls his eyes and slams the door.

Now, he won't find it odd when the light comes on during my escape. I climb over the center console into the driver's seat and roll out of the car. Without bothering to close the door fully, I hold my breath and race toward the backyard.

The fence door is broken, so I walk right into Logan's yard. There's no outdoor lighting, so it's pitch-black and quiet.

Almost too quiet.

No screams or gunshots.

That could be a good sign.

Between steps, I peek over my shoulder to watch for Raul. I shriek when I smack into someone. It's so dark that I can't make out the person. This isn't the best neighborhood, and so far, my luck tonight has been shit. The person steadies me so I don't fall.

The wind blows the smell of gun powder and a familiar cologne in my face.

"Jesus," Benny hisses.

My shoulders tense at his voice.

"Do you ever fucking listen?"

I gesture toward the house. "I can't leave my friend in there with you crazies. She's not a part of … whatever is going on."

He blocks me from walking around him. "You're not going inside, Neomi. Either turn your ass around or I will make you. And I promise, I won't be gentle."

"Oh my God." I stumble back and smack a hand over my mouth. My heart goes wild. "Did you …" I remove my hand so my words are clear. "Did you *kill* them?"

"No, I didn't kill them." Annoyance laces his words. "I shot a few kneecaps. No big deal."

"They weren't Sienna's kneecaps, right?"

"Your friend is fine. I had my guy drive her home. That's when we realized you were missing."

"Will he also take me home, or is your plan for me to walk in this dangerous neighborhood alone and die?"

"I'll take you home."

"I'd rather Uber."

"I'd rather not hear your mouth about it, but it looks like neither of us is getting what we want."

"I was just in Raul's car. He has plenty of room for me."

"I have more." He snaps his fingers. "Now, let's go. I'm sure one of these boneheads will eventually remember how to use a phone and call 911 before they bleed out."

My father chose such a great man for me to marry.

Benny places his hand on the small of my back and guides me toward the road. Raul's sedan is gone. Benny opens a black SUV's passenger door and gestures for me to get in. As much as I'd love to run off, I'd be dumb to play games in this area. I squeeze into the seat and don't say a word when he joins me on the driver's side.

I clip my seat belt and inhale the scent of rich leather and air freshener as Benny drives.

"Why were you there?" Benny asks after turning off Logan's street.

An ambulance with sirens wailing and lights flashing speeds past us and turns where we just left.

I side-eye him. "Why were *you* there?"

"They robbed one of the pharmacies we protect—Ashbury's."

I wince. "They robbed Ashbury's?"

"Sure fucking did."

"That's rude." I sigh. "I guess it deserves a kneecap shot."

Mr. and Mrs. Ashbury are the sweetest souls. They've run the pharmacy for decades. They regularly hold donation events for those who can't afford their prescriptions and always provide free suckers.

"And there you were, hanging out with them," Benny adds, like a parent scolding his child.

"The first and only time." I click my tongue against the roof of my mouth. "I was about to leave when you played a WWE character and kicked down the door."

"Don't go there again."

"First off, don't tell me what to do. Second, I wouldn't step foot in there again even if someone held a gun to my head."

I don't care how bad Sienna pleads. She'll have to deal with lover-boy Logan alone. Not that he'll last—especially if he has a blown-out knee.

The ride is quiet as Benny drives through the city and nears the suburbs.

Some people are made for silence.

I'm not one of them.

"How's your ear?" I smirk even though he can't see me. "Last time we hung out, I could've sworn it had a little injury."

"You barely grazed it."

"Bummer." I grab my phone and pretend to talk into it. "Siri, remind me to work on my aim."

My behavior is ballsy. Grown men don't speak to Benny like this, but I'm running my little ole mouth to him.

This man is a murderer.

And here I am, saying it was a bummer I failed to make him a one-eared mobster.

I claim he can't kill me, but in the back of my mind, I know Benny Marchetti will do whatever Benny Marchetti wants.

I sigh and decide to get real for a minute. "Why do you hate me, Benito?"

"My name is Benny."

"Okay, why do you hate me, *Benny*? You act like I set up this marriage ... and am super excited to marry you." I glare at him. "I had my eyes set on Jude Law as a husband, but *no*. We're both inconvenienced."

Ignoring me, Benny clicks his turn signal and makes a right.

"Where are you taking me?"

Hopefully, he'll answer that question since he seems so selective with his responses.

More silence.

"If you don't reply, I'm jumping out of the car." I play with the door handle.

"Home." He locks my door.

"Do you know where my home is?"

"Yes."

"Stalker alert."

He tightens his fingers around the steering wheel. "I do business with your father. I've been to your home multiple times."

Hmm. I've never seen Benny around.

God must be on my side, making sure I dodge any interactions with him.

"So ..." I rack my brain for another subject of conversation. "How was your day today?"

"Terrible."

"Well, I had a good day ... until you took me hostage. Want to hear about it?"

"I'd rather have your silence."

"I met this guy." I grin. "He was cute. A little on the shy side. We went back to his place and had wild sex."

Benny suddenly cuts the wheel, and my body slams into the door when he swerves to the side of the road. The car behind us honks. Benny shifts the SUV into park, jumps out, and opens the back seat door. The overhead lights flash on. That annoying *close your door* dinging hurts my brain. I attempt to see what he's doing, but he blocks my view. All I can make out is him searching through something.

The light dims, and the sound shuts off when he slams the door. He returns to the driver's seat. Just as I'm about to question him, he reaches over and slaps something cold against my wrist. A sharp pain radiates up my arm, and I pull away from him.

"What the hell?" I ask when he snatches my other hand and does the same.

I hear metal rattling ... clinking together.

When he pulls back, I realize what he did.

The motherfucker handcuffed me.

That fast.

As if he had a PhD in it.

"What the fuck is—"

I'm so wrapped up in my anger that I don't realize that was only step one. Just as I'm yelling, he slaps something over my mouth.

Tape.

In nearly ten seconds, he's handcuffed me and taped my mouth.

I guess the rumors are true.

Benny is always three steps ahead of people.

"Get this off me," I struggle to say through the tape, unsure if he can even make out my words, while fighting against the handcuffs. With how he'd handcuffed my hands, I can't manage to remove the tape.

"Much better." He turns up the music until it's blaring, drowning out my screaming.

I glare at him and shake my handcuffed hands.

But he pays no attention to me.

Getting him back for this is all I think about on the drive home.

Every few seconds, I make a failed attempt at breaking loose.

He doesn't tear off the tape until he pulls in front of my house.

There's a sudden sting when he rips it off.

I move my jaw, and my lips stick together from the adhesive. When I finally gain control of them, I snarl, "My father will murder you when he finds out what you just pulled." I jerk my arms in his direction.

Benny opens a hidden compartment beside the steering wheel and removes a tiny key. "You're not telling him anything."

I shiver when his hand circles my wrist. His palm is soft, and his knuckles are busted.

The many sides of Benny Marchetti.

I wonder what side I'll get when he becomes my husband.

He's quiet when he frees my hand.

When he releases the other, I moan and shake out both hands, air-drying-style.

Benny unlocks my door. "Now, get out of my car."

"Gladly," I hiss before sliding out of the seat. "And have fun shutting the door behind me."

Instead of slamming the door shut, I leave it open and walk up the driveway to my home. When I'm inside and look out the window, the SUV remains parked with the passenger door open.

I toss my bag onto the entryway bench and trek up the stairs to my bedroom. The second time I check a window, Benny's SUV is gone.

CHAPTER FOUR

BENNY

Twenty-Eight Years Old
Three Months Before the Wedding

These events are a joke.

But since my father avoids crowds like the plague, I was ordered to mingle with these motherfuckers at the twentieth annual mayor's charity gala. All the proceeds go to some organization that I'm sure half of these people don't give two fucks about.

It's comical really.

Mobsters invited to political galas.

But if you dig deep, you'll realize we're not that dissimilar to politicians. They just do a better job at pretending to have good hearts.

I prefer to be the villain.

This event isn't about charity or bringing awareness. It's revolved around self-interest and making connections.

My younger sister, Gigi, is my plus-one for the night. She always is when she's in town. When I told her about tonight, she jumped out of bed and then scolded me for not giving her enough time to get ready.

Hell, my father had just told me this morning.

He'd forgotten about the invite.

Gigi loops her arm around mine as we drift down the wide staircase into the ballroom. A crystal chandelier hangs from the vaulted ceiling, and a full orchestra plays classical music in the corner. Guests have migrated into small circles, having conversations in suits and diamonds, which probably cost more than the average household income.

"How long do I get before you insist we leave?" Gigi asks.

My sister loves socializing.

She and I had two very different upbringings.

As they grew up, Mafia children's lives tended to be miserable and sheltered. My mother didn't want that for Gigi. Instead of being homeschooled or attending public schools, Gigi attended Fenimore Preparatory School. She's traveled the world with family and her bodyguard. Although I think my father prefers her out of the country. It's safer that way.

Me? Fun was never in my curriculum. My father taught me this business at a young age so I'd be prepared to take over at any given time. Not that I had a problem with it. Attending private school with a bunch of rich pricks sounded like a fucking nightmare.

"An hour," I reply and rub a hand over my brow. "Max."

"That's longer than I bet Natalia," she chirps. "My guess was twenty minutes."

"You spent three hours getting ready for an event you thought you'd only spend twenty minutes at?"

She eagerly nods. "Getting all dressed up is the fun part." She releases me to twirl in her flowing red dress. "Plus, I got to buy a new gown."

I shake my head. "You and shopping."

"Are besties," she says as if finishing the sentence for me.

I hold my arm out for her again, and we stroll through the ballroom. People nod at us, shake our hands, and make casual conversation. No one talks business in front of Gigi. Instead, men hand me their business cards and ask me to call them.

I only nod and pretend to care.

Half of these people are already on the Marchetti payroll.

If they make any laws in this city, I want them in the palm of my hand.

"Benny," a feminine voice says behind me.

Gigi and I turn around to find Concetta Cavallaro, Neomi's mom, walking toward us with two women at her side.

Concetta grins when she reaches us. "There's my future son-in-law." A diamond bracelet dangles from her wrist.

I wince at her greeting but quickly compose myself.

Gigi tightens her arm around mine. She knows how I feel about the marriage contract.

"And, Gigi," Concetta says, her voice full of appraisal, "you look gorgeous. Your gown is stunning."

"Thank you," Gigi replies with a friendly grin before handing out compliments to them.

My sister is a people person. She can strike up a conversation with anyone. You put her in a room full of people, and everyone will love her. She got that from my mother. It's why my father has had so many marriage offers for her. But unlike with me, he swore to give my sister a normal life and has denied all of them.

I'm zoned out, other things on my mind, until Concetta says, "Benny, have you seen Neomi yet? She's around here somewhere."

I frown at the mention of my unwanted fiancée.

Have I thought about the little hell-raiser since I last saw her? Abso-fucking-lutely.

Do I want to see her? Absolutely not.

Anytime I see her, it's a reminder of my life being taken away from me.

Some might call my disdain over marrying her to be child-ish, especially since it's so common in our world, but the thought of a wife being chosen for me feels invasive.

I don't want to focus on marriage.

On a wife.

My world revolves around playing second-in-command to my father and smoothly running the club. There's no time for the trouble that is Neomi Cavallaro.

She's a headache I won't be able to get rid of.

We've only had a few interactions, and with each one, she got underneath my skin.

She's careless.

Can't follow rules.

Always getting in trouble.

And that fucking mouth of hers.

She drives me crazy.

It makes me want to throw her down and fuck her into submission.

My thoughts of the little terror are interrupted by the mayor. We make side conversation while Gigi keeps Concetta and her friends entertained with handbag talk.

I paid the mayor a visit a few days ago, suggesting he report a business owner I'm having issues with.

There are different ways I teach people a lesson.

Violence or ruining their livelihood.

With Saul Pollin, I decided to ruin his livelihood.

It really hurts a man when his life dream is shattered and he can no longer care for his family. But that's what you get when you don't do what's expected of you. He needs to thank me for not pulling out his teeth and sending them to his wife in the shape of a smiley face.

The mayor shakes my hand and informs me my situation has been handled.

That conversation and handshake are all I came here for.

And to write a check to show how generous us Marchettis are.

"Time to go," I tell Gigi, checking my watch. "We made it forty-five minutes."

Gigi rolls her eyes. "I need to use the restroom, then we can go."

I tip my head while saying goodbye to Concetta and the ladies. She's muttering something about finding her venomous daughter, but I pretend not to hear it. I'd rather not involve myself in whatever havoc she's bound to cause tonight.

I follow Gigi across the room until she stops and says, "BRB."

She disappears into the restroom, and I lean against the wall, crossing my arms while watching the room. It's something I always do. I always have to be aware of all my surroundings.

That's when I spot her.

Neomi is at the bar, talking with a man, and she throws her head back while laughing.

The fuck?

She consumes my interest.

I might not want to marry Neomi Cavallaro, but there's no denying she's the most gorgeous woman in this room. Other than her mouth, she's perfect in every way. Her black hair is pulled back into a tight ponytail, exposing her face in a way I haven't seen before. Every other time we've crossed paths, she's worn her hair down. Her cheeks are chubby, rolling up when she laughs at something the asshole said.

I stare at her longer than I should.

Neomi Cavallaro is a fantasy.

She isn't sweet. She's dark.

Wicked at times.

But the thing about Neomi that differs from so many women is, she understands my world. She knows the sinister cracks lingering among the glamour. Too bad I want nothing to do with her.

I blink, attempting to read their lips while maintaining my distance.

But that stops when the man she's speaking with reaches forward and runs his hand down her bare arm.

For some reason, his touch triggers me.

Time to go say hello to my soon-to-be wife.

I snarl, ready to take my annoyance out on the grimy moth-erfucker who thinks he can touch what's mine. Pushing off the wall, I charge toward them.

I don't bother acknowledging the people I run into on my path to them. When my mind is set on a victim, nothing can stop me.

Just as she's about to take a drink, I nudge myself between her and the asshole. "Excuse me."

This seems to be our thing.

She does something stupid, forcing me to intervene and save the day.

Forget husband. I'm practically her babysitter.

I don't know who the man is, but the way his face pales confirms he knows who I am.

"Marchetti." He says my name through a heavy burst of breaths. "My apologies." He abandons his drink on the bar, doesn't pay Neomi another glance, and scurries away from us.

I confiscate Neomi's drink, and she reaches for it, but I hurriedly gulp it down. The glass shatters when I set it onto the bar. Without saying a word, the bartender grabs napkins and starts cleaning it up. I pull a hundred from my pocket and slip it into the tip jar as a thank-you while Neomi glares at me.

Since this isn't a conversation I want to have in front of an audience, I capture her hand and lead her away from the crowd. Thankfully, for once in her life, she doesn't protest.

She at least knows not to create a scene in a place like this.

I don't release her hand until we're in a darkened back hallway next to a door that says *Janitor Closet.*

I stare her down in the limited light I'm provided, backing her against a wall and blocking her from running. "People know we're contracted to marry."

Neomi makes a show of picking fake lint from the shoulder of my blazer. "And?"

She wants to play games, but unfortunately for her, I never lose.

The sound of me ripping the strap of her glittery black dress echoes through the empty hall.

Her breathing falters, and she glances at the ripped strap, my face, then back to the strap, as if she'd imagined it at first. She grabs the ends of the straps and holds them together to prevent the dress from falling.

I get into her face and play with the other strap, pretending to contemplate also ripping it. "And being contracted to marry me means you don't entertain another."

She knows this.

Every person on this fucking planet knows that's disrespect.

It's common knowledge within the Mafia world that Neomi Cavallaro is promised to me, but some outsiders might be clueless. I don't publicly advertise our engagement. For years, I've preferred that no one knew I was chained to this pain-in-the-ass woman.

But tonight, seeing another man with his hand on her caused something inside me to snap.

"Or what, Benito?" she asks. "Do you plan to handcuff me again?" She uses her free hand to tap my leg over my pocket—so damn close to my cock. "Do you have duct tape in there to shut me up as well? Until there's a ring on my finger, I'm single."

My cock twitches in my pants.

I lower my head, angling it between her neck and shoulder to hiss my answer in her ear, "You let another man so much as lay a finger on you from this point forward, I'll kill him."

She seethes when I grab that ponytail of hers and tug it back to expose her entire neck.

I can't stop myself from sinking my teeth into the soft skin, and she jerks against the wall. "It's not all I'll do to punish you, though."

She scoffs. "Punish me? Piss off."

"One thing about me is, I don't play fair." This time, I tug her hair so hard that she curses. "I'll make you watch another woman drop to her knees, deep-throat my cock, and moan around my dick. You'll stand there, watching her pleasure me while wishing it were you instead. And when I fill her mouth with my cum, I'll make her spit it into your mouth."

She flinches, but her eyes darken, as if daring me to do it. Her ripped strap drops when she releases it. She sinks her long nails into my arm, trying her best to cause pain through the fabric. "I'll do the same then."

Oh, my little unwanted soon-to-be wife.

She thinks she's capable of such a thing.

Within seconds, my hand is gone from her hair, wrapping around the base of her throat. It's a loose hold, but I can still feel her pulse bumping against my palm.

"You might think that you're that ballsy," I say, running a finger along the vein in her neck. "But trust me, you don't have the guts."

She shudders, causing glee to swarm through my veins.

"Soon enough, I'll know every inch of you *and this body.*" I pull back a few inches, putting my face in hers so she sees I'm not fucking around. "Until then, I suggest you be on your best behavior, or a lot of innocent people are going to die."

Her eyes meet mine.

Even in the dimness, the anger burns from them.

The tension is thick.

"You will never have my body," she says, certain of herself.

"Not only will I have this body, but I will also make you beg me to touch you. You will plead with me to feed you my cock, inch by inch. You'll become the submissive wife you swear you'll never be." A vicious laugh leaves me as I tighten my hold on her neck, curving my hand around it like she's my favorite toy. "I can't wait to see you on your knees for me."

Another shudder from her.

Another vicious laugh from me.

"Better yet, I bet I could take you right here, right now, and this needy little body would let me."

"You'll never touch me," she says, her voice wheezy from the lack of having her full air control. "And take your hand off me right now, or I'll scream bloody murder."

"You think screaming scares me? I quite enjoy it actually."

She stares at me in defiance.

"Let me hear it, Neomi." I get so close that my lips are against hers. "*Scream for me.*"

She turns her head and looks away from me.

I release her and take a step back. She keeps her back straight against the wall.

"I'll never be a dutiful wife to you, Benito."

"Then, convince your father to break our marriage contract." I snap my fingers. "Otherwise, be prepared to have skinned knees because I'll make you beg for every fucking touch."

Stress lines cover my father's forehead when I walk into his office. It's been hectic the past few weeks, and I know it'll only get worse from here.

He has a pregnant wife, and we might be at war with another family.

This is the ramification for him murdering another don's son. His reasoning is understandable, but the other don, Vincent Lombardi, won't accept any justifications for killing the heir to his throne.

Although, if you ask me, he did Vincent a favor. Vinny Lombardi would've destroyed his empire in no time.

But what father wants to admit their son is a total fuckup, especially in our line of business?

Natalia, my father's wife, is also Gigi's best friend. Her ex, Vinny, put a bounty on her after she broke up with him. She went to my father for help. He offered Natalia protection in exchange for information on the Lombardis. But then he ended up falling in love with Natalia. When Vinny found out they were marrying, he kidnapped Natalia. My father killed him for it.

"It's time we set your engagement in motion," are the first words to leave his mouth. Those dreaded words fall from his lips so simply, but the meaning is massive.

He sets his phone on the desk, and his eyes focus on mine. "We've waited too long."

I wince and drop down in the armchair in front of his desk as my head spins. My stomach turns, but I pretend to appear composed. Something I learned from my father is to never show emotions.

This sudden wedding is because of the Lombardis.

The circumstances are similar to how my father dealt with my mother's death.

"We can handle the Lombardis without the Cavallaros," I argue. "We can convince them it was the Corobras who killed Vinny. It'd be a good way to get rid of them anyway."

The Corobras are another Costa Nostra family.

They aren't currently on my shit list, but I'm not a fan.

So, fuck them.

I don't care if we have to murder every single one of them, so long as it prevents me from having to marry Neomi.

He leans back in his chair and shakes his head. "I spoke with Severino. Prepare to marry Neomi."

CHAPTER FIVE

NEOMI

Five Days before the Wedding

Tonight is my engagement party.
In five days, I'll be a mob wife.
A Marchetti.

My engagement with Benny has been called one for the books.

A power play of two menacing families joining forces.

I haven't spoken to Benny since the night at the gala months ago. I'm still pissed he ripped my dress.

When I got home that night—and for days after—I ran my fingers over my neck where he'd bitten me, *marked me*. As if I were his to mark. But I also hate how disappointed I was when his mark started fading.

If he thinks I'll fall to my knees and worship him as a wife, he's dead wrong.

I'll be the opposite to spite him.

To spite my father for making such an important decision for me.

He stopped me from finding true love and thrust me into

the arms of the prince of darkness. Love is no longer on the table for me, thrown out with yesterday's trash.

On the ride here, I swore to myself I'd ignore Benny.

Prove he doesn't matter to me.

So, I did that as soon as I walked into the Marchetti mansion, his father's home. I've avoided all eye contact. When he approaches a group I'm in, I quickly make an excuse and hurry away.

We are not the happily engaged couple.

We are the victims of a forced marriage.

"You can run away from me all you want, but I'll always find you," he says when I walk out of the bathroom.

I slap a hand to my chest. Benny's voice caught me off guard. I turn to find him leaning against a wall, a drink in his hand, staring me down like I'm his next victim.

"But I demand respect when we're in public," he continues.

The smell of him lingers around us when I walk in his direction. My mouth waters at the sight of him.

Since I've been on my ignore kick, I haven't had the chance to appreciate how gorgeous the man I'm marrying is. Benny might be corrupt and depraved on the inside, but the outside of him is nothing but beauty.

Perfection.

It's what makes him so dangerous.

Benny doesn't hold the appearance of a monster.

Only when you dig deep inside do you realize how dark he is.

His black Armani suit is tailored to fit his tall frame. He's not wearing a tie or bow, and his cuff links shine in the light.

Black is his color.

The only color I can imagine him wearing.

My parents expect me to hand over myself to a man whose heart is as black as the night. He'll ruin it, corrupt it with his cruel hands, and leave me with nothing but brokenness.

I can't let that happen.

"You look good." He runs the pad of his thumb over his full bottom lip. "Although I prefer seeing you in ripped dresses better."

I roll my eyes. "Save your half-assed compliments, Marchetti."

"Would you rather I say you look like shit?"

"I'd rather you not speak to me at all."

"God, I can't wait to see you on your knees, that smart mouth choking on my cock."

Is that all he thinks about with me?

How he'll choke me with his cock?

I tilt my head to the side and sneer at him. "If I look so good, shouldn't *you* be the one on your knees?"

He rolls his strong shoulders back. "I'm more than happy to drop to them right now. All you have to do is ask."

"Let me make this clear." I use my finger to create an imaginary line separating us. "We will sleep in separate rooms. You won't touch me." I walk closer to drive my point through his thick skull. "Communication will be limited. We will be married strangers."

My words appear to amuse him.

He taps his fingers against his glass. "Do you remember my warning?"

"The warning of me watching you *fuck another woman's* mouth in front of me?" I flip my hair over my shoulder. "Spare me the idle threats. I'll never be jealous of another woman being with you."

He lifts his chin and spreads his legs wide. "So, you're good with me getting it elsewhere?"

I don't reply.

"Answer me."

I glare.

"Your lack of response tells me that's a yes. Glad we cleared that up." He cheers me with his glass.

He walks away, leaving me alone in the corridor.

Twenty minutes later, I'm back in the foyer, speaking with one of my mother's friends, when I catch Benny walking by. My mouth turns dry at the realization he isn't alone. He's holding a tall blonde's hand and leading her down a dim-lit corridor, screaming off-limits. Anywhere screaming off-limits in the Marchetti mansion implies death. You don't curiously wander around this home without consequences.

Yet that's exactly what I'm about to do.

I drain my champagne, drop the flute onto a server's tray, and follow their path from a safe distance. My heels are loud against the marble floor, so I stop to level myself against a wall and remove them.

If this wasn't Benny, I'd believe I was marrying the stupidest man on the planet for his lack of discretion. But Benny is notorious for his intelligence and tactfulness. This is a game to him.

I grip my heels and stop at the door he closed behind them. Without bothering to knock, I open the door and quietly slip into a billiards room. I clench my hand tighter around my heels as bile seeps up my throat.

Benny is across the room, standing in front of the massive pool table, with his black slacks dropped to his ankles. His arms are settled behind him, palms flat against the edge of the pool table, with the blonde slumped on her knees at his feet.

A low groan leaves him when she strokes his dick, lowers her head, and deep-throats him. As if he can sense me, Benny turns his head and fixes his stare on me. The woman doesn't even notice my presence.

I'm reminded of his words—*his threat*—at the gala.

"I'll make you watch another woman drop to her knees, deep-throat my cock, and moan around my dick. You'll stand there, watching her pleasure me while wishing it were you instead."

I didn't think the asshole would actually follow through with his warning.

To further provoke me, Benny slips his hand through her

hair and pushes it behind her shoulder. The move provides me with a better view of her sucking my fiancé off.

My head spins as I run through different scenarios.

There are four reactions someone in my position could have:

1. Cry.
2. Scream at him and create a scene.
3. Charge across the room, snatch a pool ball and hurl it at his head—preferably the one between his legs.
4. Play his game right back.

Unfortunately for my future hubby, playing games is one of my favorite hobbies.

He moans loudly and hisses, "Yes, just like that," before rewarding her with a soft caress to her cheek.

I'm unsure whether she knows she's being watched, and just as I'm about to say something, the perfect plan forms. My blood runs hot as I turn and rush out of the room.

On a mission, I toss my heels into a corner and strut back into the mansion's foyer, not caring that I'm barefoot. I scan the crowd of guests, clad in their best formalwear. Most of them have rap sheets longer than college textbooks, are crooked multi-millionaires, or are women married to one of the two. The guest list was weeded through three times, so my options are limited. Finding a man willing to hook up with the bride-to-be at her engagement party won't be easy, but I love a good challenge.

My gaze glosses over my father and Cristian speaking and past Gigi chatting with Natalia before landing on the perfect pawn.

Alden Barclay.

The son of a wealthy hedge fund manager my father does business with. We share a mutual hate for my fiancé. Benny banned Alden from his club, and word is, Alden is pissed.

Tugging down the hem of my dress to enhance my cleavage,

I stalk toward him. This is a dangerous idea, but my need for revenge outweighs my common sense.

I stop in front of Alden and steal his champagne flute. He stares at me in confusion when I run my tongue along the rim and finish his drink in one swig. As the liquor trickles down my throat, I slide in closer.

I clutch Alden's tie, yank him forward, and brush my lips against his ear. "You. Me. Billiards room."

Alden rears his head back. "What?"

"Come on." I nudge him with my elbow. "What better way to get revenge on Benny Marchetti than to hook up with his future wife?"

Alden runs a hand through his brown curls. There's slight mistrust in his blue eyes. Not that I blame him. Us Cavallaros aren't known for our ethics. Throw in the Marchettis, and you're just begging for trouble.

I wait for Alden to determine the fate of my night. My grin matches that of Benny's in the billiards room when Alden jerks his head toward the hallway. I hope no one sees us as he follows me.

"I didn't expect this to happen tonight," Alden says.

The billiards room door is still unlocked, and I lead Alden inside before shutting it. Blondie remains on her knees with Benny's cock lodged down her throat.

"Fuck, I'm about to—" Benny rasps, ramming his hips forward and throwing his head back.

I clear my throat.

Blondie chokes on his cock.

Benny flinches, and I grin.

Benny's attention whips to me. At first, he's unfazed. That changes when Alden steps into his view. Benny's nostrils flare so wide that I wait for fire to burst through them. His eyes burn into mine with warning. Blondie attempts to draw back, but he curls his hand around her head and holds her in place.

Alden doesn't move as his gaze pings between Benny and me.

He might be ballsy enough to hook up with the bride-to-be, but doing so in front of the groom is riskier—especially if the groom is a Marchetti.

Props to him for not running off.

His disdain toward Benny must run deep. His stupidity too.

Benny sinks his canines into his lower lip as I haul Alden toward him. I stop inches from Benny, and he finally releases the woman from his dick. She collapses onto all fours and gapes at him.

I smirk while positioning Alden in the same direction as Benny, as if they were two men standing at a row of urinals.

When I drop to my knees in front of Alden, he gasps, and Benny curses.

"Neomi, what the fuck are you doing?" Benny hisses when I unbutton Alden's slacks.

"The same as you." I smirk at him and gesture to Alden. "Technically, the other way around though."

I don't plan to suck Alden's cock.

At least, I hope it doesn't come to that.

My goal is to piss off Benny and show him I'm not a doormat.

To further push his patience, I tear Alden's pants and boxers down. His erection springs forward. It's skinny and throbbing.

Benny's strong, dark, stubbled jaw tics. "Do that, and you'll regret it."

"An eye for an eye, dear fiancé." I wink at him.

Alden shudders above me.

"You have three seconds to get the fuck out of here," Benny says, zipping his pants. "This is my only warning."

I reach for Alden's cock.

He loudly grunts.

His grunt drowns out the click of Benny's gun.

Benny doesn't count down his seconds.

I collapse backward, and the woman screams as a gunshot rings through the air. There's no time for anyone to run or attempt to dodge the bullet. My heartbeat stalls when something wet smacks into my cheek. I sweep a shaky hand over my face, and my throat tightens when I see blood.

Alden drops to the floor with a loud *thud*, and furniture rumbles at the powerful impact. Blood oozes from his head and soaks into the thick beige carpet. Blondie screams, her tone shrill, as gun smoke rises from his flesh.

My gaze focuses on Benny as I stand. He shifts the direction of his gun away from Alden to me. He savagely smiles at me as sweat beads along his hairline. I gulp when his finger plays with the trigger, but I don't run.

I stare him down and smile.

Daring him, as he did me.

"Lesson number one, unwanted wife: I don't make empty threats."

What a way to start our impending nuptials.

CHAPTER SIX

BENNY

I lower my gun from Neomi.

She's smiling.

Jesus.

I don't know if I want to fuck her or kill her.

She's not startled by the blood smeared across her cheek or caked in her hair. You'd think it was punch spilled on her, not a dead man's blood.

She's either batshit crazy or in shock.

Gretchen, the woman who was blowing me, scrambles to the corner of the room. She knows who I am and what I do, but tonight is the first time she's witnessed me take a life.

Discovered the true Benny Marchetti.

I roll my shoulders and wait for my father. Like a vulture, he's drawn to gunshots and dead bodies, especially those in or around the mansion. The mansion is a neutral area. Chaos rarely follows us here. Checking my watch, I give him a minute, max.

"Really, Benny?" Neomi gestures to Alden's lifeless body, as if she wasn't the one who pushed me enough to pull the trigger.

The motherfucker is lucky I awarded him a quick death. I'd have preferred to hear him beg on his knees, but the moment Neomi's hand brushed his shrimp dick, I couldn't stop myself. After blowing his head off, I also held back the urge to unload every bullet in my Glock into him. I did it out of respect for my father ... and my time. The less blood to clean, the better.

"Are you fucking crazy?" I scream at her.

Before Neomi can answer, the door bursts open. My father charges into the room and blocks the view from the crowd behind him. Since he's always prepared for violence, he has his gun drawn.

People behind him attempt to peek over his shoulder, around him, and in every direction they can for answers. I'm surprised he didn't make them wait outside so he could investigate the situation first. Those who see Alden's dead body gasp. But unless they recognize his clothing—the same black suit as nearly every man here—he's unidentifiable with his face blown off.

"What the fuck happened?" my father yells, scowling while taking in the scene in front of him.

This looks really fucking bad.

We have a dead Alden—his pants down, shriveled dick on display, and brains blown out. Then two women in the room. One I fuck on the regular, crying. The other, my fiancée, painted with the dead man's blood.

Severino shoves himself through the crowd and stops at my father's side. The rigid cord in his thick neck confirms he's ready for violence. He won't like what I'm about to say.

"Want to know what happened?" I pace in front of Alden's body and swing my arm toward his demonic daughter. "I was getting my dick sucked, and she—"

Neomi steps forward and cuts me off, "He was getting his dick sucked by someone who wasn't me—*his fiancé*—I'd like to add."

When Severino withdraws his gun from his blazer, I tighten my grip on mine. I'm surprised my father allowed him to bring a weapon inside the mansion. Firearms are forbidden within these walls unless you rank high in the family. But we're attempting to build a union with the Cavallaros. It shows a sign of trust.

Shows is the keyword.

Every man of ours is packing.

Snipers are hidden inside and outside the mansion.

Cameras are everywhere, and guards are watching live footage.

My father shakes his head at Severino and blocks him from me. Severino is the don of his family, but for him to threaten me would mean war.

"I didn't think it was a problem," I say to deescalate the situation.

"Why the hell wouldn't you think it was a problem?" Neomi yells.

My little unwanted wife didn't realize I make right with my threats.

A lesson learned for her.

I angle my body toward her. "You walked into the room and walked out, so I thought everything was fine."

No, I didn't.

I wanted to piss her off.

See her angry.

Neomi snorts.

"But then," I continue, "she comes in with this dead mother-fucker here." I kick Alden's lifeless piece-of-shit body. "Drops to her knees and unbuckles his pants to suck his—"

"Don't you dare fucking say it," Severino interrupts.

"An eye for an eye, Benny boy," Neomi gloats. "You don't want to be faithful in this marriage, then I don't have to be either."

"That's bullshit," I hiss, the shame of my behavior creeping in.

This conversation needs to end, pronto.

"What's bullshit is, you think it's okay for me to walk in and see this woman sucking you off." Neomi makes a sweeping gesture toward Gretchen, as I did with Alden. "You're lucky I didn't kill her." She makes eye contact with Gretchen. "Sorry, not sorry."

Gretchen cries harder.

My head throbs, and I hope to God Neomi doesn't attempt to make right with her threat. As if I'm not the only one with that thought, my cousin Luca rushes to Gretchen and escorts her out of the room.

"The party is over," my father says, straightening the lapels of his black blazer. "You have ten minutes to exit, or my security will escort you out. And trust me, they won't be gentle."

Guests scatter out of the room like roaches, and my father slams the door shut behind them, leaving only Severino, Neomi, him, and me in the billiards room.

My father stares at me in disappointment. As the next in line to the Marchetti throne, I'm supposed to represent the family respectfully. Losing my cool and murdering someone at the mansion while filled with people was a stupid move.

Severino huffs while inspecting Alden's body. "Be glad his father had to cancel at the last minute. We do millions in business. If he finds out you murdered his son, it will interfere with that."

"Alden left the party hours ago," I say matter-of-factly before locking eyes with Neomi. "I'm sure your daughter was careful and made sure no one saw them."

My jaw clenches at my words. Even though I don't want to marry Neomi, I'll be damned if she gets on her knees for any other man besides me.

Severino joins me in staring his daughter down. "Go home and clean yourself up, Neomi."

Neomi stubbornly crosses her arms and doesn't move.

"Unless you'd like to help my son dispose of this man's body, I'd recommend listening to him," my father tells her, running his hand over his jaw.

Neomi grimaces and draws back a few steps. She might

throw out attitude toward others, but my father is on a different playing field regarding disrespect.

"I guess red isn't my best color," she says, staring down at her dress.

"Have Alfonso drive you back," Severino tells her.

I raise a brow. "Who's Alfonso?"

"My bodyguard." Neomi grins. "He's hot as fuck."

"Jesus," my father says, blowing out a stressed breath.

I crack my knuckles. "I'll have to rectify that."

She smirks. "Rectify his hotness?"

"That, or you having a bodyguard not provided by your husband."

"You're not my husband," she corrects.

"Not yet."

"Alfonso has been in our family for years," Severino says. "He keeps Neomi safe."

My little nuisance has just earned herself a wedding present —a new bodyguard. I don't know who Alfonso is, don't know what he looks like, nor do I give a fuck—but I don't trust anyone who's not family.

"Why the fuck are we discussing bodyguards?" my father shouts. "Discuss how to get this body off my carpet before it further stains it."

When Neomi turns to storm out of the room, I snatch her wrist, stopping her. She grunts when I push her into the same corner where Gretchen was. Severino starts muttering bullshit, but I tune him out.

I crowd her against the wall and ignore the transfer of blood from her dress onto my tux. "Because of you, an innocent man died tonight."

I don't care about Alden. He deserved to have his brains blown out.

She arches her lips. "I didn't expect you to murder him like a psychopath."

"What'd you think would happen?"

"I don't know ..." She bites into her plump cherry-red lip. "You'd rough him up some." Her body loosens when she sighs. "There are rumors he date-raped a woman and that his father paid his way out of a felony. It's not like I chose a saint to fake suck off."

She's right about him being a predator. It's why I banned him from my club. I don't condone sexual harassment under any circumstances. He was lucky I only kicked him out and didn't cut off his slimy fingers after he shoved his hand up a woman's skirt on the dance floor.

"There's seriously something depraved about you," I snarl before slamming my hand onto the wall next to her head.

She doesn't flinch. She only smirks, blows me a kiss, and says, "I guess we're twinsies."

Severino curses while heading in our direction. I draw back, not in the mood to argue with her father. But we still have a good minute. The man hasn't seen a gym in years. He carries not only the weight of the Cavallaro crime family but also a stomach of pasta, carbs, and Italian wines.

"Welcome to our engagement, honey," Neomi says in a sarcastic tone. "It's starting so well. I prefer a man with a bigger dick, though."

Heat rushes straight to my groin. I refrain from gripping Neomi's hair, shoving her onto her knees, and telling her to watch her mouth before I fuck it in front of every man here—relative or not.

"Oh, Neomi. You have no idea the destruction my cock is capable of." I run a heavy finger down her body, and she shivers. "But you will find out soon enough."

"Benny," my father says, and I create distance between Neomi and me only seconds before Severino reaches us.

"Neomi, home, now," Severino grunts.

She sighs, and since I don't move my arm, she has to duck underneath it to escape me. I don't walk her out. The guards at the door will do it for me. If we spend any more time together tonight, it'll only end in more problems.

No one says a word as she leaves. I keep my eyes on her, watching her hips swing from side to side, and can't stop myself from licking my lips. I might think she's unhinged, but she's beautiful.

"What's the plan?" Severino asks as soon as Neomi slams the door behind her. "I don't want any blowback on this."

"If it blows back on my son, it'll be a problem for both of us." My father shoves his hands into his pockets. "I suggest you keep your mouth shut with Barclay."

We're interrupted by a knock, and everyone looks at the door when it opens. Neomi's brother, Tommaso, steps inside the billiards room, adjusting the fly on his pants.

"Jesus," he says, surveying the room and seeing Alden's body. "What happened here?"

Severino massages his temples. "You don't want to know."

Tommaso nods. "Neomi's doing?"

"I'll explain later." Severino curls his lip and points at Alden. "Help Benny dispose of the body since it's your sister's fault the idiot is dead."

"I'll do it myself," I reply, stopping Tommaso from stepping toward me.

I'm not messy with my cleanup. Involving someone I've never worked with to help cover up a crime is reckless.

Tommaso lets out a relieved breath.

There's no missing the revulsion on Severino's face at how easily his son disobeyed his orders and allowed me to boss him around. If I were Tommaso, I'd make sure the body was properly disposed of.

"My men will escort you out," my father tells them, done with the conversation. "Expect a call from me in an hour, Severino."

Severino shakes my hand and then my father's. Neither one of us even offers our hand to Tommaso. He doesn't deserve even a word from us after his delayed response to gunshots at his sister's engagement party.

As soon as they leave, my father locks the door. "Your behavior tonight was unacceptable. You have yet to marry, and you're already creating problems."

I'd rather be shot in the kneecaps than see disappointment from my father.

"I made a mistake," I say, wiping my hands down my pants.

A hint of amusement crosses his stern face. "I have a feeling you've met your match, son."

"You can't blame me for killing that motherfucker."

"Of course not, which is why I'm allowing you to dispose of the body however you see fit. Get it done. I don't want to see a trickle of blood when you finish."

After he leaves, I text my cousins Luca and Romeo and tell them to get their asses to the billiards room. I might not trust Tommaso to help with the job, but I do trust them. Luca's father, my uncle Lorenzo, trained us for years on the best ways to get rid of dead bodies.

I was eleven the first time I saw Neomi at a wedding, but I didn't know what we'd become until years later. She was in the row before me, chomping on a Jolly Rancher. I should've known she was a psychopath then. Who *chews on* Jolly Ranchers? When I asked her if she had any extras, she whipped around and told me they were five dollars each.

I scoffed, telling her I could buy an entire bag for that price.

"Then, leave and go buy a bag," she said, unwrapping a purple one and shoving it into her mouth. "And now, the price has gone up to six dollars."

I paid the six dollars—not wanting to look like I didn't have money—and requested a green one. She handed over a red one, turned around, and flipped her hair over her shoulder. Throughout the ceremony, I caught her sneaking glances in my direction, so I kept my eyes on her.

She forgot her Jolly Rancher bag in the pew when the

wedding ended. I took it, and when she returned, asking if anyone had seen it, I told her no and left.

I've hated red Jolly Ranchers since.

"Oh, fuck yeah," Romeo says, barging into the room and seeing Alden's body. He holds his hand out to Luca for a high five, but Luca ignores it. "I was hoping it'd be someone I didn't like."

"His face is blown off," Luca says. "How do you know who it is?"

"I got stuck working surveillance," Romeo says. "I recognize his tie after having to listen to him brag to a woman about how much money he had for thirty fucking minutes. No one drives a Maserati and brags about it anymore, bro."

I rub my hands together. "Let's get this done. I have shit to do."

"Goddamn, I didn't expect that slimy motherfucker to be so heavy," Luca says as we leave the funeral home and slide into my black Range Rover.

"I think I'm getting better at this cleanup thing," Romeo says with pride.

Luca whips around in the front seat to stare at Romeo in the back. "Good job not puking this time, you weak motherfucker."

Romeo smacks the back of Luca's seat. "I told you, it was the shellfish I had eaten earlier that day that made me sick last time. Not the dead body."

I rip off my gloves and start the engine.

Disposing of bodies is my least favorite part of this job.

It's not that I don't enjoy getting my hands dirty.

It's just a pain-in-the-ass job, where you must ensure every detail is covered so nothing can be traced back to you.

I chose cremation for Alden's cleanup. It's been my choice method as of late. For a couple of grand and a promise of protection, our local mortician, Viktor, fried Alden's body like he was Colonel fucking Sanders.

Alden was the first man I had to kill because of my future wife.

My gut tells me he won't be the last.

CHAPTER SEVEN

NEOMI

Once upon a time, I prayed Carla's warning wouldn't become my future. I wished I'd be that lucky girl who could marry for love, but my father shattered my dream. He promised me to a man who kills people for a living ... and also enjoys receiving blow jobs from blondes.

Marrying Benny is inevitable—like starting my period while on vacation or my sisters stealing and never returning my clothes.

"Your behavior tonight was a disgrace to the Cavallaro name," my father tells me when I sit across from him in his office.

I wince at his insult.

A *disgrace* to our name.

There's not a worse word he could've wielded at me.

My father sits in his camel-brown leather chair behind his oak pedestal desk. Like a soldier guarding an expensive statue, Tommaso stands at his side and appears just as stressed as him.

Tommaso's black hair is slicked back, and he's wearing a Gucci suit—the same as our father.

I release a forceful breath. "What did you expect me to do?"

My father opens a desk drawer, pinches his lips, and plucks

out a cigar. He flicks open a lighter and burns the tip of the cigar. "I expect you to behave appropriately."

"You're forcing me to marry a man who just murdered someone in front of me."

"If what Benny said was true, if he hadn't killed the bastard, I'd have done it myself." He points at me with his cigar, and smoke trails his words. "No more funny business. Do you hear me?"

I enact a mind-blown expression. "I swear, I'm surrounded by crazy people."

"What you did tonight proves you're just as insane as the rest of us," Tommaso comments. "You could've left the room and ignored the situation."

I cringe. "Ignore him getting a blow job from another woman at our fucking engagement party?"

This isn't a conversation I want to have with my father and older brother, but how dare Tommaso stick up for Benny!

"Watch your mouth, Neomi," my father warns as if he'd rather not speak on the subject either. He points at me with his cigar, and ashes fall from the tip, landing on a stack of Post-its.

"Why are you siding with Benny?" I ask Tommaso. "You hate him."

"I despise the motherfucker," Tommaso answers, dragging a cigarette from his blazer pocket and playing with it between two fingers. "But I respect him. As most do."

Tommaso attempted to be Benny's friend, but Benny never gave him a chance. Anytime he tried to connect with Benny, he blew Tommaso off. Instead of forming a friendship, Benny slept with one of his girlfriends. After that, Tommaso has had nothing nice to say about my future husband.

Until now, apparently.

"This is your last warning." My father taps more ashes onto his desk. "Stop creating trouble with the Marchettis. You will marry Benny, and that's final."

I nod and stand from my chair. There's no arguing with my

father. He views this marriage as best for our family, so that's what will happen.

I leave his office and trek upstairs. When I enter my bedroom, I find my sisters, Bria and Isabella, are there, uninvited. Bria lies across my bed, staring at her phone. Isabella is at my vanity, sniffing my perfumes.

The three of us are in our twenties. I'm twenty-eight years young. Bria is twenty-four, and Isabella is twenty. Since it's considered taboo for a woman to move out before marriage in this world, we still live with our parents.

"Unless one of you wants to step in as a tribute to marry Benny, I don't want to hear it," I say, shutting the door behind me.

"Look on the bright side," Isabella says, spinning around on the vanity stool.

"There's a bright side?" I interrupt.

"The bright side is, at least he's hot." Isabella sprays herself with my YSL Black Opium. "Knowing my luck, I'll end up with someone ugly and crazy."

I walk across the room and collapse on my bed next to Bria. "He's a murderer. A legit psychopath. He killed another man *in front of me.*"

"What guy isn't a murderer these days?" Isabella asks.

I glare at her. "I refuse to listen to a girl who wanted to be a Disney princess last year."

Isabella returns my glare. "Being a Disney princess is a prestigious job, thank you very much." Her glare morphs into a frown. "I'd have made the perfect Snow White... and found my Prince Charming."

Isabella was accepted into a Disney internship, but our father refused to allow her to move to Florida. He called it "the stupidest thing" he'd ever fucking heard.

Bria rolls her eyes, turns on her belly, and drops her phone. "Neomi is getting her Prince Charming without a Disney internship."

"Yes, Benny Marchetti, Prince of Murderville," I say, smacking her arm.

"It has a nice ring to it." Isabella twirls a black curl around her finger. "Your own dark fairy tale."

I shudder. Her comment reminds me of Carla's warning.

"Skip the fairy tales, Nee-Nee. True love isn't meant for girls like us."

Screw my Prince Charming.

Benny Marchetti is the villain in my dark tale.

The next morning, Isabella barges into my bedroom without knocking.

"Benny is here," she says, her voice eager.

"Okay." I draw out the word. "He's probably here to talk business with our father. Hard pass on going downstairs to greet him."

Isabella shakes her head. "He told Tommaso you and he are going out for the day."

I slam my MacBook shut and toss it next to me on the bed. "He must be on crack."

We go quiet at the sound of screaming downstairs. I jump off the bed and follow Isabella out of my bedroom. My stomach smacks into the stair railing as I look over it and take in the scene downstairs.

Benny and Tommaso are facing off. My mother is standing in the corner, her phone in her hand, most likely texting my father to alert him of the situation.

"You and my sister aren't married yet," Tommaso says, clenching his fist. "There will be no alone time until *after* the wedding."

For once, I agree with my brother.

Hell, I'd prefer no alone time, *period*—pre- or post-dreadful wedding.

A calm Benny cocks his head to the side and smirks. "You must not have heard me correctly, Tommaso." His tone is taunting, like a bully on the playground. "Either go get Neomi or I will move you myself and hunt her down in this house."

Tommaso unclenches his fist to point at the floor. "You two can spend the day here then."

"I can fix a nice lunch for you to enjoy on the patio," my mother chimes in.

"I'm taking Neomi out," Benny states like he's the final decision maker.

Tommaso raises his voice and straightens his back. "I don't know who you think you're speaking to, Marchetti, but this is out of line."

Benny flicks his hand through the air. "Go fetch her for me."

"I'm not a damn dog," I hiss. I meant for my comment to be for Isabella's ears only, but I was louder than intended.

Benny's head snaps in my direction, and a slow smile builds along his wicked face at the sight of me. "Ah, there she is. Saved you a trip, Tommy boy."

He smacks Tommaso's shoulder, and my brother stumbles back.

From the anger burning on Tommaso's face, I'm waiting for him to lunge at Benny and for them to brawl in the middle of the foyer. My brother is a hothead. He thrives on the power he carries from being next in line to the Cavallaro throne.

The Cavallaros are a strong family.

People fear us.

We've been in this city long enough to run many parts of it.

Tommaso is accustomed to being respected and has murdered men for less than Benny is pulling.

Why is he allowing Benny to disrespect him like this?

Where is my trigger-happy brother?

Benny performs a *come-hither* motion at me. "Time for us to go."

I grip the railing. "I agree with my brother about us

spending time alone pre-marriage. It's not a good look for my reputation."

Isabella snorts, and I throw her a dirty look.

Benny's eyes harden on me, like Tommaso's is on him. "Neomi, now."

I stare at him in defiance.

"Don't speak to my sister like that," Tommaso practically growls.

Benny continues ignoring him and keeps his attention on me.

Isabella and I jump when Tommaso pulls out his gun.

"Tommaso," my mother gasps.

As if Benny still had eyes on Tommaso the entire time, he slightly turns his head so the gun is pointed directly at his face.

"Did you not hear what I said, Marchetti?" Tommaso asks, thrusting the gun closer toward Benny. "You do not come into our home and disrespect me."

Benny chuckles—it's deep and cunning—and swipes his thumb along his bottom lip. "Don't pull a gun on a man unless you intend to shoot him." He advances a step toward my brother. "Do you plan to shoot me, Tommaso?"

My heart roars in my chest.

This won't end well.

Isabella places her hand over mine.

Tommaso's eyes widen at Benny's response.

Normal people tend to be scared with a gun in their face, but not Benny.

Tommaso's finger lightly brushes the trigger, and my body tenses. The disrespect is killing my brother.

"Pull the trigger," Benny says, working his jaw. "Shoot me. The consequences won't be worth the few seconds you'll feel like a tough guy."

This is my cue to stop the madness.

If Tommaso pulls the trigger, Cristian will slaughter our entire family.

"Let me change my clothes," I shout over the railing before darting down the stairway. "Then, we can go."

My stomach sinks with dread at the thought of spending the day with Benny, but I'd much rather have my family breathing.

When I reach the main floor, I squeeze between the two men. Tommaso's gun is to my back, and just as I'm about to plead with Benny to stop, he grabs my waist.

"What are—" I start but stop when he jerks me behind him, blocking me from Tommaso and the gun. He spreads out his arms like a wall protecting me.

"If your sister is ever in front of your gun, you fucking lower it," Benny sneers at Tommaso. His voice becomes a tad softer when he says, "Neomi, you have five minutes. Let's hope your brother is still alive when you finish."

I gulp, and Benny stops my attempt at confiscating the gun from Tommaso.

"Tommaso," I plead as I walk toward the stairs, "please put down the gun."

"It's best to listen to your sister," Benny says. "If you don't lower your gun in five seconds, I'll shoot your goddamn head off. Do you want your mother and sisters to watch you die?"

I rush upstairs and am nearly breathless when I reach my bedroom. Isabella steps out of my walk-in closet with an armful of clothing. I grab the floral jumpsuit on top and hurriedly get dressed. She's at the doorway with a sweater in one hand and boots in the other. I snatch them on my way out of the room.

A pent-up breath rushes from my lungs when I see Tommaso lowering the gun. He and Benny continue the stare-down game, but at least no one is threatening to kill the other.

The house is quiet now. The only sound is the *ticktock* from the grandfather clock my father gifted my mother for their anniversary last year.

"That's the only time you'll hold a gun to me and live," Benny warns Tommaso. "Consider you still breathing a wedding gift to your sister."

I hold up my boots, interrupting their conversation. "Ready to go!"

We need to get the hell out of here.

Benny gives Tommaso one last glare. Tommaso tightens his face and charges out of the house.

I glance at Isabella standing at the top of the stairs. She sends me an uneasy thumbs-up. My mother's face is tense as we near her.

Benny offers my mother a casual smile, like he just didn't threaten to kill her son. "I won't keep her out late, Concetta."

I attempt to deliver the same casual smile, but there's no hiding the anguish. My mother's cheek is warm when I kiss it.

"You two be safe," she says, refusing to look at Benny and squeezing my shoulder.

My mother understands the social graces of this world better than Tommaso and me. She knows when to voice an opinion and when to go with the flow. With Benny's status, she's aware it's risky to make waves. But from how well I know my mother, choice words are definitely on the tip of her tongue for her future son-in-law.

She'll be on the phone with my father as soon as we walk out the door. There are cameras in the foyer, so he'll no doubt watch the footage of Benny and Tommaso's altercation. Tommaso had better prepare for an ass-chewing. His little gun stunt could've gotten us all killed.

My stupid, stupid brother.

I love him, but he's reckless.

He and Benny might be the same age and hold the same level of authority in their families, but they are day and night. While Benny is confident, Tommaso is insecure. Benny makes calculated moves while Tommaso pulls his gun out on a dangerous man with no intention of pulling the trigger.

It's why so many of us dread the day Tommaso steps into our father's role. Even though I see Benny as a psychopath, I wish Tommaso had his smarts.

I'm met with a chill when I walk outside. The concrete is cold underneath my sock-covered feet. I tuck my boots underneath my armpits. Benny settles his hand on the small of my back and leads me toward a black Range Rover parked in the driveway. It's a newer model of the one he handcuffed me in last time we were in his car together.

I shiver and hug myself as we pass through my mother's flower garden. The Manneken Pis fountain provides a temporary calmness to the chaos I'm picturing will be the rest of the day with Benny. The French marigolds are in full bloom, lining the walkway in orange, red, and yellow. They match the colors of the leaves on the ground, shed by the large trees in our front yard.

One day, I asked my grandmother why the leaves fell.

Why the trees allow such a significant piece of them to wither and die.

She corrected me, "Trees aren't much different from us, Neomi. Sometimes, we must accept that parts of us will shed and change. But in time, something more beautiful will bloom. That's why you should never fear change, for what's to come could be better than you could ever imagine."

Just like the trees, I'll change.

I'm just worried something more beautiful won't come in my marriage.

That I'll fall in love and not be loved back.

Benny opens the passenger door of the SUV, motioning for me to get in, and I don't mutter a word as I fall onto the leather seat. He slams the door shut before circling the car, and the scent of black-cherry car freshener and his cologne permeates the air.

"Was that really necessary?" I ask, dropping my boots onto the floorboard and slipping the sweater on. "I'd rather not spend the day with you … *especially* after what you just pulled with my brother *and* last night."

Benny starts the SUV. "We have business to discuss."

I jerk the seat belt over my body. "We have nothing to discuss."

"You also need to see your new home." He drops his arm to the back of my seat and reverses out of the driveway.

"I like the home I live in perfectly fine." My throat goes dry. With everything happening, I spaced that I'd have to move in with Benny.

"It won't be your home for much longer."

"We don't have to live together."

"I doubt your father will appreciate me fucking your brains out under his roof."

The scoff that leaves me is dramatic and loud. "There will be no fucking my brains out."

"We also need to discuss last night. That type of behavior can't happen again. You are about to become a Marchetti, and we don't play childish games."

"*I* play childish games? You were the one who got a blow job from a random woman to piss me off. You succeeded in the *pissing me off* part, which is why I did what I did. Cause and effect."

When we reach the gate at the entrance of my subdivision, he gives the guard a two-fingered wave and exits.

"I warned you what would happen," he says.

I snort. "I didn't believe you were serious."

"I'm not a man who speaks just to speak. When I say something, it means something. If I tell you another man is not to touch you, it's not a threat. It's a promise I will kill him."

"Technically, he didn't touch me—"

He shakes his head. "Touch you. You touch him. Neither better happen, or there will be violence."

"Why do you care anyway?" I run my fingers along the button of my fleece sweater. "You had another woman sucking you off."

Benny scoffs. "Jealous it wasn't you, my little unwanted wife?"

"Possibly, but *only* because I'd have had the opportunity to bite your dick off."

"I'd bet my entire kingdom you'd never have the balls to do that, so stop wasting both of our time, attempting to prove you're some *badass*." He jerks his head toward the back seat. "I still have handcuffs back there that I have no problem using again."

I cross my arms, a bitter taste forming in my mouth. "If you're kidnapping me, at least feed me lunch. I'm starving."

My stomach rumbles at the mention of food.

I planned to ask Isabella and my mother if they wanted to go out for tacos and margaritas.

Benny suddenly makes a U-turn, and I grip the door handle to stop myself from whacking my head against the window. Instead of questioning where he's taking me, I relax in the seat and watch him drive.

He uses only one hand. His knuckles are busted, but his nails are well-groomed. His black button-up sleeves are rolled up to the elbows, exposing the tattoos stretching down his arm to his hand. His other arm is bare, a blank canvas, as if he were waiting for the next chapter of his life before painting it onto his skin. I wish I could lean in closer, take a magnifying glass, and examine every inch of the tattoos.

I'm dragged away from my thoughts when Benny enters the private parking lot of L'ultima Cena. My stomach rumbles again, but it's more in excitement this time. This is the best Italian restaurant in the city.

It's also the most favored for Costa Nostra families. The restaurant requires all employees to sign NDAs and to provide three references from those within *our community*.

Benny swerves into an open spot, and I hurriedly slip on my boots before jumping out of the SUV. We walk side by side to the back entrance. Entering this way isn't new to me. My father never uses the main entrance to the restaurant, nor have we ever dined in the public dining area. Everything is kept private.

He rings a bell, and the door swings open seconds later.

"Benny! Neomi!" Argentino, the head chef, greets like he was expecting us.

"Table for two," Benny tells him. "Magnolia room, if it's open."

Argentino nods, waves us inside, and says, "Everyone is thrilled about you two finally tying the knot," as we follow him down the hall.

Argentino's uncle owns the restaurant. He and my father go way back. He attended my christening, caters my birthday parties, and sends us pignoli cookies every Christmas.

L'ultima Cena considers itself neutral ground, but that doesn't mean it doesn't house plenty of secrets and deaths. It's why people say the name fits the restaurant so well. It translates to the *last supper*.

Light opera music plays in the background as Argentino leads us into a small, low-lit room. A hurricane of candles is spread over the white-clothed table. The windows are covered with burgundy curtains. The entire restaurant has a Tuscan feel. Classic Italy.

Argentino draws out the chair for me, and I sit across from Benny. Luigi, one of the servers, enters the room. The smell of sweet garlic and fresh tomatoes lingers on his clothes.

"Good afternoon, Mr. Marchetti and Miss Cavallaro. I'm so happy you are dining with us today," Luigi greets, handing us menus. "What can I interest you in drinking?"

"I'm actually ready to order my meal as well," I tell him.

The faster we eat, the quicker we can get out of here.

Which means less Benny and Neomi time.

Luigi peeks at Benny, as if asking for his permission, and I grimace.

Benny leans back in his chair and makes a *go ahead* gesture.

"I'll just have a water to drink and the linguine all'astice," I say without bothering to glance at the menu. It's what my father orders on special occasions.

Now, I'm not a big lobster fan.

And my father taught us it's bad-mannered to order the most expensive item on the menu if you're not footing the bill.

While lobster isn't my favorite, being bad-mannered to Benny Marchetti is.

But Benny doesn't bat an eye at my selection. He only hands Luigi our unopened menus and says, "I'll have the same."

Neither of us adds an alcoholic drink—like we both want to remain sober for whatever will happen today ... whatever this *business* is.

Luigi tells us he'll return with our drinks before scurrying out of the room, shutting the door behind him. Benny checks his phone, and I realize I didn't grab mine on my dash out the door. Which means I have no money or phone.

Great. Stuck with him with no possible escape plan if needed.

I unravel the white cloth napkin and drape it over my lap. "What is this business we need to speak of?"

Benny sets down his phone. "The business that is our impending marriage."

"I don't think I have much say in the business of our marriage." I wince at the reality of my words.

"It seems you keep forgetting the contract wasn't my idea." Benny rubs at his dark brow. "You're acting like *I'm* forcing your hand here."

Our conversation is interrupted by Luigi returning with our waters.

"You could stop the marriage," I say when Luigi leaves the room again.

"I have as much power to stop it as you do." Benny shakes his head. "Regarding contracts and alliances, my father, like yours, does what's necessary to protect his family. He makes all final decisions."

He tugs at the collar of his shirt.

Benny is second-in-command.

The prince of the most powerful Mafia family.

All that prestige and superiority and he still can't decide the fate of his life.

I gulp and go quiet for a moment before asking, "Do you think our parents are holding us back from finding true love?"

"Finding true love?" He says *love* with such distaste that you'd think he'd drunk it once and discovered it rancid. "Love runs in the opposite direction of me, Neomi. It'd be a waste of my valuable time to even look for it."

"Gee"—I play with the straw in my water—"that sure makes me eager to marry you."

He shrugs before taking a sip of his water. "I'd like to think we can make this work without being in love. As long as we're honest with each other." He leans back in his chair to make himself comfortable. "Tell me something about Neomi Cavallaro no one knows."

This is supposed to be business only.

That's a personal question, and there will not be any getting personal with Benny Marchetti.

"I'm not really in the mood for a *get to know you* session," I reply. "Follow me on Instagram or Twitter. I post what's on my mind there."

"You post *Buffy the Vampire Slayer* memes and puppy videos. None of which tells me who you are. All I have is what you've shown me—you're reckless, you have a smart mouth, and you enjoy pushing my buttons. Now, there must be more to you. So, spill."

"Stalk me much?"

"You wish I thought you were worth the time to stalk." He scoffs. "I simply want to ensure you're behaving."

I level my elbow on the table and rest my chin in my palm. "And if I wasn't?"

"It could give me an out with our marriage contract."

I thrum my fingers along my cheek. "But *you* obviously haven't been on your best behavior, Mr. I Like Blow Jobs at Public Parties."

"Neomi, I want to make one thing clear." His tone turns all business, and frustration stretches along his face. "I have an empire to help my father run. I will give you an easy life. You'll want for nothing. But I need you to stop being such a pain in my ass."

I smirk. "But what would be the fun in that?"

He presses his fist to his head, knocking on it a few times. "I'd have my fucking sanity."

I do a circle motion toward his face. "Is there any sanity lingering in there, though?"

He chuckles. And it's not one of those cruel ones he gave Tommaso. It's somewhat genuine.

"Another thing I want to make clear."

"We're doing a lot of clearing here."

His eyes are sharp as they focus on me. "I'll never love you, Neomi. I am not made for love."

There is no humor or malice in his voice.

It's sincere honesty.

A warning.

Don't come looking for what I don't have to give.

"I don't want you to love me," I answer.

"I'm glad we're on the same page."

"No love. No feelings. All business."

He raises his glass, and I cheers, tapping mine against his.

But what about sex? is at the tip of my tongue.

But I leave it there, wash it down with my water, and let it sink with dread into my stomach.

We'll cross that bridge when we reach it.

Because there's only one thing scarier than marrying Benny Marchetti.

And that's *wanting* Benny Marchetti.

Our meal is to die for.

The lobster is fresh. The pasta is made in house and cooked to perfection. No one makes food that reaches your soul like Argentino. Just the aroma of the shallots, onions, and garlic relaxes me.

The talk Benny and I shared about not expecting love loosened some tension between us. Don't get me wrong. It's not like I'm having brunch while sipping mimosas with my sisters, but we're making decent conversation.

I suck in a noodle in a not-very-ladylike slurp and then explain my reasoning behind the endless puppy videos. When I was growing up, my father refused to allow us to have a family dog. Every year for Christmas, it was at the top of my wish list. But he always refused.

They bark too much.

Piss in the house.

When I was in high school, a homeless shelter ran an auction there. Bria and I adopted the cutest puppy. Our plan of hiding him in my room failed, and poor Bruiser was sent to live with my aunt Malina and her three evil cats.

Benny tells me they've never had a pet, either. Although he doesn't seem as bothered as me about it.

He refuses to answer when I ask him what he did with Alden's body.

"The less you know, the better," he says before taking another bite of his pasta.

Understandable.

They're the exact words my father has recited to my mother countless times. We can't go to prison for something we don't know about.

After declining dessert, Benny looks at me and says, "Time to see your new home."

I don't know what I expected from my *new home*, but it wasn't this.

I'll admit. I got my hopes up.

But Benny grew up in a home rich in character.

Romanesque architecture with vaulted ceilings, arched walkways, and marble flooring. You'll never find a home like the Marchetti mansion. Yes, it's a multimillion-dollar home, but the size and cost aren't what provide the allure.

It's the details.

The life breathed into it.

I hoped Benny shared that peculiarity.

Sitting in the passenger seat of Benny's SUV, I bite into the inside of my cheek.

I don't want to appear like a spoiled brat, whining about a home that probably cost a good seven figures, but I should have a say in where I live.

"It's …" My words trail off, and it takes a moment for me to finish my sentence. I decide to go with honesty. "It looks like a white box with windows."

It's stale.

Floor-to-ceiling windows span nearly every inch, giving me a glimpse of the home's interior. The landscaping contains nothing but shrubbery and has no bright flowers. It's too modern for my taste.

Benny disregards my comment and steps out of the SUV.

I do the same.

We walk up the concrete walkway of the house, and I don't miss the security system's motion sensors following our every move. Benny keys in a code at the glass front door and signals for me to step inside first.

What I walk into is a bachelor pad.

Not a new home for a wife—even if I'm an *unwanted wife*.

Reminder: I need to correct him about his little nickname for me.

The scent of clean linen and lemon wafts in the air. The

space has no evidence of being lived in. The white couch looks like it's never been sat on, and there isn't *one* throw pillow. The walls are a gray so light that they appear almost white.

The home has good bones with its open floor plan and architecture, if that's your style. But to make it a home I'd feel comfortable in, it would need work. The maple wood flooring provides some comfort, but it still lacks a homey feel.

I stroll into the kitchen and brush my fingers along the cold quartz countertop. Benny shoves his hands into his pockets, and his gaze follows me.

The chef's kitchen, complete with a Viking stove and stained wood cabinets, will give me plenty of space to cook—which is something I love to do.

"Are we, uh … married to this home?" I ask.

Benny follows me into the kitchen. "I had it built only a year ago."

"Can I throw out the idea of living somewhere else … or is the option of separate living still on the table?"

He stares at me, unblinking.

"I'm not trying to sound like a pain—"

"You always sound like a pain," he interrupts.

I flip him off before swinging my arm out to signal toward the living room. "It's too … modern. It's like a saltine cracker. Dry and boring." I hate that I almost sound like I'm sulking.

I whip around and rest my back against the counter.

Benny's steps are loud as he walks toward me. "Is there anything you're happy with, my unwanted wife?" His strides are long, and when he reaches me, he crowds me against the counter.

"Anything I'm happy with? No." I lose a breath at our closeness and grip the edge of the counter. "But if I can make a list of what I'm unhappy with, I'll start with my little nickname. Unwanted wife? How unoriginal."

His face is only inches from mine, and our eyes meet. "What would you rather I call you?"

"Neomi." I smirk. "Your Highness."

I'd actually gag if he called me the second one.

He gives me a wry smile. "*Unwanted wife* has a better ring to it."

"So does *unwanted husband*. Looks like we're two peas in an unwanted pod."

"I don't want to be your unwanted husband."

Benny bows his head, lowering it to the curve of my neck, and I shiver when the coarse scruff on his cheek scratches my skin.

"What do you want to be?" I breathe out.

He feathers light kisses on my cheek, and a chill runs down my spine. I curl my toes, stopping myself from arching my hips forward to rub them against him. If he didn't have me pinned back, I'd collapse to the floor.

"Your undoing," he whispers before stepping away from me.

On the ride home, I request a stop for ice cream.

It's another antic to fuck with him, but to my disbelief, he whips into the drive-through of my favorite ice cream shop. I order a cherry cordial sundae. Benny orders nothing. I eat while he drives me home.

There are so many sides to him.

He'll easily kill a man with no regrets.

He'll make it clear he'd rather shoot himself than marry me.

But he'll also stop and buy me ice cream.

I always knew Costa Nostra men were complicated.

Benny is a puzzle, and I get another piece of him each time we're together. Whether that puzzle is one of a dream or a nightmare is yet to be determined.

The security guard at our neighborhood gate waves him in without bothering to check if he's a resident. I'm sure it's the same way he weaseled himself inside earlier. Everyone knows who Benny is, and people don't say no to him.

He parks in front of the two-story brick colonial I've lived in since I was ten. It has character. You walk into my family home, and you'll see it's lived in. You'll get hints about each person who resides there.

There are photos.

Nicks in the flooring.

Furniture passed down through generations.

It's *home*.

"Welp." I take the last bite of my sundae. "I guess I'll see you at our death sentence."

"Can't wait," Benny grumbles. "Until next time, my unwanted wife."

CHAPTER EIGHT

BENNY

The mansion is silent when I walk into the foyer. The only light source comes from a gargoyle sconce on the wall. My father requested I end my work early tonight since tomorrow is my wedding.

Neomi was correct in her assessment of the home I'd taken her to. There's no character because there's been no life. I haven't slept one night there.

Every night, I sleep at the mansion.

It's not like I'm crashing on the couch here. I have plenty of privacy and my own wing.

But that's about to change.

I curl my lip as I take in the silence around me.

Silence is deadly to me. I prefer chaos.

Silence makes me remember and awakens memories I want to forget.

I run a hand over my face and stroll toward the staircase before suddenly stopping. There's one more thing I need to do before my wedding.

Speak with Gretchen.

Not to fuck her. We saw the mayhem a blow job caused.

Whether it will make my night better or worse, I have no idea.

We haven't spoken since the engagement party. I've texted her a few times, but she hasn't replied. I'm sure my father spoke with her and offered a hefty bonus to never speak of what happened in the billiards room. Then, I'd bet my left nut Natalia spoke with her. Natalia has always been worried about my relationship with Gretchen. She knew it'd end up hurting Gretchen, and it did.

I take a left and stroll down the long corridor leading to the employee quarters. Most of our employees live with us—cooks, housekeepers, landscapers, and their families. We are good to our help and always will be.

Miriam, Gretchen's mother, has worked for the Marchettis for years. Gretchen grew up in her grandmother's home until we hired her here last year. The day I met her, she blushed and struggled for words. She made her crush known—arguing with her mother to clean my room and do my laundry.

One night, while she was cleaning the dining room, I stopped and said hi. We chatted for an hour and then ended up fucking right there, on the table, and haven't stopped since.

But now, the time has come.

I have to say goodbye to Gretchen.

I hear the TV playing through the door to her suite when I knock on it. It takes her a few seconds before the door cracks open, and she pokes her head through the gap.

"Go away, Benny."

A heavy feeling forms in my chest. Gretchen has never spoken to me like that. When she goes to shut the door, I kick out my foot to stop it. She blows out a long breath when I push the door open and step inside.

Candy wrappers and tissues litter the coffee table, and Reese Witherspoon is crying on the TV screen. Gretchen steps in front of me, her hands on her hips, wearing pink sweats and one of my old gym tees. Her pale face is puffy, her eyes red, and her stare is distant as we look at each other.

We knew this day would come. The problem is, we never discussed what would happen when it did.

I shut the door behind me, walk into the living room, and shove my hands into my pockets. "You knew I was engaged before I ever touched you." I remove one hand to run it over my sweaty forehead.

I made it clear from the beginning that we'd be nothing but casual sex. Gretchen became my steady fuck—my *only* fuck. I was loyal and honest with her.

Gretchen throws her arm out as tears fill her eyes. "You said it wasn't real, Benny." Her voice is scratchy. "You said the marriage was only an agreement between your families and that you and Neomi couldn't stand each other."

"We don't like each other." *Never lied there.*

"You killed a man for her."

"I killed a man for touching what's mine."

Gretchen backs up a step. "She's *yours?*"

"She will be my wife, yes."

"I won't sleep with a married man." Her chin trembles as she repeatedly shakes her head. "I told you that." She slices her hand through the air. "Once you tie the knot and it becomes official, I'm done."

"I know, and I respect it."

"You used me to prove a point to her." Hostility grows in her voice.

"I'm sorry for hurting you." I blow out a breath. "I never claimed to be a perfect man. You know I'm far from that."

She smooths her hand down her top. "I'd appreciate you allowing my mother and me to keep our jobs."

"You won't be fired."

"You say that now, but what if your wife wants us gone?"

"You won't lose your job." I stress the words with as much certainty as I can. "Neomi won't live here."

"Thank you." Gretchen bows her head. "I should've listened to my mother and stayed away from you."

I plant two fingers below her chin, raising it so our eyes meet. She squeezes hers shut. It pains her to look at me.

"Take care of yourself, Gretchen," I say, and tears slip down her face when I kiss the top of her head.

She's quiet as I turn away, and just as I'm about to walk out, she whispers, "Goodbye, Benny."

I grit my teeth as I shut her door behind me.

Anger swells through my body.

I need to get the fuck out of here.

It's not that I'm in love with Gretchen.

Or that I want to marry her.

It's just … the reality of what's happening tomorrow has finally hit me.

No matter how I feel about Gretchen, about Neomi, or about my life, it doesn't change anything. I will be a married man tomorrow, and nothing I can do will change that.

I won't only have to worry about my family's safety, the club, and my work, but also a woman I'm tied to. And not just any woman. Neomi Cavallaro. The biggest pain in the ass to ever step into my life.

I storm through the mansion and toward the garage while dragging my keys out from my pocket. The Range Rover beeps as I unlock it. I wait until I'm away from the house before I blare my music and drive to Seven Seconds.

I need to fuck or hurt someone.

Some people pray about their problems.

Or talk to a therapist.

I screw women and shoot men to cope with my stress.

Call it unhealthy. I call it fun.

I lower my speed as I pass the front of the club, noticing the long line and the packed parking lot. I swerve to the back, rolling down my window to give my guys a thumbs-up to allow me entry, and park in the back lot.

When I make it inside, I charge into the security room, where monitors line the wall. Three of my men are inside, watching footage spanning every inch of the club.

I grab a chair, turn it backward, and straddle it. "Find someone stupid. I need violence tonight."

"You got it, boss," Raul says.

CHAPTER NINE

NEOMI

An ear-splitting roar of thunder cracks outside as I stare down at my mother fussing with my dress.

Carla's words have haunted me to this day.

"Prepare yourself, sweet cousin," she told me. "Arranged marriages are all we get from this life. And whatever you do, don't fall in love with your husband. He'll rip your heart into pieces."

But unlike Carla, I won't cry and beg my mother to stop the wedding.

I've felt numb all morning, completely disassociating from today's events.

My hands are shaky as I run them down the lace of my dress.

I don't feel like a bride.

I feel like a sacrifice.

Other than my sisters and possibly Benny, no one else sees it that way.

My mother and father's marriage was arranged.

So were their parents'.

My gown is simple, just as I wanted it.

White lace with a square neckline and a sweep train.

My hair is down in loose curls, and the comb of my veil is tight against my scalp, giving me a headache. My veil was hand-stitched by my great-aunt and mailed from Italy. It's layered to the floor and the same length as my train.

I was adamant not to have the veil cover my face. The thought of the theatrical moment where the groom slowly lifted the bride's veil made my stomach curl. It'd be too romantic. Too real. My mother argued over my choice and said it was against tradition. So, I knew she'd lie about sending my aunt the request. To prevent that, I made sure to tell her that if any *miscommunication* occurred, I'd cut the face out. She stared at me in horror. But the veil arrived exactly how I'd requested.

My mother cups her hand over my trembling one. "Relax, sweetheart. This is the happiest day of your life."

"Yes," Isabella says, fastening the strap of her rose-colored heel around her ankle. "It's not like you're being forced to marry a man you don't love."

My mother's head turns so quick to glare at Isabella that you'd think she almost snagged the role of the possessed girl in *The Exorcist*.

She squeezes my hand. "Even if you don't believe it now, when you look back at it later, when you and Benny are as in love as your father and I are, you'll want to remember this day forever." Her voice cracks at the end.

There's guilt inside her.

She probably had the same dread on her wedding day. She and my father barely knew each other before they said *I do*.

"Or she'll forever remember it as a nightmare," Isabella says, shrugging while grabbing her other heel.

My sisters are my only bridesmaids, and I have no maid of honor. They're really all the friends I have. Sienna got married to a guy she had met online, and we lost contact after.

"I can find you some sedatives," Bria says. "I know a guy."

"No one is getting sedatives," my mother says. "We can't

have her walking down the aisle like some zombie—or worse, *dying*." Her lips are tight as she looks at Bria. "And you *knowing a guy* had better be a joke."

"Why not?" I ask. "You're pretty much killing me anyway."

"And here I thought having girls would be easier than boys," my mother mutters under her breath before retreating a step to take a good look at me. "You look gorgeous, my dear."

Tears form in my eyes, but I shake my head to get rid of them. "Let's get this over with."

My father waits for me at the cathedral.

"My first daughter to marry," he says, his smile reaching his eyes. "You look beautiful, sweetheart."

He blinks away the wetness in his eyes and holds out his elbow for me to loop my arm through it. My mother hands me my bouquet of purple roses before ushering Bria and Isabella down the aisle. She crouches behind them, trying to appear discreet in her pink dress, and sits in the front pew. The bridal chorus starts—my signal to go—but I hesitate.

"You can do this, Nee-Nee," my father says. "You're the strongest woman I know. If he does anything to hurt you, I'll kill him."

I tighten my hold on my father as he proudly walks me down the aisle. He has no concerns about handing me over to a murderer. My heart races, warning me to make a run for it. I hold the bouquet firmly to my chest to calm it.

I'm doing this for my family.

As I walk down the aisle, the music fades. Faces in the crowd blur. When this is over, I'll have lost the last of my freedom. All I can focus on is Benny, standing at the altar, waiting for me in his fitted tux with his hands clasped behind his back. At first, he appears detached, but the closer I get, the more that changes.

Those dark eyes of his drink me in. His gaze overflows with caution, but a spark of excitement also lingers. Like he's preparing to rise to the challenge of becoming my husband.

I wobble in my heels when we reach him. He doesn't abandon eye contact and hardly pays my father a glance. They shake hands, and my father kisses my cheek before sitting next to my sobbing mother. Cristian stands behind Benny, his hands hanging in front of him, and Luca is next to him.

Bria helps hold my dress up as I stand before Benny. The music stops. The priest steps forward and asks Benny and me to join hands. Benny captures my hand in his, holding it tight, worried one of us will make a run for it.

My voice is low, nearly a whisper, as I recite my vows.

Benny says his loud and clear, as if he wants the entire city to know I'm now his. My hands shake, and his fingers flex when we exchange rings. I gasp when he slips the ring on my finger. Benny never proposed, and we never discussed a ring.

I don't get much time to admire it before the priest says, "You may now kiss the bride."

Benny runs his tongue over his bottom lip, and I shut my eyes. I gasp when he tugs me toward him and smashes his mouth to mine. His lips are soft and perfect.

So different from what I expected from him.

Our kiss isn't a quick peck.

It wraps me up, hugging me, and consumes me.

I forget about the people around us. About the contract. About others making this decision for me.

Benny slips his tongue into my mouth, desperate for a taste, and I allow it.

We don't kiss like two people forced into a marriage.

We kiss like we're soulmates.

Like we've done this our entire lives.

Benny doesn't kiss me like an unwanted bride.

He kisses me like I'm all he's ever wanted.

I'm not sure how much time passes as we stand there and kiss.

But reality shatters through us as the sound of gunshots breaks our moment.

CHAPTER TEN

BENNY

I was so wrapped up with my mouth on Neomi's that it took me a moment to knock myself back into reality and realize I'd heard gunshots.

A rarity for me since I'm always on guard.

I should've known not to expect a calm wedding.

But weddings never concern me. They tend to be safe spaces. The receptions are usually where trouble arises. Most of us prefer not to create violence in places of worship.

Neomi gasps, the bottom of her dress ripping when I tackle her to the ground and use my body to shield hers. Gunshots fire around us.

"Take the back exit," I tell her, and she wheezes under the heaviness of me. "Do not fucking stop for anyone."

She nods. "Back exit. Got it."

I roll off her, stand, and continue blocking her from harm while drawing my pistol from my blazer pocket. Even though the gunfire has ceased, I grip it tight.

Neomi shuffles toward the back hall, her dress creating a struggle, and her sisters are behind her.

My uncle Lorenzo slams the cathedral's double doors shut.

Our guests are ducking behind their pews or gripping guns in their hands to return fire.

The shots don't last long.

Merely a few seconds before ceasing.

Then, there's yelling.

A baby crying.

People rattling off questions while others argue over who will clean up the dead bodies.

There's a dead body in the aisle. I'm not surprised one of our guests killed him. Every person in this room is affiliated with the Marchetti or Cavallaro name. If we hear gunshots, we return gunfire and ask questions later.

Tommaso appears defeated, his shoulders slumped, as a gun hangs from his hand. The veins in my neck pulse as I stalk down the aisle to the motherfucker who interrupted my wedding.

Interrupted my first kiss with my wife.

He's lucky he's already dead.

The man is facedown, and blood has puddled around his body. His arm is out, as if he fell and attempted to reach for his gun next to him. I smirk while taking in his bullet-ridden body with too many shots to count.

When I look past the dead moron, I spot another man slumped against one of the cathedral doors with a bullet between his eyes. The bastard didn't even make it far enough to cause destruction.

Who sent their amateurs to fuck up my wedding?

"Has anyone seen my daughters?" I hear Concetta call out at the same time a scream comes from the back hallway, where Neomi and her sisters fled.

I sprint in that direction. My father and Severino are on my heels. We find Isabella at the end of the hall in front of the exit door.

Why is she blocking it and not running?

Her eyes quickly flash to us before returning to her left. I step farther, leveling my finger on the gun trigger, and follow in the direction Isabella is looking. I can hear the blood rushing through my head when I see a man restraining Neomi from behind. He has one hand over her mouth, and the other holds a gun against her head.

Neomi's eyes are wide with horror as she struggles to fight him off. When the man's eyes land on me, panic grows in them, matching Neomi's. Severino attempts to push past me, but I stop him.

"That is my goddamn daughter," he grunts, fighting me.

"Who is now my wife," I say, holding out my arm while keeping my eyes pinned on the motherfucker who threatened my wife and ruined my wedding. "I'll handle this."

"Lower your gun and release her before I blow your head off," I sneer at the man. I'm gritting my teeth so hard that my jaw aches.

The man, who appears more experienced than his dead coworkers, grinds the muzzle of the gun harder into her skull. "And I'll do the same with hers. You pull the trigger, I'll pull mine."

Neomi winces at his remark.

Concetta cries out her daughter's name behind me.

"I have a clear shot," my father says, his voice low.

"If someone hurts my wife, they die at *my* hands," I tell him. "No one else's."

My eyes meet Neomi's, and a tear spills down her cheek. A rage I've never experienced courses through me, and for a moment, I refuse to look away. She needs to see in my face that she will not die here today. That I will protect and save her from this man. And anyone else who tries to hurt her.

As much as we push and pull, she's mine.

She carries my name and will forever be protected.

My life will always be on the line before hers.

"You do know crazy men with guns surround you," Isabella tells him with a snarl you wouldn't expect from her, given how innocent she appears. "You won't leave here alive, so let my sister go."

"If I don't bring this bitch where she needs to go and finish the job, I'll die," the man hisses, and sweat clings to his brow. "Either way, I'm a dead man."

Just as I'm finding the perfect angle to shoot him, he screams when Neomi bites into the palm of his hand. When he pulls back his hand and shifts his body, I shoot him in the head. His body jerks back at the impact, and his brain matter spatters onto Neomi. He slumps against the wall behind him as he collapses to the floor.

"Forgive me, Father, for I have sinned," I say sarcastically.

Severino opens his arms as Neomi rushes toward us. But she doesn't go to him. Her body smacks into mine as she wraps her arms around my neck and shoves her face into my chest. She breathes me in like she's been searching for breaths and I'm finally providing them to her.

I run my hand down her back, soothing her and pleading with her to know she's safe. When she calms, I create enough distance to grab her face with both my hands.

"Are you okay?" I stress, running my hand along her cheek and not giving a shit about getting blood on me.

She nods, but her entire body trembles. "I just want to get out of here."

"Um, does anyone know where the priest went?" Bria asks, and I notice she's been stuck next to Isabella, just out of view.

"He ran out as soon as he heard gunshots," Natalia says, and that's when I remember we have people around us. "He's probably praying for forgiveness for allowing us to use this church."

Severino chuckles.

Nothing like a little bloodshed at your wedding.

Now, I need to figure out who created it.

CHAPTER ELEVEN

NEOMI

"Are you *positive* we have to cancel the reception dinner?" my mother asks. "We shouldn't allow a few dead men to ruin such an important event."

Leave it to Concetta Cavallaro to be upset that my almost kidnapping has interfered with the wedding reception she planned for months.

We're in the cathedral's choir room. A few moments ago, Benny grabbed my hand and brought me inside, only allowing my father, mother, and Cristian to join us. Tommaso attempted to come, but Benny slammed the door in his face. My father's face was red. No doubt, he was ready to argue, but he stopped when he realized Tommaso hadn't attempted to fight Benny's dismissal.

Tommaso sure is backing down from Benny.

Even in my father's presence.

"It's not like anyone from our families died," my mother continues her argument, hell-bent on making this party happen. "We have no one to mourn."

One thing this life does is smear nonchalance over death.

The longer we're in, the more empathy we lose.

She has a point though.

But I don't back her up since I'd rather not have the reception. I shift from one foot to the other, staring at the ripped skirt of my bloody dress while masking the vulnerability percolating through me. I rub at my body in all the places the man touched me. I feel exploited, a person punished for someone else's wrongdoings. I haven't done anything to piss off a group of men with guns. It was those around me, and I was the easy target to seek revenge on them.

Years ago, my father told me it isn't a rarity for men to target family members to get revenge. I've heard stories where they make a man watch as they kill his family, saving him for last. The more suffering, the better. But today really punched reality in my face.

I'd been so nervous about the wedding, but there'd been a sense of ease when we kissed.

Maybe we could do this marriage thing without killing each other. But that positivity died at the sound of gunshots.

Benny and I marrying will always be a bad idea.

"I'm taking Neomi to the mansion," Benny tells the room before glancing at my mother. "You can hold the reception dinner there … for you and the girls." His tone is all business as he turns his attention to my father. "Why would someone want to kidnap Neomi?"

My throat thickens, and I desperately want to say, *because of one of you.*

"No idea." My father runs a hand over his sweaty face. "Both of us have enemies in this city."

I shiver, hugging myself, and Benny removes his blazer before draping it over my shoulders.

For a man who didn't want to marry me, he's sure worried about my safety.

And for a woman who didn't want to marry him, I sure ran straight into his arms.

Benny stands tall, staring harshly at my father, as if he wants to read any lies on his face. My father's face hardens—a dare that he won't find what he wants.

No one will own up to anything until they know all the details.

"Can we go?" I ask. "I'd like to change out of this dress and" —I run a hand through my ratty hair, thickened with blood and brain matter—"shower this off me."

Benny ushers me through the back exit and helps me into the passenger seat of his Range Rover. He doesn't allow anyone else to ride with us.

As he drives, I want to shrivel into the heated leather seat and vanish. This is exactly what I didn't want to be—helpless in front of Benny.

I jerk on my seat belt. One of Benny's men drives in front of us, and three more tail the SUV.

"Why didn't you let them take me? Kill me?" I ask, my throat raspy. "It would've solved our 'being married to each other' problem," I say with air quotes.

"Our problem?" He keeps his attention on the road. "Had he killed you, it would've solved mine, absolutely. But I wouldn't consider you dying or kidnapped a solution to *yours*. I hardly think marrying me would be worse than whatever they had planned to do with you."

Fair point.

"Now, I need answers from you," he adds.

"What do you mean?"

"You—or your family—need to tell me what's going on."

"How would I know?"

He shoots me an accusatory glance even though I should be questioning him. His phone ringing stops his possible interrogation.

He answers the call, listens for a moment, and says, "I'm gonna make sure Neomi is comfortable at the mansion, and then we'll talk."

The sun is setting as he drives. When we arrive, three guards with guns thrown over their shoulders wait at the mansion's steel gate. They approach the SUV, and Benny rolls down his window.

"I want eyes on every inch of this place," he instructs them. "Every fucking inch. Do you hear me?" Spit flies out with his last three words.

The man in front, who seems to be around Benny's age and has a long scar on his cheek, rapidly nods with Benny's every word before saying, "We're on it."

The gate slowly opens, and Benny hits the gas. He swerves around the circular driveway with a massive fountain in the middle and parks at the front door. He jumps out of the SUV, and I open my door—an attempt to beat him from helping me out.

When my heels hit the ground, I stare at the mansion and remember what happened the last time I was here.

"Come on," Benny says, signaling me to walk. He stays behind me and watches our surroundings.

The front door flies open before we reach it. Gigi and Natalia stand at the entrance. Most of our guests left when Benny and I went into the choir room to speak with our parents.

Natalia leaps forward, hugs me, and practically drags me inside the mansion.

"Neomi, I am so sorry you had to go through that," she says, her pregnant belly creating space between us as she hugs me.

I tense at the sudden affection. Sure, my parents have hugged us, but we've never been a doting family. We save this type of affection for holidays. I pat Natalia's back in an attempt to appear normal.

"I have to say," Gigi says, standing next to Natalia, still wearing her gold dress, "blood seems to be your color, but let's get you out of that dress."

"I think, after the engagement party, we should've learned black is the best color for you," Natalia says.

Gigi nods in agreement. "It hides blood better."

"Just get her some fucking clothes, Gigi," Benny snaps.

"All right, all right, cranky," Gigi mutters, rolling her eyes at her brother. "Come on, Neomi."

When I step forward, Benny grips my elbow, stopping me. I turn to face him, and his expression is tense. He swipes his thumb along my cheek, taking bits of dried-up blood, and I shiver.

"You'll be safe here," he says, his voice deep.

"I know," I whisper.

The mansion is said to be the safest place in the city. It has better security than most federal prisons. Anytime the Marchettis have encountered trouble, it's always been outside the gates. If there's anywhere you'll feel protected, it's within these stone walls. There are guards at the gate, on the roof, and at every entry into the mansion.

"I'll be back." Benny kisses the top of my head.

That simple touch from him is like a relaxant injected inside me.

As soon as he leaves the mansion, Gigi captures my hand and leads me upstairs.

"I have to say, that was my favorite wedding I've attended thus far," she says before glancing over her shoulder to Natalia behind me. "No offense."

"None taken," Natalia replies. "I also quite enjoyed the engagement party."

Gigi throws her head back and laughs. "I'm just loving this for my brother."

"I don't think he is," I mutter.

She shakes her head. "Oh, don't let him fool you. He's definitely loving it."

I follow her down the hallway before she stops at a door, opens it, and flips on the light.

"Are you going for a more casual look, dressy—" Gigi starts to ask.

Natalia interrupts and says, "Sexy? It is the night of your

wedding, after all. I'm sure you and—"

I cringe and stop her. "Our marriage is strictly non-romantic."

Gigi holds up her hand and shoots Natalia an annoyed look. "There will be no talk of my brother's … romantic life."

My mouth falls open when I enter the bedroom. Gigi Marchetti's bedroom is exactly how you'd imagine a Mafia princess's room would look like. A sparkling chandelier hangs from the high ceiling, and purple paisley wallpaper decorates one wall. White drapes are hung along her dark canopy bed, complete with a purple velvet comforter.

Just like with her bedroom, Gigi fits the profile of a Mafia princess. Sure, my sisters and I do as well, but she is to the extreme. Her hair is black with hints of purple in the wavy curls. Her tanned skin matches her brother's, and she has an Italian nose—long with a prominent bridge.

My gaze moves from Gigi to Natalia.

While Gigi is shorter, Natalia is tall.

Natalia oozes sex appeal with her straight jet-black hair and hourglass curves, while Gigi bleeds high-maintenance and *fun aunt* vibes. She's attractive but not *in your face* sexy.

Gigi opens a set of French doors to a dream closet.

"All right, new sister-in-law," Gigi says, "what are you in the mood to wear?"

"Something casual," I say, admiring her handbag collection. "Comfortable."

She nods and points toward the opposite end of the room, where another set of open French doors leads into a bathroom. "Shower is in there. Use all the products you want. I'll grab some things and leave them on the bed for when you're ready. You can leave the dress in the bathroom. I'll have it dry-cleaned and send Benny the bill."

I clasp my hands together, and my voice cracks with sincerity. "Thank you so much."

"Let me know if you need anything," she adds.

I walk into the bathroom and shut the door behind me. I hate nothing more than being emotional, so I hold in a breath to keep myself together as I change out of my dress. I need to do it quickly because if Mom or my sisters get here, they'll want to help. But I need to do this alone to process all that's happened and give myself space.

While I wait for the water to warm, I attempt to shed my dress, but it's too hard. Tears hit my eyes as I search through Gigi's drawers for scissors.

I cover my mouth as a sob leaves me and cut one strap of the dress.

It falls loose as I do the other.

I held in my tears until this moment. I stare at the blood-stains as the dress pools at my feet. My mother was right. My wedding will forever be a memory—only one I wish I could forget.

I collect the dress in my hands, worried I'll get blood on Gigi's floor, and drop it on the closed toilet seat.

I have the blood of a man who wanted to hurt me on my dress.

In my hair.

On my skin.

A tear runs down my cheek, mixing with the blood, and I throw my head back. I place my hand on my chest to calm my heart, and that's when I notice my ring glistening under the vanity light.

I've never seen a piece of jewelry so breathtaking. The band is rose gold, and the color of the salt-and-pepper diamond is so translucent that you can partially see through the stone. A halo of white diamonds is at the top in a geometric shape, the ring almost appearing crown-shaped.

When I step into the shower, I scrub my body harsher than I should. I'm at a crossroads. I want to keep the memory of when Benny and I shared our kiss, but I also want to erase when a man attempted to kidnap me. Even though it was a wedding I didn't want, I still wanted it to be good, goddammit.

I take the longest shower of my life while attempting to relax, and when I'm done, I don't bother blow-drying my hair. I snatch a scrunchie from the counter and throw my hair into a ponytail.

When I get out, a stack of clothes is waiting for me on the bed. A panty and bra set with the tags still on them. Three leggings and four top options. I get dressed, choosing Lululemon leggings and a loose sweater before heading downstairs. Isabella and Bria are waiting for me in the foyer.

Right before I hit the bottom step and approach them, I freeze. A pain forms in the back of my throat when I come face-to-face with the blonde from our engagement party. Her blue eyes widen when they meet mine. She turns, not giving me a moment to speak, and speed-walks down a corridor.

Oh, hell no.

I can either chase after her or yell at Benny.

"Where's Benny?" I snap, rushing down the last stair.

Bria and Isabella look straight at a shut door.

I march toward it and bang on the door without considering the consequences.

"Benny Marchetti!" I yell through it. "You'd better get out here right now!"

It's a ballsy move.

But after what happened today, I deserve to be ballsy.

I hear voices on the other side, and the door swings open just as I raise my hand to knock again. Benny's jaw is tight when he appears in the doorway and gives me a questioning glance.

I signal to where I ran into the woman even though she's no longer there. "What the hell is she doing here?"

He steps out of the office and pulls me into a corner. "She who?"

I push at his shoulder, ready to take today's emotions out on him. "The girl from the night of our engagement party."

Understanding dawns on him.

He rubs his forehead. "Gretchen lives here." Before I can rant, he presses a finger to my mouth. "She *works* here, and, no, I won't touch her again. But I can't do this with you right now."

I glare at him. "This conversation is not over."

He scrubs a hand over his stressed face. "Trust me, I'm well aware."

"Neomi! Where is my gorgeous bride?!"

I turn at my mother's voice singing through the room, and she struts toward me. Behind her is Alfonso, my old bodyguard. After the engagement party, where I claimed Alfonso was hot as fuck, my father informed me Alfonso had been assigned elsewhere.

Not that my sisters and I keep a regular bodyguard. We like to maintain some freedom. I have a feeling that part of my life will change now that I'm a Marchetti. Rumor is, Gigi and Natalia can't even step outside without a bodyguard. Gigi's bodyguard even travels with her across the world.

"Come on, honey," she continues, her tone sugary-sweet. "Everything is ready." Her attention slides to Benny. "Are you sure you can't stay *at least* for dinner?"

Benny shakes his head.

My mother grins. "I'll save you and your father a plate then."

Benny nods.

When my mother walks away, I start to follow, but Benny's hand closes around my arm.

"I'll be out late," he says, only loud enough for me to hear. "You can sleep in my bedroom until I return, and we can go home." He doesn't allow me to tell him I'm not sleeping in his bedroom before walking away. He reenters the room he was in and slams the door shut behind him.

Ten minutes later, when I'm in the dining room with my sisters, my mother, Gigi, and Natalia, I spot Benny and his father leaving the mansion.

I pick at every course of our meal.

Even my favorite ravioli doesn't spark an appetite.

I don't even touch the wedding cake I spent six hours contemplating the flavor of.

My mother went all out with the caterers to create the perfect meal for our reception dinner. Even though only sixty guests were invited to the wedding, she sent out one hundred fifty reception dinner invites.

The wedding was a personal affair.

The reception would have been a party.

How most nuptials go in my family.

I taste metal with every bite, as if the man's blood were still in my mouth. To add to my anxiety, my mind won't stop racing after seeing *Gretchen*. I never questioned Benny about her because I didn't expect to see her again. I thought she was a random woman he'd used to taunt me.

My mother makes most of the conversation. She offers Natalia baby advice and talks with Gigi about her travels through Italy over the summer. Surprisingly, like me, Bria and Isabella are on the quiet side. I'm sure they are processing what happened as much as I am. Even though they kept brave faces as the man held a gun to my head, I know my sisters. They were holding back fear and tears.

"Alfonso is going to take us home when we finish," my mother tells me. "But I want you to call me first thing in the morning."

My father insisted Alfonso stay at the mansion with us. My mother made him a plate, and he told us he preferred to eat in the car. Alfonso is a man in his fifties, who insists on listening to Bob Dylan during every car ride and keeps to himself. My father said he's silent but deadly.

"Benny instructed me to show you to his room when you're ready," Gigi tells me.

"Oh, you don't have to worry about that," I reply. "I can sleep in a guest bedroom."

Gigi cracks a smile. "Trust me, babe. Benny will drag you out of there and throw you in his bed if you go anywhere else."

My head throbs, and all I want to do is collapse into a comfy bed, so I nod.

Benny's bedroom in the mansion is nothing like his plain home.

It's dark, sophisticated academia, and it fits him better. Instead of hospital white, the walls are warm-toned. Dark leathers instead of minimalistic white furniture. There's a TV on the wall above a brown leather ottoman. Aesthetic, old photos in bronze frames hang on the walls.

I skim my fingers along the wood shelf lined with books before opening a door leading into a walk-in closet. Since leggings are uncomfortable to sleep in and I don't want to ask Gigi to borrow pajamas, I steal one of Benny's black shirts.

What's his is now mine.

I button it halfway and wiggle out of the leggings.

With each step I take toward the bed, I feel like a zombie. My exhaustion grows heavier and heavier. I yawn a few times as I slide into the crisp sheets, and I quickly doze off.

My sleep doesn't last long.

A gasp bursts from my lungs when someone rips the blanket off my body.

CHAPTER TWELVE

BENNY

"I want an explanation as to why my goddamn wedding was shot up," I sneer at Severino, staring at him from across his desk.

My father and I spoke before driving to Severino's home. If the wedding violence were our fault, it would've been at the hands of the Lombardi family. The murdered men at the church weren't Lombardis. We're still unsure who those motherfuckers were, but Raul has been digging into their identities.

Besides the Marchettis, three families are active in this city— the Cavallaros, the Lombardis, and the O'Connors. So far, we've found no affiliation to any of them.

I promised my father I'd have restraint and provide Severino the benefit of the doubt, but who was I kidding?

I left all that promised restraint at the door.

Tommaso stands next to Severino with his back against the bookshelf and arms crossed, looking guilty as sin. He's hardly muttered a word since we walked in. We decided to hold our meeting at their home so as not to bother those celebrating our reception dinner at the mansion.

Severino gestures for us to sit in the two leather chairs situated in front of his desk.

I don't. Neither does my father.

Severino massages his temples. "It could've been the Lombardis."

Vincent Lombardi, the head of the Lombardi family, would never attempt a move so risky. His son might've been stupid, but Vincent isn't. It's why his son died in his twenties, and Vincent is pushing seventy.

"Bullshit," I hiss, balling my hands into fists. "We know everyone who works with and for the Lombardis, and those two dirty fucks who tried kidnapping my wife—and your daughter, might I add—were not one of his men."

I'm not sure why I'm suddenly so protective over Neomi. Months ago, I'd have been happy to hear she was kidnapped. But after exchanging our vows, something has shifted. No one fucks with what's mine.

Speaking to a don in this matter is disrespectful, especially when you're not one yourself. But frankly, I don't give a fuck.

Severino slams his hand onto the desk, and Tommaso winces.

"I don't know what you want me to tell you, Marchetti," he grunts.

"Someone had better tell us something," my father says, his voice layered with accusation.

I glance at Tommaso. "What about you?" My eyes harden. "Why don't you explain it to us then?"

Tommaso's Adam's apple bobs, and he refuses to make eye contact.

His actions tell me everything I need to know.

While some fathers spent their weekends teaching their kid sports, mine educated me about human behavior and body language.

"I have no idea," Tommaso finally says, each word slowly leaving his mouth. "But we're looking into it." He places his fist to his mouth and clears his throat. "Our men are looking into it."

I glare at him, certain he's keeping something from me. "You have until the morning before I raise hell."

This is the last shit I want to deal with.

I have a new wife to get home to.

"We'll discuss this in the morning," Severino says with a slow nod.

My father and I leave the room. Two guards are at the front door, and I give both a head nod as we exit the home.

"Tommaso knows something," my father says when we climb into my Range Rover.

I clench my hand around the steering wheel. "He doesn't just know something. He knows why it happened and is scared we're going to find out."

The mansion is quiet when we return.

It's late, and it was a long day, so I wouldn't be surprised if everyone is passed out. Hell, I think sleep is a waste of time, and I'm ready to collapse into my bed.

My father also prefers quiet, especially now, with Natalia being pregnant. I can only imagine how insufferable he'll get with the rules once my baby brother is born.

I say good night to my father when we hit the top of the stairs. He retreats toward his wing, and I make a left toward mine.

My bedroom door is shut, but unlocked. A corner lamp shines when I enter the bedroom to find Neomi sleeping and snuggled on my side of the bed. I step to the edge and appreciate the solitude of taking her in without hearing her mouth.

Her hair is a wild mess, strands lying in every direction on the pillow and her shoulders. I run a hand along my jaw as my gaze travels down her body and grin when I find she's wearing my shirt.

There's something about seeing a beautiful woman in your bed, wearing your clothes. It awakens something inside me.

My cock jerks in my pants.

So, I do what every romantic groom does.

I rip the blanket off her.

Time to wake up.

CHAPTER THIRTEEN

NEOMI

I jerk forward, nearly pushing myself into a seated position, when a rush of cold air smacks into my body. After what happened at the wedding, my brain's immediate thought is, *This is bad.*

My legs tense when hands clasp around my ankles. I curse, attempting to kick my legs free as someone drags me to the foot of the bed.

"Neomi, it's me."

I stop my fighting at Benny's deep voice. I blink and remember where I am.

"Time to go home," he says, squeezing my ankles.

I shake my head. "I'm cozy here. You go home, and we'll chat in the morning."

Surprisingly, I'm comfortable in Benny's space.

The sheets are like heaven against my skin.

The room is the perfect temperature.

And I feel safe.

"Nice try." He frees my ankles but remains at the foot of the bed.

My jaw drops when he spreads my legs and positions himself between them. His outer thighs against my inner ones.

"I'm not above dragging you out of this bed, wife," he says.

My head spins, and shivers spread over my body as he lazily dances his fingers along my skin. As bad as I wish I could pull away, it's as if my body were paralyzed. His hands ease up my thighs. I turn my head in shame when warmth builds between my legs.

My body comes alive at his simple touch. I attempt to rub my thighs together, but Benny's hands are in the way. The lighting is limited as I rise up onto my elbows and stare down at Benny. He doesn't bother looking up at me. His focus remains on my bare thighs.

His face hardens, and his gaze lingers between my legs. The shirt is short and unbuttoned on the bottom, exposing my black panties. What a stupid move it was to choose this as my bedtime attire when I knew Benny would return to the mansion some-time tonight. My little outfit of choice is as risky as the lingerie Gigi offered me earlier.

The mood changes.

Gone is the Benny who wanted to teach me a lesson.

Enter Benny who looks like he wants to eat me alive.

In the best way.

The erotic way.

A way that makes me want to give him full control of my body.

"Does this turn you on, my wild wife?" Benny's voice is hoarse as his fingers start a slow trail toward my center. "I bet if I slid my fingers into your pussy, they'd come out drenched. Wouldn't they, Neomi?"

He says *Neomi*.

Not one of my nicknames.

I love the sound of it.

I also hate how right he is.

That I'm soaked for him.

I hiss, my body tightening when he runs his thumb along

the hem of my panties. His touch is a slow torture. My heartbeat turns frantic when he slips his finger beneath my panties.

"I'm as dry as the Sahara," I say around a heavy breath while trying to maintain my pride.

He chuckles when the tip of his finger meets my core. "Maybe you don't hate me as much as you claim." His teasing touch runs up and down my slit.

I raise my knees, scooting them back, stupidly allowing him access.

A phone ringing snaps me out of my trance.

Benny freezes.

I suddenly shut my legs, trapping his hand there, and he peers up at me.

"You'd better get that," I say since the ringing is coming from his pocket. I slowly open my legs and pull away, not giving him the opportunity to ignore the call.

The interruption was proof I'm not supposed to let Benny touch me.

The universe sent me a reminder.

He ignores the call, and I roll off the bed, practically falling onto the floor. Benny remains in place and doesn't offer a helping hand. I groan while gripping the edge of the bed and pull myself up.

It's like I have a hangover, and I didn't even take a sip of liquor at dinner.

Benny watches me, his gaze controlled yet full of hunger.

I clear my throat to stop his eye-fucking.

He smirks. "I like you in my clothes."

I roll my eyes and attempt to tug down the shirt, wishing I could make it longer. "This isn't yours."

"Where'd you get it then?"

"Some random guy."

He runs his finger over his bottom lip. "Act like you hate me all you want, but your drenched pussy tells me otherwise, you filthy liar."

"Anyway," I say, dragging the word out, "you said we're leaving."

I speed-walk past him and out of the bedroom, apparently having no regard that I'm not wearing shoes or pants. I'm not sure if it's from the sleepiness or if I'm struggling with the overwhelming desire coursing through me.

I don't look back but can hear his footsteps behind me as I walk downstairs. When I reach the front door, I stop, noticing the alarm keypad with a red light blinking. Benny turns off the alarm, blocking me from seeing the passcode, and we walk out into the chill of the night.

Benny tugs me close to his side as we walk to the Range Rover parked in the driveway, the engine still running. Three other vehicles with bright headlights are parked around it. He assists me into the passenger seat, blocking anyone from seeing me in my lack of decent clothing, and shuts the door behind me.

Like on the route to the mansion after the wedding, one vehicle drives in front of us and two follow. I rest my head against the window, the cold a relaxant against my cheek, and doze off.

The sound of a garage door opening wakes me. I lift my head, wiping drool from my chin, and look around as the door shuts.

"Where are we?" I rub my eyes. "A safe house?"

My family owns several safe houses. It's not uncommon to go to one when there's a threat.

"This is your new home," Benny replies.

"New home? You bought another house?"

"It was my grandparents' home. I'm renting it from my father until we find something else. You weren't a fan of the first place I showed you. What did you call it, a *saltine cracker* home?" There's no animosity in his tone as he repeats my insult.

He moved us into a new home because I didn't like the other one?

I scan my surroundings. An old Mercedes is parked next to us. The garage is full of old Coca-Cola memorabilia, and an old wooden bench is pushed against a wall. Birdhouses—some of them complete, some not—line the bench.

"What about the saltine cracker?" I ask around a yawn.

"I'll sell it." He shrugs and turns off the SUV. "Keep it. I haven't decided."

"Why?"

"My wife doesn't like my house, so I have to buy her a new one," he replies, like it was a simple task, as if I'd asked him to pick up something from the store. "Until then, we'll stay here. The home was approved by your mom, and we'd already installed a security system."

My bare feet slap against the concrete floor when I step out of the SUV and follow Benny through a door with chipped paint leading into the home. A cherry-wood staircase takes up most of the space in the narrow foyer.

The house is older.

Outdated.

But homey.

I don't need a mansion.

I only need comfort.

"I like this." I run a hand over the railing, and my fingers brush against the nicks in the wood.

"My mother grew up here." He shuts the door and turns the lock. "My father promised her he'd never sell it."

I love that there's a memory of his mother here.

History makes a home cozy—as if everyone who lived here left a piece of their heart.

"I'll give you a tour tomorrow," he says. "But for now, I'll show you the bedroom." He jerks his head toward the stairs.

A wave of nausea hits me.

It's our *wedding night*.

Those words hold such significance for newlyweds.

I nod and pretend my knees aren't wobbly as I walk up the creaky stairs. "Which bedroom is mine?"

Benny is so close behind that his chest brushes my back with every step. "First door to your left."

As soon as I hit the doorway of the room he pointed out, I turn to block him from entering. "Good night. See you in the morning." The words leave my mouth so fast that they sound as if they were one. "Good job at the wedding today ... and thank you for saving my life."

I curtsy.

I fucking curtsy.

What is wrong with me?

Benny holds out his hand to stop me from shutting the door in his face. "This is *our* bedroom, Neomi."

I perform a dramatic sweeping gesture toward the hallway. "Then, what other bedroom is for me?"

He grinds his teeth. "We're not spending our wedding night in separate bedrooms."

I'm caught off guard, and I stumble back a step when he walks into the room. I glare at him as he turns on the light and shuts the door.

Just like downstairs, the bedroom is outdated, but the linens are new. I run a hand over the white duvet on the cherry-wood sleigh bed.

We're quiet as we face each other.

It's our wedding night, in our new bedroom, and neither of us knows what to do.

What do you do with a man you don't love on your wedding night?

Crack jokes? Play dominoes?

Sleeping in separate rooms is off the table, apparently.

The tension in the air is thick as we stand inches from each other. He focuses his stare on me, as if I'm the only thought in his mind. When he advances a step, I retreat one. We repeat the dance until I'm backed against a tall dresser, and the knobs dig into my back. A heaviness forms in my stomach when Benny crowds me.

"I'm going to ask you this again," Benny says, his voice callous but calm at the same time—the opposite of what it was when he told me about the home. "Why would someone want to kidnap you?"

I grip the edge of the dresser. "I have no idea."

"Don't bullshit me, Neomi."

"I'm not bullshitting you."

"Do you not understand the severity of the situation?" He slams his hands on top of the dresser, caging me in, and I jump. "Their failed kidnapping won't end at our wedding. They'll keep trying. It could be you next time, one of your sisters, or they could kill someone." His lips are so close to mine that they're nearly touching. "This isn't a game."

I gulp as the reality of his words sends a chill down my spine. "Why do you care if I'm kidnapped?"

He winces. "I care because you're my wife."

I shiver at his response. At the raw truth in his voice and eyes.

He genuinely does care.

Just when I think he'll pull away, he lowers his hand and toys with a button on my shirt. Well, *his* shirt. Desire crashes through me when he turns his hand and shoves it through the opening. Buttons scatter at our feet, but neither of us looks down at them. The shirt falls open, exposing me, and my heart skips a beat when Benny curses.

We don't speak when he brushes his thumb along the curve of my breast, under my bra. I shut my eyes, my nipples tightening when he cups my breast over my bra.

He lowers his hand, and I whimper when his fingers graze over my panties. Benny's face is packed with desire and what appears to be contemplation. So many times, he's made a point to tell me I'd have to beg for his touch, but twice tonight, he's touched me without so much as a please from me.

It scares him he might want me.

That I could be the one to make him beg … to make him weaker than he thinks he is.

I grip a drawer knob when he cups my mound the same way he did my breast. He groans, shifting so his leg is against mine, and I feel the hardening of his erection through his pants. My body begs me to move against him, to thrust toward him, feeling my core against his cock.

Benny drags his lips over my cheek before pressing kisses along my jaw and neck—each one sending a sharper spark through my body.

Such gentle kisses, coming from a dangerous man.

I tighten my grip on the knob to hold myself up when his lips brush my earlobe. He slowly eases a finger under my panties.

"Has anyone touched this pussy, Neomi?" he whisper-hisses. His hand inches closer to my clit, and he presses his thumb on it.

It's not rough, but not soft either.

My head spins so fast that I'm shocked I can form words when I answer, "None of your business.com."

Yes, there's seriously something wrong with me for answering like that.

My words don't stop him from playing with me.

"Everything about you is my business." He separates my thighs farther, using his knee to give him better access, before shoving a finger inside me without warning. "Especially here."

"What about my OB/GYN?" I breathe out. "Are you going to kill him?"

He thrusts another finger inside me, rougher this time, shoving me into the dresser. "Your gynecologist is a woman. Dr. Katherine Merlow."

"Stalking is against the law, you know," I say between pants while holding back the urge to ask him for more when he slows his pace.

I won't give in.

If he stops, he stops.

He'll never hear me plead.

He roughly bites my ear. "I keep an eye on what's mine."

"I'm not yours," I say around a moan.

"Every fucking inch of you is mine, Neomi."

I circle my arm around his neck and dig my nails into the skin beneath his hairline.

His fingers slide in and out of me, his thumb pleasuring my clit. "Now, who has touched you?"

I'm proud of myself for not falling apart, for continuing this game we play, which has now suddenly grown more physical … more intimate.

"Every man in New York City." I peer up at him for his reaction to my words.

His sharp eyes meet mine—so full of animosity, like a predator keeping his eye on his prey.

"I wanted you to have their sloppy seconds," I add.

For that comment, he roughly shoves another finger inside me, causing my feet to practically rise off the floor.

He chuckles. It's not a happy chuckle. It's laced with venom, like the devil he is. "You drive me fucking crazy."

He lowers his head and bites my lip before devouring my mouth. We kiss, our tongues fighting each other.

What's happening proves how fucked up our dynamic is.

We swore we didn't want each other, yet here we are.

He's finger fucking me against a dresser while I talk shit.

An intense rush of pleasure sweeps through my body, puncturing itself into my veins. I jerk my hips forward. The first time is slow, but I quicken my pace within seconds, and he meets me, thrust for thrust.

"God, I can't wait to slide inside you."

And for some reason, those words hit me, as if I were woken up from a dream.

My body hates me when I smack a hand over his between my legs. "Wait."

He pulls away from me, his eyes widening in question.

"I'm not having sex with you, Benny." It's never been so hard to force words out of my mouth.

He thrusts his hips forward and gives my clit another stroke. "You sure about that?"

"Positive." The one word comes out in three stutters.

Neither of us moves for a moment.

"You're so wet for me, Neomi." His voice is full of seduction. He doesn't continue touching me, but he doesn't pull away either. "Us fucking doesn't mean you have to like me. In fact, I think our hate fucking would be better than lovemaking could ever be."

My voice is low and stern when I say, "Benny, stop."

My body aches for him.

My pussy walls are still tightening around his fingers.

I'm so close to falling apart in his arms.

So close to giving him something I've never given anyone.

I have to stay strong.

I quiver when he pulls away, taking his touch with him.

He stares at me, silent and focused, as if wondering if I'll change my mind. I yank the shirt together, hugging it to my body so it covers as much as possible. I can't stop myself from lowering my gaze. I swallow when I notice a wet spot where I was practically dry-humping him. The fact that it's noticeable on black pants proves how much I was worked up.

"I'm going to, uh …" I stop and release a long breath. "Find a guest room now."

I need to get out of here.

I feel like such a fool.

When I go to pass him, Benny captures my elbow to stop me. "You're sleeping in here."

I violently shake my head. "I'm not having sex with you, Benny."

"I wasn't aware we could only share a bed if we were fucking."

"I don't trust you—"

He releases me and pushes me forward, as if my response had burned his skin. "I don't fucking rape women." He stares at me in disgust, as if he's never been sicker of me. "Get in bed. I won't touch you ... not even if you fucking beg for it."

Turning, he stalks toward an open door in the corner of the room, where I assume the bathroom is. He slams the door shut, and I hear something shatter.

Now is the perfect chance for me to dart out of the bedroom, to go somewhere else and lock him out, but I don't. I don't because even though Benny is dangerous, I trust him. The bitterness on his face at my insinuation made it clear he won't touch me against my will.

I take slow steps toward the bed and sit on the edge, bowing my head. I'm not sure how much time passes before I lower myself onto the bed, throw the blanket over me, and lie in the fetal position. The shower turns on in the bathroom.

The light is still on, and my back is to Benny when he returns to the bedroom. I don't bother getting up to brush my teeth or to use the bathroom. All I want to do is stay on my side of the bed and forget this day happened.

Benny's touch still lingers on my skin as he shuts off the light and joins me in bed. When I peek over my shoulder, I find his back is to me.

A wall between us—the truth of our fake union.

His breathing is hard as he lies there.

I shut my eyes and count to ten, hoping it will help me fall asleep.

But all I can think about is Benny.

Even though I'm his wife, I refuse to be a woman he uses.

I want him to worship me.

When my husband touches me, I want him to love me enough that he'd choose to marry me over any other woman, forced or not.

But Benny won't give me that.

So, I won't give him my heart.

CHAPTER FOURTEEN

BENNY

I quietly slide out of bed and walk to the bathroom the following morning. The house needs work, but it'll do for now. My father refused to give me permission to renovate anything. He wants to keep it as authentic as possible.

I might be the only man who didn't get laid on his wedding night.

Not only that but my wife also swore she'd never fuck me.

I'd put my inheritance on the line that she'll change her mind about that. Eventually, my little wife will cave, but, fuck, I must've pissed God off for him to deal me this hand.

But I'm pissed right now. The thought of Neomi insinuating I'd force myself on her had me up all night. I wanted to crawl out of my fucking skin at what she'd implied. I'm not a rapist dirtbag. I've never in my thirty years of living had to force myself on a woman. I love pussy, but I don't steal it.

Neomi faked sleep just as much as I did, but I knew when the exhaustion finally hit her. She scooted in closer. Not enough to cuddle, but the brat was stealing my body heat as if it were hers to take. I almost pushed her away but stopped myself.

I text Luca and tell him to come over before I get dressed. Neomi will most likely be pissed when she wakes up and finds him here, but I don't care. She should consider herself lucky that I don't have a man guarding every room in this house.

"If something happens to her, I'll cut off your arm," I tell Luca when he walks into the house, a tied plastic bag in his hand.

He takes off his black Ray-Bans and holds up the bag. "Leftover wedding cake?"

I shake my head, brush past him, and leave.

I have business to take care of.

And by business, I mean beating the shit out of my new brother-in-law.

Tommaso lives in a two-story brick townhome out of his pay grade. I'm sure Severino pays a chunk of the rent, if not all of it.

I park the SUV in front of the house, take two stairs at a time, and knock on the door.

No answer.

I knock again.

No answer.

I raise my foot, prepared to kick the door in, but stop myself.

I need to keep my cool.

He's my brother-in-law.

Instead, I pound on the door with my fist until it swings open. A half-naked Tommaso stands in the doorway, rubbing his sleepy eyes and yawning.

He's too relaxed for my liking.

So, I punch him in the jaw.

It's all about balance.

He stumbles back, allowing me room to walk through the doorway and into the townhome. My pulse speeds up. His younger sister was nearly kidnapped—which was most likely his fault—and here he is, showing no signs of stress. In fact, it looks like he even had himself a good night's rest.

"What the fuck, Marchetti?" Tommaso shouts, curving his hand over his nose to stop blood from running. "It's too early to deal with your anger issues."

He hasn't seen anger issues.

My reply to his question is another punch to the face.

He's a good pick to take my anger out on.

This time, he stumbles backward into a wall. A picture of a half-naked woman falls, shattering on the tiled floor.

"I want every detail of why my wedding was shot up," I demand, slamming the door shut. "Start speaking."

He topples forward before gaining his balance, and I follow him into the living room. He grabs a black shirt draped over a cushion and holds it to his face before collapsing onto the couch. The coffee table is littered with cocaine, weed, and liquor bottles. Two open condom wrappers are on the floor.

My anger surges.

Just as I'm about to scream at him, I notice a woman wearing only a bra and panties peeking around the corner.

I snatch one of the alcohol bottles and throw it across the room. It hits the wall, and liquor splatters against it.

"Do you know what would've happened had they succeeded in kidnapping her?" I scream, stepping in front of Tommaso and widening my stance. "They would've tortured her, raped her, and then killed her."

This dumb motherfucker needs a reality check, stat.

Tommaso hunches his shoulders forward, and his gaze cuts to the woman.

I do the same and snap my fingers toward her. "Blondie, is your car here?"

She shakes her head, dragging her long nails through her curls.

"I brought her here," Tommaso says, refusing to look at the woman, no doubt embarrassed by what's happening.

"I'll have one of my men drive her home." I jerk my head toward the hall and tug my phone from my blazer pocket. "Go get dressed."

She shoots Tommaso a questioning look, and he waves his hand in agreement. Neither of us wants her to overhear the conversation we're about to have. She timidly nods, her eyes watery, and retreats down the hall. I call Romeo since he lives around the corner and tell him to get his ass here. He says to give him five minutes, and I end the call. Tommaso takes care of his bloody nose while I wait for the woman to leave.

"Wait outside," I instruct when she returns, wearing a tight pink dress and holding her heels. "A guy will pick you up in a black SUV. Make sure his name is Romeo, and he'll take you home."

She purses her lips. "How do I know he isn't, like, a serial killer?"

I glare at Tommaso while answering her, "You were just fucking him. I think you're okay."

She nervously nods and waves to Tommaso, and he tells her he'll call her before she disappears from the townhome. The girl would be dumb to take that call. Tommaso didn't offer to drive her home or call one of his men to do it. He couldn't have cared less whether she made it home safe.

What a joke.

My men can be trusted. I know she's in good hands, but it shows what kind of man Tommaso is. He doesn't care about anyone but himself.

As soon as I hear the door click shut, I crack my knuckles and approach Tommaso. He drags the shirt away from his face and has blood smeared across his cheek, but there isn't much bleeding.

"What did you do, Tommaso?" I stand tall, and my voice turns harsher with each word.

He stares at me, wide-eyed, as if racking his brain for a lie.

I check my watch. "I'd prefer not to spend the day beating

the shit out of you for answers since I'm a busy man, but I'll cancel my entire schedule if that's what it takes."

Tommaso jumps to his feet, as if suddenly growing a pair of balls. "Do you know who you're talking to?" He smacks his hand on his bare chest, as if preparing to fight me. "I'm also the son of a don. Show some respect, Marchetti."

"I show respect to those who deserve it." I smile wickedly. "I'm speaking to the man who put his family in harm's way. The idiot who's putting my family, my wife—who's also *your sister*— at risk."

He scoffs and shakes his head. "You've been married to Neomi for less than twenty-four hours, and suddenly, you're her protector? My sister is more at risk from being married to you than anything."

Bullshit. As soon as we said *I do*, Neomi became one of the most protected women on this planet.

I curl my upper lip and step into his space. "Start talking, Tommaso."

He's quiet for a moment and backtracks a step as if ensuring there's enough distance that I can't right-hook him when he replies. "It's Sammie Karpenko. I owe him money. The day before the wedding, one of his men threatened they'd make an example out of my family if I didn't pay up."

Sammie Karpenko is the largest loan shark in the city. He's known to loan large sums of cash and charge outrageous interest. He's also vicious if you don't repay him.

"Easy fix," I say. "Pay him back."

His face turns grim. "My debt is over a million dollars."

"Fuck," I hiss under my breath, holding myself back from punching him again. "How did you get yourself in debt for a million dollars?"

"Gambling." He does a sweeping gesture toward the coffee table. "Drugs ... sex."

What a fucking idiot.

"It should be easy for you to get pussy without having to pay for it, Tommaso," I say in annoyance. "From now on, find some poor girl who is stupid enough to fuck you. And make a pit stop at rehab while you're at it."

"I tried to stop, but it's addictive." His arms fall slack at his sides. "I messed up, Benny. You don't think I know that?"

Anyone else would probably feel sorry for him.

But I don't.

I don't have one bit of sympathy toward him.

I fix my glare on him. "You or your father needs to pay him every cent you owe—today."

"My father doesn't know." He shuffles his feet. "And it's not like we have a million dollars just lying around."

"You'd better find it then."

"I've tried, trust me."

"Try harder. If you continue to endanger my wife, I'll hand you over to Sammie myself."

"Do that, and you'll have a war with my father." Tommaso straightens his stance, as if his words will scare me.

"I don't mind starting a war over my wife." I cock my head to the side and deliver an evil smirk. "I'm sure you heard what my father did to the man who threatened his." I form a fake gun with my hand and imitate shooting myself in the head.

Tommaso recoils at my response.

"Get Sammie paid, Tommaso. Or there will be hell to pay."

I call my father and tell him what Tommaso told me after leaving.

"I'm surprised Sammie allowed him to rack up that much debt," my father says. "We need to tell Severino. He's the only one who can help his son."

"I'd like to put a bullet in the motherfucker's head for being that stupid," I grind out. "I don't want him near Neomi. Who knows who else he's pissed off?"

If you're in trouble with one loan shark, you owe others.

Always.

Men like Tommaso accumulate anywhere they can.

"I don't think Severino has a million dollars to hand over," I add, hitting my turn signal and cutting a right.

My father sighs. "I'm sure Tommaso has already gone to him with past debts and drained as much cash as he could from his father. Watch over your wife; if all else fails, we might need to step in."

"I'm not about to pay a million dollars for a man who will only continue to put himself in more debt."

"I know." He's quiet for a moment while the two of us brainstorm. "I'll see if I can talk with Sammie."

"No," I rush out. "Don't get yourself involved."

"It seems we're already involved. They attempted to kidnap your wife."

I scrub a hand over my face. "Thanks for the reminder." It makes me want to turn the car around, return to Tommaso's, and beat him senseless.

I swore I didn't give a fuck about Neomi, but now, all I want to do is protect her. And I'll bring hell onto this earth if I have to while doing it.

CHAPTER FIFTEEN

NEOMI

The bed is Benny-less when I wake up, but it's not like I expected a passionate morning with my new husband. His absence is a relief and allows me time to process the changes in my life.

I got married.

Was almost kidnapped.

I want answers as much as Benny does.

The sheets smell like Benny. I rise and stretch my arms. My toes sink into the Persian rug when I step out of bed, wander across the room, and open the curtains. Sunlight spills into the room, and the house is quiet.

I smile when I open the closet and find my clothing hanging inside. I snag a sweater and a pair of leggings and get dressed. Then, I head downstairs to find Luca eating at the kitchen table.

His attention flicks to me, and he drops his fork. "Oh, hey, Neomi."

I smile before pointing at the table. "Are you eating my wedding cake for breakfast?"

He nods. "Your mom gave me a plate last night. Good choice on the lemon curd. It's my favorite."

Luca reminds me of a not-so-intense Benny. He shares the same Marchetti genes as Benny, but Luca's aren't as prominent.

You know not to mess with Luca, but he isn't as terrifying as my husband. Luca has more humor laced into his personality, but that tends to always be the case. He doesn't have as much expectation held over him. If you're next in line to take over the family, you don't get a life outside that. Your days are consumed with being educated on maintaining this life and caring for your family.

There's no having fun, like your cousins and friends.

It's something Tommaso has always struggled with.

It's also why my brother isn't cut out for the responsibilities my father plans to give him someday.

I stroll into the kitchen, pull out a chair, and sit across from him. "Why are you here?"

Luca scratches his clean-shaven cheek. "I'm your—"

I cut him off, "Don't you dare say it."

"Your bodyguard." He now seems amused as he shoves a bite of cake into his mouth.

"Call yourself that again, and I'll cut out your tongue."

"Fine. I'll call myself your babysitter then."

"Do that, and I'll cut off your entire head."

He leans back and blows out a breath. "Why do I always get stuck with the crazy ones?"

"Hey, you chose to work for crazy. Who'd you think they'd marry?"

"I was *born into* crazy," he corrects. "Cristian is my uncle, so I had no other career options."

I frown, hating that for him. "I was also born into crazy."

This is the first conversation I've shared with Luca—other than the simple hellos when we randomly crossed paths. His mother, Helena, who's also Cristian's sister, sweetly told me I looked beautiful four times at my engagement party.

I've also heard Luca's name a good fifty times since the engagement party. He seems to be Isabella's new favorite topic of discussion. Not that I blame her. He has the Marchetti charm—dark hair, sun-kissed skin tone, and a bloodline bleeding with power and authority.

"Sooo … where's my husband?" I reach forward, snatch a chunk of his cake from his plate, and drop it into my mouth.

"No idea."

I furrow my brow. "Where'd he go, Luca?"

"He just said he'd be back." He shrugs. "That's it."

"Can you drive me to my parents'? I need to get my car to run a few errands."

He shakes his head. "I was instructed to keep you here."

Of course, he was.

I'm surprised Benny didn't have bars installed on the windows while I was sleeping.

As if on instinct, I reach into my pocket for my phone but realize I didn't grab it before we left the mansion last night.

I stand when my stomach growls, walk to the fridge, and open it. All that's inside are three lonely bottles of water, one of them half full. No wonder Luca's breakfast of choice was leftover wedding cake. I grab a water and shut the fridge.

"There's no food here," I tell Luca, as if it were a problem he'd care about.

"The home was pretty much vacant until a few days ago," Luca replies. "Make a list, and I'll ask my mom to bring groceries over."

"We can go to the grocery store."

"Let me text Benny and see if that's okay."

I throw my head back. "And now, I have to ask permission to shop."

Luca pauses mid-texting on his phone. "Neomi, you grew up in this life. You know it's not always like this. Everyone is on high alert right now. What happened at your wedding was serious."

My shoulders slump. "I know."

"We were up all night, worried our families would be the

next target. My mother even has escorts." He glances at the doorway, as if verifying Benny isn't here. "Benny's biggest fear is losing someone close to him. Losing his mom was hard, and when shit like this happens, it drags that memory back up. Take it easy on him." He offers me a kind smile. "Don't fault him for keeping you safe."

Benny declined Luca's request for us to go grocery shopping.

He told him *he'd* come home and drive me.

When Benny returned to the house, he graced us with bloody knuckles and an attitude problem. When I questioned him, he blew off answering me and said we'd talk about it later. Then, when I mentioned forgetting my phone at the mansion, he declared that was also a *later* situation.

So, I'm living in the Stone Age until then—having to manually write down my grocery list on a pad of paper and not scroll Instagram while pretending the silence between my husband and me isn't uncomfortable in the car.

Benny has hardly spoken to me. He's on edge—no doubt from our conversation last night. I insinuated he was a man capable of taking a woman against her will. I shouldn't have said it, but I've heard too many stories of women in our lifestyle being raped.

But I understand how such a serious accusation could hurt someone.

Rape is the only crime committed for selfish purposes—no matter who you are or the circumstances.

People can kill in self-defense.

Steal for survival—food and clothes to protect them from the cold.

But there is never an exception for rape. It's purely selfish.

I decide the best way to start my apology is to make a nice meal.

Benny whips into the parking lot of Guzzi's Meat Corner, the local market. Painted on the window in neon-pink lettering are this month's specials.

Benny rests his hand on the small of my back as we walk into the market.

"There're the newlyweds!" Louisa calls out, moving around the register and skipping toward us.

She wraps me into a quick, tight hug and gently smiles at Benny after pulling away.

Louisa and her husband, Ralph, own the market.

"You are glowing." Her wrinkles show as she jumps in excitement and stops a random customer. "Isn't this gorgeous newlywed just a-glowing?"

The woman stares at me and slowly forces herself to nod. Neither Benny nor I are *a-glowing*.

"I'll let you two get to your shopping." Louisa shoos us away. "Ralph has great specials in the back. Make sure you stop by and say hi!"

I offer her a similar smile she gives to us while Benny grabs a cart and stares at me for our next move.

"Have you ever gone grocery shopping?" I ask, heading toward the produce.

Benny pushes the cart. "No."

"Never?"

"Never. I can arrange it so you don't have to either."

I shake my head. "I enjoy grocery shopping."

As soon as we could walk, we helped my mother in the kitchen. She passed down her love of creating delicious dishes to my sisters and me. Okay, me and Bria. Isabella is the queen of burn town.

I select my products and gather essentials. Benny doesn't mutter a word or grab anything for himself until we reach the cereal aisle. While I snatch Cheerios, he tosses a box of Lucky Charms into the cart.

I raise a brow. "Lucky Charms?"

"What?" He smirks, a hint of his animosity chipping away. "They're magically delicious."

This seems so … domesticated.

Not what I expected from him.

I check items off our list and play with the pen in my mouth as we walk to the meat counter. Ralph makes small talk while cutting our order. I answer most of the questions. Benny is like his father. He doesn't speak much in public. I don't miss the curious glances from other customers. Some even creep along our aisles just to be nosy, pretending to be interested in an item before placing it back onto the shelf. No wonder Benny doesn't like grocery shopping.

"You ready to go?" I ask, glancing back at him after checking the last item off my list.

He nods.

"Why aren't you two lovebirds on a honeymoon?" Lorna, the clerk at the register, asks when she begins scanning our items.

I pause.

I never considered a honeymoon, nor was one mentioned by Benny or my family. They probably knew it was for the better.

My only response is a warm smile.

It's not until Lorna rattles off the total that I realize I don't have a purse. Benny immediately slides into my space and hands her cash.

"Add the change to the donation box," he says.

I have money. Not as much as Benny, but sometimes, I'll fill in at my father's alterations shop that one of his men runs for him. The pay is decent, but my father doesn't care much about the cash flow it brings in. It's an easy business to launder money through and pay all of us.

The teenage boy bagging our groceries stares at Benny in awe and drops a few items on the floor. I hold back the urge to tell him not to idolize this life.

Benny wheels the cart out and doesn't allow me to help load the bags into the back of the SUV.

"I can pay you back for the groceries," I tell him when we're in the car. "I would've offered, but I don't have my purse."

Benny reverses out of the parking spot. "You'll never pay for our groceries."

I shake my head. "I make my own money, Benny."

"Cool. Buy yourself something nice with it then."

"That's not what I meant, *Benito*." I don't know what motivates me to randomly call him by his full name.

"Oh, she's pulling out the full name now." He smirks. "Not going to lie. I kind of like you calling me Benito."

I throw my head back. "I just wanted to shop in peace."

He brakes at a stoplight and reaches over to squeeze my knee, and his voice turns rough when he says, "Peace doesn't belong in my world, Neomi."

We make a quick pit stop at the mansion.

The only people there are employees and guards. I stop Benny from coming inside with me, dash upstairs, and grab my phone and purse. We need to get our groceries home.

When I'm back in the car and Benny drives off, I unlock my phone to find endless notifications.

Texts.

Missed calls.

Tagged wedding pictures, which irks me. I told my parents I wanted a strict no-photos policy. Not that I can complain because when I click on the notifications, I realize most of the photos are from my mother's profile.

I check my texts next.

> Bria: I need all the details from last night.

I ignore hers and move on to the next.

> Isabella: How many times did you do the dirty? Bria and I made a bet. Tell me now, and I'll split half my winnings with you.

I roll my eyes and open my mother's.

> Mom: Good morning, my beautiful newlywed daughter! Please call me when you get a moment. Your father and I love you.

And lastly, I hit my brother's name.

> Tommaso: Your maniac husband barged into my house this morning and went nuts. Reel him in!

I glare at Benny. "Did you go to my brother's this morning?"
"Yes."
I glance at his knuckles. "Did you hurt him?"
"Yes." He holds up a finger to prevent me from speaking and to allow him to explain himself. "He deserved it, and he's lucky I didn't do more than punch him a few times."
"You *punched* him?" I can only imagine how Tommaso reacted to that.
Benny works his jaw. "Did you know your brother owes Sammie Karpenko over a million dollars?"
I drop my phone onto my lap. "What?"
"I take it that's a no."
"Why … why would he go to Sammie for money?"
Sammie and his crew are dangerous. My father once said anyone who makes a deal with Karpenko is an idiot with a death wish. He charges astronomical interest and isn't understanding about late payments.
"Your brother has a gambling addiction … among other vices."
I cringe. Any appetite I had is gone. Tommaso has always indulged in the perks of this world—the good and the bad. I

once overheard my mother promising my father he'd grow out of it, but he hasn't. I'm scared he never will.

No wonder Tommaso was adamant I marry Benny when we were in my father's office. He no doubt sees Benny as an opportunity to escape his mess. The Marchettis are the most feared in this city … and extremely wealthy.

I pretend to pick at my French manicure. "Do you think Sammie sent his men to our wedding for Tommaso's debt?"

"It wasn't someone in a rival family, so they're my best guess."

"What's your plan to stop them?"

"Tommaso will pay them back. It's that simple."

"My brother doesn't have money like that."

"He'd better find it. Ask your father. Sell something. I don't care how he does it, so long as he does."

"What if he doesn't?" My throat turns sore.

"I'll make it clear to Sammie he doesn't touch you."

"And Tommaso?"

"I'm not married to Tommaso."

I don't reply to Tommaso's text.

I have nothing nice to say.

A bottle of Dom Pérignon with a Post-it attached is on the kitchen counter when we return from the grocery store.

> To the newlyweds!
> I'm sorry your reception didn't go as planned.
> Drink this and enjoy your night!
> Love,
> Cristian and Natalia

Thank you, Natalia. No way Cristian would ever use an exclamation mark.

"Dom, nice," Benny says, picking up the bottle and playing with it in his hand.

He sets the bottle down, helps me unload the groceries, and then retreats to his office after I shoo him out of the kitchen. I take a quick bathroom break and peek at Benny in the office before returning to the kitchen. The office is on the main floor. It's small and cramped. Most of the room is occupied by the brick fireplace and metal desk, providing just enough space for Benny's MacBook and water. I'm surprised he managed to squeeze the chair behind it.

Benny is here because of me and what happened last night. Otherwise, I have no doubt he'd be in his fancy office at the club instead.

When I return to the kitchen, I open all the drawers and cabinets, taking a quick inventory of what we have.

Like the rest of our temporary home, it's outdated.

But, hey, a kitchen is a kitchen. I'll make do.

I've never worked with an oven so old. I look up at the ceiling and send God a silent prayer I don't burn down Benny's mother's childhood home.

Would that be grounds for a divorce?

As the oven heats, I slip my AirPods into my ears, turn on my favorite playlist, and start cooking. I sway my hips to the beat of Beyoncé and move around the kitchen. I'm in my zone, forgetting where I am and belting out song lyrics while dropping the cooked chicken onto a plate.

I turn, the plate of chicken in my hand, and nearly drop it when I catch Benny standing in the doorway, watching me.

"How …" I place the plate on the Formica countertop and pluck out an AirPod. "How long have you been standing there?"

Benny leans his shoulder against the doorframe, and his lips twitch in amusement. "Long enough to confirm your dancing is incredibly sexy." His gaze drifts down my body—from my messy hair to my sweater that falls loosely off my shoulder, black leggings, and bare feet.

I gulp, my cheeks burning, and do the same to Benny.

He has his sleeves rolled to his elbows, and the top three buttons on his shirt are undone. That seems to be his thing. The only times I've seen him with his sleeves unrolled was at our engagement party and wedding, when a blazer covered them. His dark hair is messy, as if he was stressed and spent his time running his fingers through it while he worked.

Benny pushes off the wall and tucks his MacBook underneath his arm. I fix my gaze on him, biting my lip when he enters the kitchen instead of returning to his office.

"Uh … what are you doing?" I ask when he drops the MacBook onto the kitchen table and sits.

"Working." He opens the MacBook.

"Why aren't you working in your office?"

I need to finish cooking, and he's a major distraction.

"I'd rather work in here."

"*Why?*" I stress.

He scrubs a hand over his scruffy jaw and makes a show of resting his gaze on me. "Initially, I came here to keep you company while you cooked." He runs his tongue over his straight white teeth. "And after the free show I just got, I'm definitely staying."

Shivers zip up my spine.

Benny stares at me like he wants to eat me alive.

I'm sure the look I'm sending him in return is similar.

I reach down and dig my nails into my leggings.

Living with my husband is becoming dangerous.

The more time we spend together, the more these walls of mine will come down. Walls I thought I'd plastered, nailed, and bonded together.

"Do you know how to cook?" I blurt out, in need of a subject change.

It takes him a moment to register my question since his mind was elsewhere. He gives me an *are you serious* expression.

I park my hands on my hips and try to sound like my mother. "If you want to be in the kitchen, you have to help." I give him a serious look. "It's a rule." When the last word leaves my mouth, I cringe. That was actually a bit too similar to my mother for my liking.

But it's one of the tricks she used with my father and Tommaso. They'd attempt to linger around the kitchen when we cooked, their intent more to steal food before it was ready, so that was her way of kicking them out.

Benny motions toward the stove. "It appears you have it covered."

I hold up two fingers. "Two options, Benito."

A smile hits his lips at my use of his full name.

"One: you help me cook." I lower a finger. "Two: you return to your office." I drop the second finger.

"Two minutes ago, you didn't want me in here. Now, you want my assistance?"

"Go back to your office. I'll deliver your dinner when I'm finished." I grab a knife and start dicing the chicken.

"Deliver my dinner?" Benny taps his knuckles against the table before shutting his MacBook. "Not happening, *wife*. We eat dinner here *together*. Our first meal as newlyweds."

I tense, waiting for his next move, when he stands.

He pushes his chair in and rubs his hands together while strolling toward me. "Word of caution, Neomi. I'd assign me the easiest job here because I'm bound to fuck something up. Cooking isn't my strong suit."

Shit.

Apparently, Benny isn't as easy to manipulate as my father and brother.

I don't want Benny's help. Someone who doesn't know how to cook is worse than having no help.

There also isn't much more to do.

I glance around the kitchen, taking in all the ingredients, and point toward the basil leaves with my knife. "Wash those under cold water and then tear them."

It's an easy task my mother had me do at three years old.

But I also hope it scares him off.

Benny has others service him while he runs the hottest club in New York and bullies those he doesn't like. Helping his *unwanted* wife in the kitchen and ripping basil don't fit into that persona.

I pause my cutting and wait for him to leave the kitchen.

My plan backfires when he takes a handful of the basil and carries it to the sink, dropping a few in the process. The man can hit a running target but not carry a few leaves across a room.

I dump the chicken into a pan with pasta noodles, tomatoes, and chicken broth. He finishes rinsing the leaves and drops them into a pile on the counter beside me. I shiver when he stands behind me and peers over my shoulder.

"Listen," he says, as if suddenly having an issue with our meal. "We can order delivery."

I wince. "Excuse me? Dinner is about finished. Why would we order in?"

"Those noodles … they're not cooked." He says the words slowly, as if it were something I forgot to do and he feels sorry for me.

I roll my eyes. "I'm well aware."

"Who the fuck eats uncooked pasta?" He digs his chin into my shoulder. "I can hire a chef. It's no biggie."

"You don't have to precook the pasta in this recipe." I glare back at him. "Now, complete your task and let me do my work."

He pulls away, stands beside me, and starts tearing the basil leaves.

I realize giving Benny a tearing job was a mistake.

The sound of him tearing echoes through the kitchen. He rips them apart as if they were the limbs of a man who owed him money with no intention to pay him back. I shudder, my stomach dropping, and I hate that my mind immediately goes to Tommaso. That will happen if he doesn't pay his debt to Sammie.

I cover the pasta and chicken with minced garlic and mozzarella, and I wiggle my fingers in a *give me* gesture toward Benny. He hands over the basil, and I add it to the top.

I cover the pasta bake with foil, shove it into the oven, set a timer on my phone, and start cleaning my mess. There isn't a dishwasher, so the dishes have to be washed by hand.

It might be the suckiest thing about old, unrenovated homes.

The appliances—or lack thereof—aren't updated.

Give me a home with history but add a dishwasher and a new stove.

I open a drawer, snag a dish towel, and flatten it on the counter next to the sink. While the water is running, I roll up my sleeves, and as soon as the sink is full, I start washing dishes. After I clean a bowl, I place it on the towel.

I furrow a brow when Benny opens a drawer, removes a towel, and dries the bowl. It takes me a moment to wrap my mind around what he did as he places it into a cabinet.

The urge to tell him he doesn't need to help is on the tip of my tongue, but I stop myself. My mother would be horrified if her husband helped in the kitchen, but I don't mind. If Benny stays in the kitchen, he might as well make himself useful.

"Thank you," I say, placing another dish on the towel.

He dries it.

We keep doing that, like a Benny and Neomi dishwashing assembly line.

We appear so domesticated.

We don't speak much, but it's not an awkward silence.

It's a comfortable one.

That silence stops when a loud whack reverberates through the kitchen. I jump at the sudden sting on my ass and drop my towel. I lower my wet hand to my ass, getting my sweater wet, as if to confirm that's where the pain is coming from.

"Did you …" I wipe my face with my arm and glower at him. "Did you just smack my ass?" It's a struggle to keep my voice serious.

Benny grins and twirls the towel, as if preparing to do it again.

I'm thankful there's at least a pull-out faucet. I tug it out and point the sprayer toward him. "Do that, and you'll get a shower before dinner."

"You get me wet, I'll get you wet right back." A *pleased with himself* smirk takes over his entire face. "Although, mine won't involve water, and it'll be a bit more hands-on."

Oh-my-fucking-God.

I thought my face was warm when he complimented my dancing.

This is a new side of Benny.

A playful side.

A side that doesn't scream, *I have no personality but Mafia psychopath.*

Publicly, he plays that role as if he had been born for it.

Okay, technically, he was.

I'm beginning to realize Benny isn't as one-dimensional as I thought.

And, well, I kind of like it.

Ugh, okay. I love it.

I return the faucet to its place and spin around to face him. "I'm definitely getting you back for your little ass-slapping— when you least expect it." Unable to stop myself, I make a spanking gesture … which I'm later mortified by.

His face remains smug, and he tilts his head to the side. "I have to say, spanking has never been one of my kinks." He strokes his chin. "But with you, I'm willing to try everything once."

I don't believe that.

Benny will try what *he* wants once.

I snort. "You'd *so* not let me spank you."

"You're right." He relaxes against the counter, crossing his arms and ankles. "I'll stick to being the one who does the spanking."

"You sure aren't spanking me, so your spanking days are over." I scrunch up my face at the thought that, at one point, he had women he spanked.

"We'll see about that." He straightens himself and erases the distance between us. "Remember how I said I couldn't wait to hear you beg for my cock—"

I open my mouth to tell him to fuck right off with that talk again, but he presses his finger against it.

His voice turns deep and husky. "I've added something higher on the list."

My body trembles. "Me not begging?"

"Me bending you over my knee, smacking that ass of yours, and absolutely loving it."

He adds another finger to my mouth and inserts them between my lips.

Enter the Benny who makes me want to forget the promise I made to myself and straddle him on this floor.

I never thought I'd be turned on by someone's fingers inside my mouth.

Remember, no sex with Benny.

Remember, he's bad news.

He'll never love you.

Those reminders babble through my thoughts, but I can't seem to reach them now—can't seem to pull away from Benny's trance. My breathing seems to be stuck, trapped behind Benny's fingers, and it becomes a bigger struggle when he rams them down my throat, causing me to choke.

He removes them just as fast as he put them there.

"We'll need to work on your gag reflex," he comments, as if he were an employer giving me a yearly review. "So, I can fill your pretty little mouth with my dick and watch you choke on it."

Lust, the need for this man, pumps through me.

Everything he does seems so erotic.

Yet effortless at the same time.

I draw in the breaths I was missing while staring at Benny.

He stares back while exhaling controlled breaths.

The room seems smaller and the air thicker while we stare each other down.

Benny's eyes are a storm that drags me in.

I inch closer to him, as if being dragged with no control of myself.

Then, the timer goes off.

Saving me from being reckless and giving myself to him.

"This is actually pretty good," Benny says, directing his fork toward the pasta bake on his plate before shoving another bite into his mouth.

"*Actually?*" I scrunch up my face. "Did you think it'd not be good?"

Thankfully, my phone's timer pulled me out of my Benny haze earlier, and I rushed to the oven to take the pan out. Then, I attempted to bail on dinner, trying three different excuses— sudden headache, loss of appetite, and need to wash my hair.

None of them worked.

Instead, Benny walked me to a chair, shoved me into it, and told me to keep my ass there. I pouted but did as I had been told while he strolled across the kitchen. He popped open the bottle of Dom, pulled two antique champagne flutes from the cabinet —from their design, my guess was that they were his grandparents' wedding flutes—and poured us each a bubbly glass.

He handed me one before dumping pasta onto two plates and delivering mine to me, as if he were a server.

"The uncooked pasta scared me for a minute," he replies.

"The *I struggle with tearing leaves* scared me for a minute." I take a sip of champagne and shoot him a pointed look.

He leans back in his chair and motions toward me with his glass. "You know, I didn't think I'd like your smart little mouth, but I have to say, it's growing on me."

His words cause me to massage my throat, as if I could still feel him shoving his fingers down it.

I rest my arms on the arms of the chair. "Do I get something for that?"

"What do you want?"

I jerk my head toward the sink. "I'll start with a dishwasher."

He shakes his head. "My father would have my ass if I made one renovation to this place. He swore to my mother that he'd never change it."

"That's sweet of your father."

He scoffs. "My father is far from sweet."

"For him to keep a promise like that to your mother is sweet—Mafia king or not." The table grows quiet for a moment, and I lower my voice before saying, "I'm truly sorry about your mother, Benny."

A grave expression flashes across his face.

Uh-oh. I said the wrong thing.

Any playfulness he had dissolves.

I attended Benita Marchetti's funeral with my parents. It was before our marriage contract was created. I sat in the back of the cathedral and listened to the priest, and my heart hurt for Benny and Gigi. I told my mother I loved her every hour of the day after we left the funeral.

Benny had done his best to hide the pain as he went to the podium and spoke about how great of a woman his mother was. He told two stories about her loyalty and love without shedding one tear.

Me, on the other hand? I had cried as if I'd known her personally.

It was tragic. Devastating. Her death brought us together even though we didn't know it yet.

I gulp down my champagne and pucker my lips. I'm more of a mimosa gal.

Benny grabs his glass and moves it in circles, watching the liquid splash, but doesn't take a drink. "My mother would've liked you."

His voice is somber.

His words shocking.

My heart pounds at the compliment.

That he'd say such a thing to me.

I rack my brain for the perfect response, but can't find one.

"I don't know," I say, my tone as low as his. "I'm not exactly a traditional Mafia wife."

"My mother asked my father not to allow Gigi to become a traditional Mafia wife." He returns his glass to the table and locks eyes with me. "She didn't want obedience when it came to love. If my mother were alive today, she'd approve of you."

Wow.

Out of all the versions of Benny I've experienced, this is my favorite.

The one where my husband cuts open a piece of his soul for me.

This is how I imagined marriage would be.

Secrets unfolding.

Confessions.

Words only shared between the two of us.

Benny clears his throat and shakes his head, as if wanting to erase every emotion he's shown. "You'd better eat. We don't want our food getting cold."

That version of Benny burns out.

A quick commercial break, and he slips his mask back on.

"Benny"—there's a twinge of nervousness in my tone—"can you make me a promise?"

He finishes chewing his bite before replying, "It depends on what it is."

"Promise me you won't hurt my brother." I sigh, and my voice turns almost pleading. "And please help him get out of his mess."

He stays quiet.

I clutch my fork. "Benny."

"If he puts you in harm's way, I make no promises, Neomi."

I look away from him.

"Don't you dare get angry with me for ensuring you're protected!" He rests his elbows on the table. "You are my priority. Not your brother. *You.*"

I swallow. "You could've at least lied."

"I'm not a liar."

"All men lie."

He clenches his jaw. "The only time I won't be one hundred percent honest with you is if the truth will hurt or put you in trouble."

My stomach tightens, and all my appetite is gone as I bring up another subject that's consumed my thoughts. "Or if that truth is you sticking your dick inside another woman."

Why not throw it all on the table?

"No, I'll be honest about that too." He wipes his mouth with a napkin.

"Does that mean you'll cheat on me?"

"What is our relationship, Neomi?" He leans in closer—so close that our mouths are nearly touching. "Do you want to fuck me like you're my wife … or do you want me to fuck someone else because you only want to be my wife on paper?"

"I don't know." Goose bumps travel up my arms, and my sweater slips farther off my shoulder. "I'm still trying to figure that out."

"Once you have your answer, let me know." He stands from the table and drops his napkin onto his hardly eaten food. "But we need to work out the dynamics of this relationship because I'm not a man who plays games."

"What do *you* want our relationship to be, Benny?"

"We're stuck in this together, Neomi." He throws his arms out and raises his voice. "You asked what kind of relationship I want. I want a real one. A *real* wife who doesn't question every single one of my intentions. Divorce isn't an option. We can either make the best of it or we can drive each other fucking insane. You decide and let me know."

He shakes his head, curses, and leaves the room.

CHAPTER SIXTEEN

BENNY

I take a swig of Jack Daniel's straight from the bottle, and then rest it against my forehead. I found the dusty, nearly empty bottle shoved in the bottom desk drawer.

Thanks, Grandfather.

The whiskey is most likely a few decades old and tastes like it, but I hoped it would take the edge off.

I've almost dragged my ass out of this chair six times to say fuck it and talk with Neomi, but I stop myself every time.

It's an unfortunate situation we're in.

But we're in it—locked with the key thrown away.

There are no divorce papers.

Death is the only method of leaving this marriage.

I've watched arranged marriages thrive while seeing others turn into nightmares. I dreaded this marriage from the beginning, but my chest tightens at the thought of it being a nightmare. I'd rather give a little than live with a wife who despises me ... or who I despise.

I'll take thriving for three hundred, please.

Hell, I'll even take half thriving at this point.

But if your wife doesn't trust you, you'll never have a healthy marriage.

I understand her reasoning. I haven't made the best decisions, but neither has she. Her concerns are valid and seem
natural for women in this world.

Natalia came to me with reservations about my father and if
he'd be faithful.

My father might be a wicked man.

But he's a damn good husband.

That's how I want to be.

Wicked in the streets and loyal in the sheets.

I refuse to be a husband to a woman who won't be my wife
though.

It's either all or nothing.

I look away from my computer when a knock comes on the
half-shut office door. Neomi appears in the doorway, wearing a
black lace nightie.

My back instantly straightens, and I pull at my shirt collar.

This is what I want from her.

My wife stepping into my office, wearing lingerie.

The nightie pushes her ample breasts up, and I want to run
my tongue between her cleavage. It's nearly see-through, so hints
of her nipples show through the thin fabric.

God, I want to suck on them too.

The nightie—or whatever the fuck its technical name is—
flares at the waist and splits at the top of her thigh. I suck in a
breath, and she doesn't say a word, allowing me to appreciate
every inch of her perfect body.

My cock aches to peel the remainder of the fabric off her
body to see all of her. I roll out my chair, spread my legs wide,
and wait for her to explain the purpose of her visit.

She nervously runs her hand down her nightie, and I smile
at the sight of the wedding ring on her finger. "I want you to set
up marriages for my sisters, each with a Marchetti."

"Excuse me?" I reach forward and slam my MacBook shut.

She shoves a strand of wet hair falling from the clip holding the rest of it up behind her ear. The strand gets caught in her hoop earring, but she ignores it.

"You've made it clear I have the protection of the Marchetti family because I'm married to you."

"Correct." I fall back in the uncomfortable chair, and an old spring digs into my back.

"I want my sisters to have that protection."

So, this is my little wife's manipulative plan.

Come in here, looking mouthwatering, to ask me to give two of my men the same fate as me?

Right now, a Cavallaro is the last thing I want to stick one of my men with. They're proving to be quite the headache.

I exhale a long breath and rub my forehead. "I can't force a family member to marry either of your sisters."

She balks. "We were forced to marry."

"Our marriage was different."

"How?" she cries out.

"It was a contract between families. Not to mention, my father's only other available son has yet to be born."

I also doubt Natalia would be comfortable with promising him to a woman over two decades older. She already hates the logic of arranged marriages.

Neomi steps farther into the room. "Is Luca married?"

"No," I snap. "Nor does he want to be."

Luca has made it clear he dreads the day he'll have to tie the knot.

She wrings her hands together. "Can we fix that?"

"Luca isn't marrying one of your sisters." My tone is sharp, like my father's when he makes a final decision.

She inches closer. "Is he promised to someone?"

"Not either of your sisters." I open a drawer and pretend to rifle through its contents.

"I want to protect my sisters, Benny." She sits in the rickety wooden chair in the corner of the room. "Please give me that."

"There's nothing I can do, Neomi." I slam the drawer shut.

"End of discussion. If that's all you came here for, there's the door."

My headache is intensifying.

As soon as she leaves this room, I'm calling Luca—not to inform him to start searching for groomsmen, but to tell him to get his ass here so I can leave. I need a break from this infuriating woman.

Neomi is quiet as she stands, and I grab my phone, waiting for her to exit. Instead of walking toward the doorway, she rounds the desk toward me. When she unclips her hair from the back, it falls onto her shoulders, and water droplets hit the wood floor.

My cock stirs when she reaches me. Turning, I wheel my chair out farther, and it smacks against the wall. Neomi steps between my legs, as if I'd invited her.

Not that I'd kick her out though.

The scent of her coconut shampoo envelops me. Raising my hands, I clasp them around her waist, holding her in place. Her breathing quickens, goose bumps crawling up her skin as a reminder of the trouble she's starting.

She clutches my shoulders. "Please, Benny."

A gasp leaves her when I pick her up, settle her onto the desk, and switch positions. Now, I'm standing between her open legs. Half her ass is hanging off the edge of the desk. I lick my lips when I look down to see her nightie pushed up her thighs, showing off her black lace panties that barely cover anything.

My little wife wandered down here to seduce me.

It's time for a little payback.

What a stupid, stupid woman to think she can pull my strings.

"I don't accept pussy as payment for a contract." I capture her chin, push it up, and force her eyes to meet mine.

She squeezes her eyes shut. "What will you accept then?" She cringes harder with each word escaping her plump lips.

My thumb brushes along her bottom lip. "What happened?"

Her eyes shoot open. "What?"

"You came down here, offering your pussy on a platter, out of nowhere." I lightly slap her cheek a few times. "But I'm not like other men, Neomi. I'm not thirsty enough to sign away people's lives to get a taste of your sweet pussy."

I lower my hand from her cheek to her jaw, caressing it before shoving my hand down. I'm rough as I clutch her throat.

She glares at me, but doesn't attempt to break free.

I'm not choking her.

Asphyxia is only my kink when I'm murdering someone.

Not in the bedroom.

"Now"—I squeeze her neck—"be a good little wife and answer me."

She narrows her eyes at me and licks her lower lip.

I press my thumb into her windpipe, applying more pressure, and her body jerks. Her knees buckle, rising from the desk. I use my free hand to capture her leg and wrap it around my waist.

"I'm still waiting for an answer," I taunt, squeezing her neck again.

I don't play games.

I don't get used.

I'm not easily manipulated.

I don't care if it comes from a breathtakingly gorgeous woman who most likely has the best pussy I'll *hopefully* get to taste.

She clasps her clammy hand over mine on her neck, swallowing a few times, and I loosen my hold.

"My mother called with bad news," she rasps, and she removes her hand from mine.

"And?" I keep my hand on her neck.

"Riccardo"—she exhales a long breath—"Tommaso's right-hand man, was murdered tonight. Shot in his house. Execution-style."

She attempts to turn her head away from me to hide her emotions, but I don't allow it.

"Ah." I pull my hand away from her throat and slip it between her legs. "So, you thought offering this pretty pussy to me would make me play knight in shining armor to your family?"

My loss of hold on her neck allows her to turn her head away from me this time.

"Don't look away from me." I raise my free hand to clasp a chunk of her hair in my palm and force her to face me. "You came in here, ready to give me this"—I run a finger over her panties, right over her clit—"if need be. Should I sample it first? See if it's worth me possibly considering your request?"

Her knees lock up, and she pushes at my hand. "Forget it, Benny."

When she tries to move out of my grasp, I tsk, press a hand to her chest, and push her flat on her back.

"I'd rather not forget it." I return a hand to her panties, scraping my fingers over the thin fabric, and she shudders. "In fact, I don't know if I'll ever forget the sight of you laid out for me like this."

I snatch a rusted pair of scissors from the drawer I opened earlier and don't bother being gentle as I cut through her panties.

"What the—" she starts, but I grab what remnants of the panties I can and shove them into her mouth, stopping her from speaking.

My mouth salivates at how bad I want her pussy.

How bad I want every inch of this woman.

I run a finger over her slit, playing with her juices. "Now, I won't marry one of my men to either of your sisters. I want to make that clear right now."

She shudders at my touch and ever so slightly grinds her hips forward.

Ah, my little wife wants to feel the friction of my cock against her.

She likes to play games, but I'm much better at them.

"If you only wanted me to pleasure your pussy in exchange for that, get your ass up right now and leave." I tease her swollen clit and apply pressure with my thumb, but the touch is only temporary. I pull away, not giving it more of what it's throbbing for.

She doesn't leave the room.

No, she rotates her hips forward, this time more obvious than the last.

A silent plea for more.

Silent is the keyword.

She won't beg.

Without warning, I shove a finger inside her, and her body thrusts up the desk, causing it to shake.

"Jesus, fuck, you're tight," I hiss, gliding my finger in and out of her warmth.

When I add another finger, she whimpers, as if somewhat in pain, and grounds her hips into my touch.

I tease my bratty wife.

Play with her selfish pussy as it begs for more and more.

It doesn't take long until she's ready.

She's close—*so close*—to coming on my fingers when I hit her G-spot and toy with it. She spreads her arms out, desperate to grab something, and clutches at a random pencil on the desk.

Oh no. She thinks I'm going to let her have fun?

Silly little wife.

I remove my fingers and hurriedly step back before she's fully satisfied. It's hard, taking all my willpower because I'm dying to know what she looks like when she comes. The sounds that she makes.

But she needs to be taught a lesson.

She spits out her panties and spreads her legs wider.

The distance between us gives me a better view of her dripping pussy.

How wet and pink it is.

How smooth it is.

How it's still needy for my touch.

All my life, I've prided myself on my willpower, but Neomi Cavallaro—no, Neomi *Marchetti*—just fucking incinerated it.

I take one long step to her, drop to my knees, and throw her legs over my shoulders. Her back arches off the desk as I flatten my tongue against her slit, licking her slowly.

I've never tasted pussy so goddamn good.

Never wanted to devour a woman as if I'd been starved for years.

And here, I didn't even make her mutter the word *please* once.

I play with her clit, squeezing it, pinching it, rubbing it while pleasuring her pussy. It doesn't take long until she's falling apart—*and I allow it*, not taking it away at the last minute, as I tried moments ago.

She cups my head, holding me in place, as if she's worried I'll stop, and her body trembles as I lick up every inch of her sweetness. I lick until there's nothing more to consume before dragging myself away.

I run my tongue across my lower lip, collecting her juices and getting one last taste of her as I stand. She presses a hand to her chest, catching her breath, and slowly slides off the desk like a rag doll. I'm shocked she manages to stand on her feet and doesn't collapse to the floor.

As she gains better control of herself, a relaxed smile is on her face.

The anxiety over her sisters being in harm's way has dissolved … at least for now. I'm sure I'll get asked the same question again relatively soon.

"The answer is still no," I remind her.

Her eyes are sleepy as she squints at me. "But—"

I sit back down, roll my chair forward, and kick my feet onto the desk. "I told you to leave the room if that's all you wanted. You stayed and came on my face."

She straightens her stance. "You're a dick, Benny."

"No, I'm your husband"—I hold my finger up and lick it— "who finally knows what his wife's sweet pussy tastes like."

After giving myself a moment to calm down, telling my dick it won't be inside Neomi, I call my father and tell him about Riccardo's death.

"Who the fuck is Riccardo?" he asks.

"Tommaso's right-hand man." I lick my finger that was inside Neomi. "You met him at our wedding. Tall. Chipped tooth. Talked like he was Robert De Niro."

"I couldn't give two fucks about Tommaso's men," he says, his tone bored. "Nor do I appreciate being interrupted with calls about him. Find someone who cares."

"Normally, I wouldn't care either," I say. "But unfortunately, I'm affected by his actions because I'm married to his sister, who just asked me to marry each of her sisters off to a Marchetti so they don't die."

"She's that worried?"

"It seems so."

"Please inform her we're not a fucking drive-through line for marrying women to protect them from her brother's idiotic actions."

"I think it's time Severino is informed of his son's troubles."

"I'll call him tomorrow, set up a meeting."

I'm no snitch, but someone needs to handle Tommaso at this point ... or pay his debt since he seems incapable of doing so himself.

We end the call, and I head upstairs to the master bedroom, only to find it empty. When I return to the hallway,

I notice a light shining under the crack of a guest bedroom door.

It's the room I'd stay in when I slept over with my grandparents.

The same bed too.

I throw my head back while heading in that direction. I've been married two days, but it feels like two fucking centuries. I wiggle the door handle, finding it unlocked, and walk in without knocking.

Neomi is lying in bed, her knees brought up to her chest, with her phone in her hand. The nightie is gone and replaced with an oversize tee. The words *I Love New York* are scrawled across it.

She drops her phone and glares at me when I enter the room. For someone who just orgasmed, she's in a sour mood. All because I won't pimp out my family members.

I stop at the edge of the bed, slipping my hands into my pockets, and feel too much like a father scolding his daughter. "What are you doing in here?"

She picks at the worn plaid comforter. I hope it still smells like me so she's wrapped up in my scent—no matter where she tries to hide in this house.

"This is my new bedroom," she answers as if it were obvious.

"Wrong." I remove a hand from my pocket and gesture for her to get her ass up.

She slaps her hand onto the bed in frustration. "This is where I'm sleeping, Benny. End of discussion."

"Fine." I storm out of the bedroom and into the bathroom to brush my teeth, and then I snatch my pillow from the master bed.

Neomi eyes me warily when I return to the guest bedroom, and those eyes harden when I toss the pillow next to hers on the bed.

"I guess this is also where I'm sleeping." I dump the contents inside my pocket onto the nightstand, drop my gun next to the pile, and then strip out of my clothes. "I doubt this bed will be as comfortable, given it's probably a century old."

The only furniture my father allowed me to swap out was the master bed. I was adamant I wasn't sleeping in my late grandparents' bed. I promised to store the bed in my air-conditioned garage and return it in pristine condition.

Her breathing hitches when I tear back the comforter and join her in bed.

She shifts onto her side, digs her elbow into her pillow, and dramatically glares at me. "Keep your hands to yourself."

The bed squeaks as I rest my back against the headboard.

I give her a mocking smile. "You know, I won't be so nice next time."

She blinks, her long lashes fluttering. "Excuse me?"

"Because of your attitude right now, recent orgasm or not, next time, I'll make you beg me to eat your sweet pussy." I click my tongue against the roof of my mouth and shake my head in disapproval. "The things I will make you do before I allow you to ride my cock will be amazing."

And I can't wait.

CHAPTER SEVENTEEN

NEOMI

Boundaries.

My husband has none.

Last night, while I was dreaming of running away to Hawaii and falling in love with some rando surfer, Benny picked me up and carried me to our bedroom.

He dropped me onto the bed with a thud—not gentle, of course—and told me, "Keep your ass there unless you want to sleep outside instead."

Then, he shut off the light and joined me in bed. Since he was right about our bed being more comfortable and because I was tired, I kept my ass there.

Like yesterday, my bed is void of Benny when I wake up. I didn't hear him leave this morning. When I reach for my phone on the nightstand, I realize it's still in the guest room.

I slap my arm over my eyes and groan when I remember what happened in his office. I plead temporary insanity for my behavior. And desperation.

After cleaning the kitchen after our dinner last night, I showered and called my mother. She answered the call, frantic and sobbing, and it took me five minutes to calm her down before I could make out her words. Someone had murdered Riccardo, and she was scared about who was next.

Then, her request came.

"Neomi! You have to convince Benny to find someone to marry your sisters! He is our best bet to protect them!"

I argued and told her the Cavallaros were a strong family, but her voice was unsure whether Tommaso would be fit to take over the family.

I changed into the ridiculous nightie someone had hung up in the closet and performed the walk of shame into Benny's office. I intended to sleep with him to fulfill my mother's wishes.

That sure didn't work.

Thrill shoots through my veins when I remember what happened in his office—play-by-play. Even if it was a bad idea, it will forever be a memory I'll appreciate.

I stretch my legs, relax into the mattress, and lower my hand between my thighs. As my fingers slip into my panties, I'm already soaked.

I think of Benny and how he touched and pleasured me with his tongue.

Sweat builds along my forehead as I remember how much I liked it.

I pretend my hand is his as I play with my clit.

I wish my fingers were his when I slide them against my slit.

And he's the only thought on my mind when I plunge two fingers inside myself.

I'm quiet as I masturbate, just in case someone is in the house. I doubt Benny would leave me home alone. It doesn't take me long to come. I bite into my lip and hiss Benny's name.

I give myself time to come down from my high before slipping out of bed, brushing my teeth, and getting ready for the day. I shuffle out of the bedroom and into the guest room to snatch my phone from the nightstand.

I unlock the screen to find a text from Benny.

Benny: I'll be out late. Don't wait up.

I glower at my phone, wishing he could see the expression on my face, and reply.

Me: Out late where?

Benny: The club.

Me: Can I come and hang out?

Benny: No.

I exit out of my texts and call him instead.

"Let me get this straight," I say as soon as he answers. "You get to hang out in a club all night, doing God knows what, while I sit at home?"

He blows out an annoyed breath. "I won't be doing *God knows what*. I'll be *working*."

I scoff.

Working.

Right.

It's the same generic excuse my father tells my mother to hide his affairs.

"Why don't you have your sisters over today?" Benny suggests, as if wanting to appease a child. "Luca will keep an eye on you guys."

Ah. So, Luca the babysitter is here.

"Hmm." I tap the side of my lips. "Having my sisters over sounds like a great idea. Talk to you soon."

I end the call and grin.

My husband doesn't know inviting my sisters over isn't the best idea if he wants me to behave.

"And why can't I go to the club with you?" Isabella whines while glaring at me from across my bedroom.

I snatch a pair of heels from the closet. "You're not old enough to get into the club."

"Plus, you need to keep Luca occupied," Bria adds.

Isabella grins from my bed and runs a hand through her

curls. "He is cute."

After I hung up with Benny, I called my sisters and set up the perfect plan. They arrived two hours later, and we've been preparing for the night since.

I check my makeup in the mirror one last time before peering at Bria. "Did you bring what I asked?"

Bria nods, jumps up from her seat on the floor to grab her purse from the bed, and shuffles through it. "If Dad flips his shit because I stole this, I'm blaming it on you."

She hands over the device, and I slip it into my bag.

"Dad doesn't inventory them." I zip my bag and shift my focus to a gloomy Isabella. "Go downstairs and keep Luca company."

It's not like I'm throwing my sister out to the Mafia wolves. Luca has been the topic of at least one discussion a day after she spotted him at my engagement party. Now, instead of talking about him to every person in our family, she can speak to him while covering for Bria and me. It's a win-win.

"And what should I tell him when he asks why I ditched my sisters to hang out with him?" Isabella raises a brow.

"Tell him we got into a fight," Bria answers. "You're giving us the silent treatment."

Isabella rolls her eyes. "Gee, that'll make me sound like a grown woman."

Bria grabs a pillow and tosses it at her. "Oh, shush. Go flirt with the man and have fun."

Bria helps me gather what we need, and I groan while shoving open the heavy window. A sudden gust of wind smacks me in the face, holding me back for a moment. I snap my fingers and gesture toward the open window. Bria searches the room, attempting to find something to hold it open for us. I'm grateful the windows don't have alarms on them.

"Ugh," Isabella groans. "I'll shut the window behind you."

I blow Isabella a kiss, and Bria smacks her lips against her cheek.

"I expect a Vegas trip on my twenty-first," Isabella says as I crouch against the windowsill with Bria behind me.

"Yeah, yeah," I say, waving off her comment.

"I can't believe Benny thought you'd just sit at home," Bria says.

"I pegged him for being smarter," Isabella adds.

Goose bumps form along my skin as I peer back at Bria. "Do you want to go first?"

"Hell no!" Bria shakes her head. "This is a window we've never jumped out of before. I'm not about to be the guinea pig." She gives me a gentle shove to where my body is halfway outside.

I toss my heels and bag out the window before smiling at Isabella. "Have fun. Go flirt. We'll text if there's an emergency."

I wiggle my fingers. I'm a little rusty with my *sneaking out of windows* skills. I crawl out of the window and hang by my hands. The first advice I read from Google years ago when I researched sneaking out of windows is, you want your feet to be as close to the ground as possible. I slowly lower myself, inch by inch, and attempt to roll when I hit the ground.

My fall is anything but graceful.

I collapse onto the ground. Freshly mowed grass sticks to my skin, and I'm flicking it off as Bria comes down next. Since she witnessed my *how not to do it* demonstration, her jump is more agile.

"Be safe," Isabella calls out, cupping her hand around her mouth while keeping her voice low.

I wave to her, and she slams the window shut.

"I can't believe we're in our twenties and sneaking out windows," Bria says, flipping dirt off her foot before slipping her sneakers on. "How sad are we?"

"I think the better question is, how sad are our lives that we have to do this?" I grumble as we rush through the backyard.

Benny said the home has security cameras, but I don't know their locations.

For all I know, he could be watching my subpar window acrobatics from a camera monitor and stop us from leaving. So far, we're in the clear.

We pass the playset, which is missing a swing, and I nearly break a nail as I unlatch the fence.

We did it.

Bria and I circle the block, wearing our tennis shoes, and walk to where her white Mercedes is parked. I'll change into my heels later. Her car beeps when she unlocks it. The loud sound is a reminder to my brain that I need to collect my car from my parents' house.

Isabella and Bria left our parents' separately, but before they got here, Bria parked her car here and got into Isabella's. We needed it to look like they came together.

I grab the junk from Bria's passenger seat and toss it in the back.

"Seven Seconds, here we come," she says, starting the car.

Before Bria came over, I had her rifle through my closet and find my fake ID from high school. I'd bought it from one of Sienna's boyfriends. I haven't used it in years, given that I can now legally drink, but I don't want my name to stand out to the bouncer.

I hug myself to keep warm, and the fall breeze whips into us while we wait outside Seven Seconds. Twenty minutes have passed, and the line has barely moved an inch.

And why did I think wearing a black minidress was a smart move?

My legs feel so numb that I'm waiting for them to fall off.

The college-aged guy in front of us has offered us blow four times, and the couple behind us won't stop making out.

"Screw this," Bria says, snatching my elbow. "I know you want to be incognito, but I'm not freezing to death for it. I've never had to wait in line to get into a club, and I'm damn sure not starting at my *brother-in-law's*."

I swat at her and inch closer. "You can't let people hear you say that."

She opens her wallet, plucks out a hundred-dollar bill, and marches us toward the bouncer blocking the entrance. The music spilling out of the club and the crowd chatter around us drown out the click of our heels against the concrete.

The bouncer has been a real hard-ass tonight, turning away people left and right, even if they offered to pay their way in.

He pauses mid-check of a man's ID when Bria approaches him, her hold still latched to me. His eyes do a slow roam of her body, like he's deciding whether she meets the hotness requirement in her ribbed maroon cutout dress and strappy heels.

Bria is gorgeous. Her hair is thick and black, like mine. Her body is toned and her ass tight. She's a gym junkie, and she considers squats a way of life.

When he's finished with his approval, he yanks the bill from her hand.

"Just me and my sister here," Bria says, pouting her lips as she signals back and forth between us.

The bouncer grins and unhooks the rope. "You didn't even need to pay me, sweetheart. I'd have let your sexy ass in for free."

Bria holds out her hand. "Then, give me my—"

I push her forward, midsentence, and he steps to the side to allow us entry into the club.

We're in.

It's a small feat, I know.

Bribed with one hundred dollars and a hot sister.

But I feel like I climbed Mount Everest over here.

That I outsmarted the smartest Mafia man.

The rave music slaps us in the face when we walk in. Colorful lights flash from every corner of the room. A half-dressed server passes us with a tray of drinks. It's a job, dodging people as we move deeper into the packed club. We pass a group snorting a substance I'm sure is illegal off a pub table, then two men arguing over who fucked Michelle first.

Dark red leather booths line the walls, and the decor is similar to Benny's room in the mansion.

The club is three stories high, and a guard stands at each stairway. The higher the level you're at, the better your status.

My stomach knots as sweaty people grind against others on the dance floor. Their hands, lips, and tongues are everywhere on each other. The lights are low, so I wouldn't be surprised if a few people were fucking each other.

Yes, this is exactly where I want my husband every night.

I stand there, people bumping into me as they move, and my mind wanders to last night. I gulp down a tinge of vomit that my husband would grab a woman from this dance floor, take her to his office, and be intimate with her. Just thinking about it makes me want to burn down the building.

I shake my head, wondering when I became this insecure.

Since Benny—that's when.

It's as if the man tore out that jealous, raging monster I never knew I had.

"Time for a celebratory drink for not being caught," Bria screams at me over the music.

I give her a side-eye. "Pretty sure you just jinxed us."

We hold hands as we head toward the bar so we don't get lost in the crowd.

A man steps in front of us, only inches from the bar, and cuts off our path. "Hey, sexy girl. Want to dance?" He performs an offbeat version of the running man.

"Dancing gives her hives," Bria answers for me.

I nearly fall when she tugs me around the man and storms toward the bar.

"Hives?" I ask when we reach the bar. "Really?"

"It's one thing being here, but dancing with another man will poke the murderous bear," she explains, squeezing us between two men at the bar. "That guy seemed a little weird, and his dance skills were definitely sketchy, but he doesn't deserve to die at the hands of your murderous husband." She tilts her head to the side and gives me a *remember your engagement party* expression.

"Fair point," I mutter, wiping my hand along the wet bar while Bria waves down a bartender. "I want to drive Benny insane, but not at the expense of someone else."

Bria steps on her tiptoes and swings her arms in the air, a twenty between her fingers. People yell their drink orders to the poor bartender, screaming over each other from every inch of the bar.

Thanks to my sister's hotness, he takes our order third.

She orders a round of tequila shots. He takes her money and hurriedly pours them. When he shoves them down the bar, a man tries to intercept one, but I whack his hand away.

We cheers before draining our shots.

The drink soothes my parched throat.

I wonder how long it'll take Benny to find me.

CHAPTER EIGHTEEN

BENNY

"Did you speak with Severino?" my father asks while wandering around my office at the club.

I shake my head and click the pen in my hand. "He had a colonoscopy and is out of commission for the day."

"At least he'll have a clean asshole when you tell him what an idiot his son is." He picks up a gold paperweight from my desk and plays with it in his hands.

I nod in agreement.

That's a positive way to look at it.

"Did you speak with Sammie?" is his next question.

"Over the phone."

"Why not in person?"

"He refuses to meet with me."

My father scoffs. "He probably thinks you want to kill him."

"I do want to kill him."

"What'd he say?"

"At first, he denied that the wedding shooting and kidnap attempt were his men's work." I toss the pen on my desk. "When I laid out the evidence, he changed his tune real fucking quick."

"And what did his tune change to?" He returns the paperweight.

"He claims his men went rogue. He'd fired them days earlier. A few men have personal problems with Tommaso for reasons other than money. All Sammie cares about is money, but they want him for another reason." I relax my elbows on my desk and groan before scrubbing a hand over my face to ward off the impending headache.

My father stands in front of my desk. "Do you believe him?"

I move my hand. "Surprisingly, yes."

He shakes his head in frustration. "I wish we could kill the brother. It'd easily solve the problem."

"Him paying his debt would solve the problem."

"Temporarily, but then he'd rack up more loans in no time. History would repeat itself." He clicks his tongue against the roof of his mouth. "A dead man can't accumulate more debt."

He's right. That's why I refuse to pay Tommaso's debt. I'm not parting with a million dollars with no guarantee he learned his lesson. I know the cycle as someone who deals with men not paying their debts. Ninety-five percent of them acquire more debt, which eventually leads to their death.

I drum my fingers along the desk. "The problem is, I'd have a wife with a dead brother."

"Surely, Neomi knows her brother is a liability."

I nod. "But that doesn't make her love him less."

I think of what she asked me to promise her last night—not to hurt him and to help get him out of the mess he created.

"What a pity." He shakes his head in disdain. "Did Sammie at least promise Neomi's safety?"

"Sammie won't lay a finger on Neomi. There was fear in his voice when I told him what happened at my wedding."

He throws his hands out before wiping them together. "All is done then."

"But he won't promise the safety of anyone else. Tommaso owes them a lot of money, and Sammie wants it."

"Understandable." He smirks. "How's married life?"

I lean back in my chair and massage my neck. "More stressful than single life."

That is the understatement of the fucking year.

All day, I've thought about Neomi.

About the taste of her sweet pussy on my tongue.

How she squirmed and moaned beneath me.

Fuck, I want to taste her again.

It's like she's a drug and I'm her addict.

His voice breaks me out of my thoughts. "It gets better with time."

"Your advice might work with other men but not with my marriage and the little demon you handed over to me."

He cracks a smile. "And how is the club running?"

My father and I co-own Seven Seconds. I came to him with the proposal. I'd run the club, and he'd put up the funds to start it. He remains behind the scenes—how he likes it—and I handle everything on-site. The club is easy to launder money through, and we pay our men through the company, making them appear as tax-paying, law-abiding citizens.

I allowed him to choose the name, and he went with Seven Seconds. Only a few people know the meaning behind it. Seven Seconds is my father's favorite game. He came up with it when he became bored with torturing and killing men. So, before he takes their last breath, he allows them to run.

They get seven seconds to dodge his bullet.

He's never lost a round.

It's pretty morbid, naming the club after a murderous game.

I learned everything I know about business and life from my father. He's ruthless but a good man to his family. Since my grandfather passed, he has dedicated his life to this family and our businesses.

My father was only in his midtwenties when the weight of controlling the city, companies, and our enemies fell onto his shoulders.

Cristian Marchetti will go down as one of the most

successful crime bosses in history. He's ruled the family and lived a life of crime for decades without being charged with a single felony.

The same goes for me. I have plenty of arrests under my belt, but no charges. Much of that is thanks to my aunt Celine's husband, Santos. Santos is one of the top defense attorneys on the East Coast and handles all our legal problems.

A knock on the door interrupts our conversation.

"Come in," I call out.

The door swings open, and Raul steps inside the office.

"We have a problem." His gaze lands on me. "Well, *you* might have a problem."

I rise from my chair. "If I have a problem, we all have a problem."

"Then, you'll probably want to see this."

He waves us forward, and we follow him down the hallway to the security room. Everyone turns in their chair, all eyes on us when we enter. The monitors show how packed the club is. Night after night—whether it's in the middle of the week or on holidays—patrons fill the club.

It's New York's hotspot.

I worked my ass off to earn that title.

Raul points at the middle monitor. "I think she belongs to you, boss."

I step in closer, squinting as I stare at the screen, and Diesel, one of our security men, hits a button to zoom in.

Motherfucker.

Sure enough, my pain-in-the-ass wife is enjoying a drink with Bria in the bar. She laughs at something Bria said while sucking on the straw inside her glass.

I see red as anger sears through me.

"Beat the shit out of the bouncer," I snarl to Raul. "Then, fire his ass and make sure he never gets another job in this city."

Raul gives me a thumbs-up, and his face brightens, as if I'd informed him of a raise. "Yes, sir."

"I'm still waiting for the *it gets better* part," I tell my father, brushing past him on my way out of the room.

"I was attempting to lighten your mood," he says before checking his Rolex. "I have a wife to get home to. You need to go collect yours."

We turn in opposite directions.

Me toward the club.

And him headed straight for the back exit.

Three men follow me as I charge through the club. I push people out of my way and zero in on my wife's back. Bria notices me first, and her eyes widen. She smacks Neomi's shoulder and signals toward me. Her face shines with amusement, like she knows the show of a lifetime is about to start.

I'm damn sure not finding another Cavallaro a husband. Not one of my men deserves to go through this hell.

I grab Neomi's shoulder and whip her around to face me. "What the fuck are you doing here?"

"Oh, you didn't hear?" Neomi asks, her voice dramatically chirpy. "It's Visit Your Husband at Work Day."

"That's not cute," I deadpan before pointing Raul in Bria's direction. "Grab the sister and take her to the waiting room. And keep an eye on her." I motion between my troublesome wife and her sister. "These ones don't know how to behave."

Neomi shrugs and downs the remainder of her drink.

"Whoa," Bria says, holding up a hand in defense. "I'm an innocent bystander."

"You are in my club, unwanted," I reply. "Now, either go with Raul nicely, or he'll throw you over his shoulder and escort you where I want you."

"Go, Bria," Neomi says, rolling her head back. "They won't hurt you. You'll probably get popcorn and a ride home. *I'll* be the one dealing with the crazy."

She shoots me a look, and I crack a cruel smirk.

She has no idea.

Bria performs an *I'm watching you* gesture before Raul

grabs her arm and guides her through the club toward the back. She makes small talk with him. Neomi, on the other hand, talks shit the entire time. I'm reminded of the first time she came to my club, and I had to deal with her stabbing a man.

My little wife never fails to bring trouble everywhere she goes.

In my club.

My house.

My motherfucking brain.

I gulp.

And possibly my heart.

Raul escorts Bria into the waiting room, where there are drinks, snacks, and a TV.

I loosen my hold on Neomi but don't fully release her until she's shoved into my office, and I slam the door shut behind us.

"Where is Luca?" I scream.

Neomi wrinkles her nose and drops her bag to the floor. "I believe he's at our house."

"So, my idiotic cousin just allowed you to walk right out the front door?"

I'm cutting my cousin's tongue out and then nailing it to his bedroom wall to remind him of this mistake. Luca doesn't make errors like this. That's why I assigned him to watch Neomi.

Dumb and Dumber had to have schemed some plan to sneak out.

Neomi crosses her arms as a sly smile plays on her cherry-red lips.

What I'd give to see them around my cock.

My wife wears a short black dress that cuts down the middle of her chest, her cleavage on full display. The dress shows off her tanned legs—legs that were around my head while I ate her sweet pussy last night.

She looks delicious. So fuckable. So *mine*.

Now, if only she could behave like it.

"We used a distraction device," she tells me with pride in her voice.

"Did you *drug* my cousin?"

"Sure, if you call Isabella a drug." She steadies herself on the edge of the desk and unstraps one of her heels.

"You won't find this funny when Luca hates you for him being in deep shit over this."

"I'll have Isabella kiss him and make it better."

Anger ignites through me at her response.

"This isn't cute, Neomi." My ears pound, and I raise my voice as I begin pacing. "My job is dangerous. Your behavior is distracting not only me but also my men—putting all of us in harm's way. They could get killed. You could get killed." I pause my pacing to meet her eyes. "So, please, for the love of God, can you fucking behave?"

"I refuse to be your hostage, stuck in a house, Benny." She removes her other heel.

"Hostage?" I return to my pacing to stop myself from throwing something through the floor-to-ceiling window behind my desk. "You've been in that house for a few days and left several times. It's not like I've kept you locked in some tower, like Rapunzel."

She cracks a smile and plays with a strand of her hair. "How do you, of all people, know who Rapunzel is?"

I glare at her. "I have a younger sister."

"You watched princess movies with her?" Her face softens. "That's so adorable."

I exhale a long breath, not in the mood for her games. "You know what isn't adorable, Neomi Marchetti?"

Yes, I use her full name.

She's a Marchetti, so she needs to act like one.

She taps her nails together. "Loan sharks?"

"You dead." I bolt toward her, capture her waist, and jerk her toward me. My head bows, and she flutters her lashes while staring up at me. "You're driving me fucking crazy."

Neomi gasps and slowly blinks, as if processing my words through her brain again. If it takes being honest with her to keep her safe, then that's what I'll do.

If I have to open my damn heart up and spread it out for her like a platter for her to realize she will die if she doesn't stop her antics, I will.

She slowly raises her hand and drags her palm across my cheek. "Are you afraid to lose me, Benny?" I've never heard her voice so soft.

Like me, Neomi isn't a gentle soul.

But right now, that's what she's giving me.

Am I afraid of losing her?

Is this me playing the role of a dutiful husband, or do I honestly not want to lose her?

I cup my hand over hers on my face, and my brain spins.

I'm not a man who speaks his feelings.

Or one who believes in love.

But I am a man who protects his wife.

Who *wants* his wife.

I clear my throat, but my voice is still raspy. "I don't have the perfect answer to that, Neomi. All I can say is, if someone hurt you, there wouldn't be a large enough army to stop me from massacring them." I slide in closer, our bodies brushing together, and run my lips along her cheek. "If that's what being afraid to lose someone is, then, yes, Neomi, I'm fucking afraid to lose you."

A faint whimper leaves her before my lips smash into hers.

I cup her face as we devour each other's mouths.

It doesn't start slow.

Or timid.

It's desperate.

Needy.

It's our first private kiss—not forced or done in front of an audience. I suck in her every breath as if it gives me life and back her into the desk as we make out. Our tongues slide together, and I roll my hips forward.

The room grows warm.

My breaths turn into desperate pants.

"Benny," Neomi moans when I move my mouth from her lips to rain kisses along the soft skin of her neck. "I want you. *I need you.*"

I pull back, understanding her words aren't simple.

My wife needs me.

And what kind of husband would I be if I denied my wife the very thing she needed?

CHAPTER NINETEEN

NEOMI

"I want you. I need you."

Six words I swore I'd never speak to Benny.

It's becoming clear—no matter how many promises I make to myself, when it comes to Benny Marchetti, he'll make me break every single one.

He doesn't have to use force with me—unlike others who fall to his mercy. All he has to do is offer me a glimpse into his soul and mutter words that make me fall apart, and I'm a goner.

"Fuck, Neomi," Benny hisses through clenched teeth as his chest presses into mine. His hand delves into my hair, and he pulls the strands tight. "You have no idea how much I want to be inside you."

My heart races at his words.

He swiftly drops his hand to my waist and hauls me onto the desk. My body aches for him when he parts my legs and steps between them.

Desk action 2.0.

The original was good. Five stars.

But fingers crossed, the sequel is better.

I want more than his tongue tonight.

I want all that is Benny Marchetti.

My husband.

I can feel his erection through the material of his pants. My eyes widen when it brushes against my thigh, and he rotates his hips forward. I moan, my heart beating against its cage when he reaches down and hitches my leg over his waist.

I've never wanted something so bad.

I squeeze my hand between our bodies—my movement uneasy—and my fingers shake as I attempt to unbuckle his belt.

Benny presses a quick peck to my lips, brushes his nose against mine, and backs away. Rejection smacks me in the face. I reach forward, attempting to grip his shirt and pull him back, but he shakes his head.

"Our first fuck won't be in this club or on a desk," he says, his breaths ragged as he stops me from tugging him closer again.

I frown but can't help but laugh at his words. "You made that romantic by not wanting it here, yet also unromantic by referring to it as *our first fuck*. You need to work on your vocabulary skills, hubby. Add some romantic words in there."

A devious smirk forms on his lips. "I can only be halfway romantic, baby."

I yank the hem of my dress down and slip off the desk.

Benny is right. When I give him such an intimate part of me, I don't want it to be in his office or at the club. I want it to be somewhere private.

"What about Bria?" I press my hand on my chest to calm my frantic heart. "We need to take her home."

I can't ditch my sister for some husbandly dick.

"I'll have Raul walk her to her car and follow her home." He adjusts his pants in an attempt to conceal his erection. "I'll be right back. Don't go sneaking off. I'm not in the mood to chase you around."

I nod. He kisses the top of my head and leaves the office.

As soon as he disappears out the door, I scramble toward my bag. I rifle through it for the camera Bria brought me. I'm out of breath as I scout the office for the perfect spot to stash it. It wasn't wise for Benny to leave his sneaky wife in his office unattended.

Scanning the office, I play with the camera in my hand until my gaze lands on the bookshelf. I scramble toward it, shove a copy of *The Art of War* to the side, and plant the camera between that and a business encyclopedia.

I retreat a step and am admiring my work when Benny returns.

"You ready?" he asks from the doorway.

I nod as I grab my heels and bag, and he captures my hand as we leave the room. Our fingers interlace as if we're finally becoming one while we walk down the hall. His hand is cold and callous but offers a sense of security.

We walk into a room where Bria is relaxed on the couch. Her bare feet are kicked up onto the table as if my mother raised us in a barn, and a plate of pizza sits on her lap while she watches TV.

She peers over at us and grins.

Raul joins us, and Benny tells them the plan.

"Can I stay here a bit longer?" Bria asks with a pout.

"No," Benny says firmly.

"Oh, come on!" She throws her arms out toward the TV. "I like this episode!"

Benny cracks his neck. "Either Raul walks you to your car or I call your father and request he picks you up here."

I wrinkle my nose at Benny.

Bria scowls at him.

No one likes a snitch.

"Fine," Bria groans. "But I'm taking a slice for the road."

"Take the whole fucking pizza for all I care," Benny replies.

"Don't tease me with a good time." And because my sister is like me, she grabs the pizza box and tucks it against her chest. "I'm ready to go, then."

She winks at me while we stroll down the hallway toward the exit. Another security detail joins us when we step into the night. A bright spotlight shines over the back parking lot, and I hiss at how rough the concrete is against my bare feet.

At my second ouch, Benny scoops me up and carries me. I wave goodbye to Bria, who's tiptoeing on her bare feet.

"Can one of you follow his lead, please?" she asks them.

Raul looks at the other guy. "My girlfriend will kill me if I tote another chick around. She's all yours, Myles."

Myles shakes his head before throwing Bria over his shoulder.

Bria squeals, pulls her dress down to cover her ass, and waves at me. "I'll text you when I get home!"

If these men were anyone but Benny's, I'd never allow my sister to walk down a dark street with strangers. But I trust Benny.

Benny hauls me toward a row of black SUVs. A pair of headlights flashes, and his Range Rover beeps when unlocked. He opens the passenger door with one hand, drops me onto the heated seat, and shuts the door.

We're quiet as he exits the parking lot and turns onto the street. Benny turns the radio on low volume, and I don't recognize the song. There's no containing my smile when he rests his hand on my bare thigh. He cups me tight, as if he fears I'll run away. I sit back, loosening my muscles, and attempt to part my legs discreetly.

A silent invitation since I'm not forward enough to grab his hand and shove it into my panties.

Benny keeps his hand in place, not moving an inch, and I narrow my eyes at him. I rub my thighs together, hoping he'll get *that* signal. It's dark in the car, so I can barely make out his features. He keeps his eyes on the road, and just when I assume this will be a no-action car ride, he slips a single finger beneath the hem of my dress. That simple touch sends excitement shooting through my veins.

I lose all sense of my surroundings, focusing only on the two of us.

My breathing is heavy. I roll down the window and allow cool air to fill the car.

Heat pools between my legs, and my skin burns for more of him when I feel the faintest touch across my covered center. My eyes roll to the back of my head. Momentarily, I forget we're in a car. We're so caught up in each other that neither of us notices the car riding our ass until it revs its engine. I fly forward at the blunt force of the car ramming into the Range Rover's bumper.

Benny removes his finger out from underneath my dress and slams his foot on the gas, flooring it. He drapes his arm on the back of my seat and peers over his shoulder while he controls the steering wheel with his free hand.

The car's wheels screech as they follow us.

"Fuck!" Benny shouts, slamming his hand against the steering wheel. He reaches out, cups the top of my head, and pushes it down. "Get on the floor. Don't fucking come up until I tell you."

"What—" My sentence is interrupted by gunfire.

Benny reaches down, covering what he can of me, and swerves onto a backroad. A gunshot whips through the back of the Range Rover, shattering the rear window, and barely misses Benny's head.

I scream, and my side smacks into the door when Benny makes another turn, trying to lose the bastards.

Benny controls the steering wheel with his knee and one hand and uses the other to open a hidden compartment in the car's dashboard. My thoughts race when he retrieves a gun and turns off the safety.

Since I'm not one to listen, I rise from the floor.

"Neomi!" he yells at me, curling his upper lip while pointing the gun toward the shattered glass window. "Get down!"

"Do you have another gun?" I frantically yell, searching the car's back seat while hoping a bullet doesn't smoke me in the face. "I can shoot back."

"Get down!" Benny repeats, attempting to shove me to the floorboard, but I fight him off.

His protecting me, driving, and shooting back will only kill him. He needs help.

"Benny!" I say, my voice almost pleading. "I know how to shoot a gun!"

Another gunshot whizzes by, hitting my side mirror.

"There's one in the glove box," he says.

Sirens wail around us, and I'm sure someone called the cops, alerting them of a road-rage situation.

My heart beats so fast that I can feel it in my throat as I open the glove box. I grab and grip the gun tightly, precisely how my father taught me. Benny continues to steer with one hand and returns gunfire with the car.

I shut one eye and aim my gun out the window.

"There are two men in front," I shout, only able to make out their figures. "The passenger is the only one shooting."

My breathing is ragged as I focus on my target, and just as the man aims to fire again, I pull the trigger. It's like time stands still as I wait. The man's body jerks back against the seat. The driver suddenly veers to the right and then corrects himself.

When we pass a streetlight, I catch a peek at him attempting to grab what I assume is the passenger's gun. I don't give him a chance to find it. I aim the gun at his head and pull the trigger.

I'm too frustrated to realize I killed two men. These assholes have ruined the night I finally decided to sleep with my husband.

The man's head snaps forward, and Benny swerves to the side of the back alley we entered. The other car darts ahead, plows straight into a dumpster, and immediately catches fire.

Benny shifts the Range Rover into park, jumps out, and sprints toward the car.

"Benny!" I shriek, dropping the gun on the center console. "Get away from there!"

It could blow up.

I could lose him.

No. No. No.

Panic surges through me, and I roll out of the Range Rover, not caring about my bare feet. I dash toward him as Benny peers into the car like he's searching for something. He dips low, snagging something from the driver, and shoves it into his pocket while returning to me.

When he reaches me, he circles his arm around my waist and holds me at a distance to check me for any harm.

Sweat cakes his forehead, and there are glass cuts on his face from the shattered window. I attempt to brush them off his skin, but he catches my hand and presses a kiss to my palm.

My lower lip trembles. "Are you hurt?"

He shakes his head and tugs me into his chest. "I'm good."

I shove my face into his shirt while he runs a hand down my hair. As my shoulders relax and my heartbeat tames, I push at his chest.

I point at him sternly. "Don't you dare run toward a burning car again. Do you hear me? You could've died!"

More fear swarmed me when he ran toward that car than when a man held a gun to my head at our wedding.

Benny's mouth twitches into a smirk.

I smack his chest. "You're not untouchable, Benny!" My voice catches in my throat. "You can be killed. And I don't think I can lose you!"

When I go to shove his chest again, he stops me and drags me back into it instead.

"You're right. I'm not untouchable." He brushes his fingers along my back to soothe me. "I told you I don't make promises I can't keep. Here's one I can: I won't leave you alone in this insufferable world, my dear wife. I'll always come back to you."

Benny holds my hand on the ride home as he talks to his father on the phone. Cristian's voice flows through the Range Rover's Bluetooth speakers and turns angrier the longer Benny explains what happened.

I declined Benny's offer to call one of his guys to take me home. He didn't think it'd be comfortable for me to ride in a shot-up SUV with no rear window on a chilly night. I don't care about those things and said no. I want to return to the safe space of my home, and I need to be sure Benny is with me.

So many emotions are running through my mind that I can't clutch a single one and focus on it. It took this for me to understand that even though I thought I had Mafia life figured out, I hadn't scratched the surface. It's more dangerous than I ever thought it could be.

"Come to the mansion," Cristian instructs. "We'll switch your vehicles, and you and Neomi can sleep here for the night."

Benny glances at me in question and squeezes my hand.

I shake my head, just wanting to go home.

"We're going home," he tells his father. "The house is secure."

Cristian scoffs. "Your wife snuck out only hours ago."

Benny shoots me an annoyed glare, and I mouth, *"What?"* while shrugging.

"Luca is there with Isabella," Benny continues. "I'll have him take her home. We all need to keep our guard up."

They end the call, and I press my hand on my heart to calm it as Benny drives. Ten minutes later, we pull into the driveway of the two-story brick home, and Benny parks in the garage. The interior door inside the garage swings open, and Luca comes into view, gripping his gun.

He lowers the gun and tucks it into his pants when he sees Benny. "What the hell happened to the Range Rover?"

"Some dumb, *now-dead* motherfuckers shot at us," Benny explains, stepping out of the SUV. "Now, get out of my house and take Isabella home. I'll deal with you later."

Luca winces at Benny's response, runs a hand over his stressed face, and returns through the doorway. My posture slumps in guilt as I climb out of the SUV. The Range Rover makes weird noises as I pass it. Benny waits for me to walk ahead and follows me into the house.

As soon as I walk into the foyer, Isabella rushes forward and hugs me tightly. She's now wearing a pair of my plaid pajamas I might never see again, and her eyes are sleepy.

"Oh my God, are you okay, Nee-Nee?" she asks in a shaky voice.

I nod, shoving my face into her shoulder.

Thank God she or Bria wasn't in the SUV with us.

My gaze slips to Luca when we separate, my cheeks reddening in embarrassment as I offer him an apologetic smile. "I'm sorry, Luca."

His face is unreadable, and he only looks away.

I'll understand if he hates me. What we did was stupid and reckless.

Benny jerks his head toward Isabella. "Take her home."

Luca waits at the door while Isabella gathers her belongings, hugs me again, and kisses my cheek. When she's finished, Luca ushers her out the door.

I follow them and linger in the doorway as Luca helps Isabella into the Suburban.

"Call or text when you get home," I call out to her. "Bria should already be there."

She gives me a thumbs-up, and I wait until they disappear down the road before returning inside. Benny shuts the door, and the click of the lock is the loudest sound in the house. We came here with the hope that we could finally give ourselves to each other, but all that has been replaced with fear.

Benny lingers at the bottom of the stairwell and holds out his hand. "Come on. Let's get you cleaned up."

"What?" I peer down at my body. Sure, my dress is wrinkled, my hair wild, and I have some back-alley grossness on my feet and ankles. But I'm not *that* bad. "Are you saying I'm too dirty to touch, Benny Marchetti?"

He flashes me a megawatt smile. "Neomi, I'll touch you any way I can get you—clean, dirty, ripe, you name it." He licks his lips. "I'm absolutely game."

My heart spasms.

All the heat in my body rushes to my core.

Benny advances a step and hoists me into his arms, like he did in the Seven Seconds parking lot. The movement is so sudden that I nearly whack my head on the railing. The smell of his cologne and sweat soothes me, and I rest my head in the crook of his neck as he carries me upstairs.

I want to forget tonight.

Forget about the high-speed chase.

Forget that I killed not just one, but *two* men.

And I want my husband to help me do that.

Our bedroom is messy since Bria and I didn't clean up before leaving for the club. Benny doesn't say a word about it, only passes through and deposits me onto my feet in the bathroom. The tiled floor is like ice against my heels.

Benny runs the bathwater, and I'm at least grateful I'm not washing someone's blood off me this time. He signals for me to sit on the edge of the tub. My dress rises, and I grimace, the porcelain tub just as cold as the floor. He snags a washcloth from the cabinet. Goose bumps appear on my skin when he kneels at my feet. Running the washcloth under the water, he squeezes a drop of my bodywash onto it before capturing my ankle. Tingles sweep up my spine as he cleans my foot.

It tickles, and I can't help but giggle and attempt to pull away.

He clamps his hand around my ankle to hold me still.

But moments later, he tickles my toes, and I smack his shoulder.

My heart swells at his sweet gesture while he washes my feet, ankles, and up my legs to my knees.

He dries my feet before helping me to them. My knees are wobbly as I reach for another washcloth and wet it. I lift my hand to his cheek and brush away remnants of glass with the washcloth. The bathroom is small, forcing us closer, and his breathing is rough against my shallow ones.

Benny eases the washcloth from my hand and tosses it into the bathtub. I shiver when he skims the edge of his pinkie along my cheekbone.

He grips my chin between his thumb and forefinger, holding it still as our eyes meet. "Are you ready to finish what we started, Neomi?"

Excitement rips through my bloodstream, seeping inside me with need for him. I don't answer him with words because I can't form them. My desire has possessed my every thought.

So, instead of speaking, I slam my mouth onto his.

It takes him a moment to gather what I did until he fully kisses me back. My heart thumps wildly as he devours my mouth, like I've taken a shot of morphine straight into my veins.

This kiss is different from any we've shared.

It starts slow and gentle, but quickly heats.

I shove my tongue into his mouth as if it holds every secret I need to keep living. Nothing has ever felt as perfect as his mouth on mine.

Wait, I take that back.

Feeling him inside me will be.

Benny groans my name like his favorite song and lowers his hands to my ass. He cups each cheek while crushing our bodies together. We don't break our kiss as he guides me out of the bathroom and into the bedroom. He stops me from collapsing onto the bed, and I gasp at the loss of his mouth.

I whine like he took my favorite toy away.

"Take off your clothes," he tells me, palming a hand on his slacks over his cock. "Strip for me."

His gaze turns almost feral while he waits for me to obey. My heart jumps as I slowly lower my hands, pull my dress off, and watch as it puddles at my feet.

His Adam's apple bobs as I stand before him, offering myself while wearing only a black lace bra and a matching thong, leaving little to the imagination.

"I said to take your clothes off. I want to see all of you, Neomi." He starts unbuttoning his shirt.

My experience in stripping for someone is a negative three, so each move I make is overanalyzed.

I might talk a lot of shit, but I don't want to ruin this moment.

A hunger yearns inside me for my husband to want only me.

To desire only me.

I suck in a breath of confidence, wrap my arms around myself, and unclasp my bra. It drops to the floor, and my breasts spill forward.

My attention latches on Benny.

He dances his fingers along the outside of his erection and bites into the corner of his lip. I keep my movements slow as I slip out of my panties, bend at the waist, and toss them in his direction.

He catches them with one hand.

His gaze roams down my body. "You are gorgeous, Neomi. Absolutely breathtaking."

Those tender words said by such a cruel man ignite a fire inside me.

I rub my thighs together, in need of any friction, and wait for his next move.

He shoves my panties into his pants, sheds his shirt, and slowly walks toward me while unbuckling his belt. As soon as he reaches me, his mouth is back on mine. I drag my hand along his bare chest.

Benny has touched me several times, but this is my first time putting my hands on him like this. His chest is solid muscle with a few tattoos scattered along it, and I run my fingers over the ink.

A rose on his chest with the Marchetti name.

Loyalty scribbled inside a shattered heart on his side.

He doesn't offer me time to appreciate his body before shoving me onto the bed. My breath hitches when he drops to his knees like he did in his office. He tosses my thighs over his shoulders and levels his face between my legs.

Surprisingly, I have no insecurity as I bare my most intimate place to him.

I don't fight.

There's no power play.

I'm giving myself to him—consequences be damned.

He skates a finger along my slit. "Want to know a secret, sweet Neomi?"

I slowly nod as he teases me.

Then, without warning, he plunges two fingers inside me.

"I've been dreaming about the taste of your pussy since you came on my tongue last night." He makes one slow lick between my folds. "I think I'm addicted to the taste of you."

I gyrate my hips forward as he pleasures me.

I briefly lose his tongue when he pulls away and says, "That's my girl. Feed your sweet pussy to me. I'm not stopping until you come on my face, and I taste every bit of you."

Ohmigod.

Ohmigod.

1-800-dying.

I slam my eyes shut as he plays with my clit, works me with his fingers, and eats me out like he's a starved man. My back arches off the bed when he covers my entire mound with his mouth, breathing on it and sucking.

And for the first time, I behave like a good little wife and do what my husband ordered.

Feed him my pussy.

Shove my core into his face.

The more contact, the better.

My nipples are hard, aching with need, and I play with one.

Benny doesn't let up or give me a second to calm myself, and I'm *almost there*. I grip his hair, yanking it so tight that I'm shocked I'm not pulling it out, as bursts of pleasure shoot through me. He waits for me to come down from my high before placing a gentle kiss on my clit, standing, and returning to where he was when he ordered me to strip.

He lowers his pants all the way. I rise onto my elbows. The sheets are wet from my sweat. I blow out a breath as his erection springs free.

It's huge.

Engorged.

Pointed straight at me.

He strokes it once. Twice. Three times.

"Do you want me to pleasure you with this cock, Neomi?"

I nod so hard that I'm waiting for my head to break.

He stops stroking himself. "Before I do that, remember what I told you?"

"Uh, nooo?"

"I want to hear you beg." A crooked smirk flashes on his face. "I won't make you do it too much tonight since I'm dying to be inside you, but before I feed that tight pussy my cock, I want to hear those words fall from that fuckable mouth of yours."

Arousal has taken over my brain, but there's still a twinge of awareness there.

Can I do that?

I swore I wouldn't.

Made it clear I'd never give him that.

But apparently, I'm a liar because I look him dead in the eye and say, "Please, Benny," when he returns to jerking himself off.

"Please what?"

"Please fuck me."

"What was that?"

Oh, he's pushing it.

I dig my nails into the sheets. "Please, fuck me."

I expect him to come charging toward me and do what I pleaded for, but he doesn't.

"Make yourself comfortable on the bed," he says. "I want us to do this right."

My juices spread along the bed as I edge off it enough to pull the blankets back and situate myself where I sleep. Benny takes two long strides to the bed, crawls over me, and settles between my legs.

Neither of us says a word as he holds himself up with one arm.

He doesn't bother grabbing a condom, and I don't bother asking him to.

This is my husband.

I want him to take me raw.

He grips the base of his erection and circles the head at my entrance. "Is this what you want, Neomi?" He nudges the head in *just a little* before removing it.

"Yes," I stammer, nearly falling apart—and he isn't even inside me yet.

His every movement is so slow that it's almost painful.

He continues his teasing. "Has anyone fucked this tight little pussy?"

I turn my head, looking away from him.

"No answer?"

I toss my head from side to side.

"I guess I'm about to find out myself then."

He eases his hips forward and enters me.

My body pulsates, my nails digging into his back as he impales me. A sting surges through my body. My knees buckle, but I'm proud of myself for not crying out in pain.

Benny freezes.

His eyes meet mine in question, but I don't mutter a word as he gently pulls out of me.

I buck my hips forward to prevent him from stopping and moan, "More, Benny. Give me more."

A slow smile builds on his face at my pleading.

He slowly pushes himself back inside me.

"God, you're tight," he says, shoving his face into my neck and sucking on my sensitive skin.

Our chests rub against each other's, our sweat mixing as one, and I part my legs wider as he thrusts inside me.

The bed squeaks with each stroke.

Then, he suddenly stops.

He draws his dick out of me and replaces it with two fingers. His eyes fixate on his fingers when he slowly drags them out. I nearly strain my neck to get a good look at what he's doing.

He holds up his fingers and sees the answer to the question I refused to answer before looking down at his aching cock.

There's blood on the head.

My jaw drops in mortification, and if he wasn't on top of me, I'd jump off the bed. Then out the window for the second time tonight.

"I am the only man who's been inside you." There's no playfulness in his tone.

It's soft.

Intimate.

Pleased.

"That's my period," I ramble, suddenly feeling insecure.

Benny rubs his fingers together, playing with the blood and staring at it, as if he's entranced. "You are a terrible liar."

My shoulders slump. "That little sucker has the worst timing."

"My little lying wife." He drops his head to press a single kiss on my thigh. "You saved yourself for me. That's my girl." He inches down the bed until his face is between my legs again.

He takes one long lick down my core.

Licks up *my blood.*

It's so hot, so fucking carnal, so *good.*

A dose of pleasure, need, and infatuation with him sparks through me.

"No, I saved myself *for me*," I correct because it's the truth.

He plunges his tongue inside me, licking me a few more times before rising forward to kiss me. His tongue slides into my mouth as he says, "Taste what you just gave me, baby."

Then, he slips his cock back inside me.

I slam my eyes shut. Never have I felt so on top of the world.

He settles himself onto his knees and takes long, deep strokes inside me. "Watch me while I fuck you, Neomi."

I make the most intense eye contact with him we've ever shared.

Our moaning, mixed as one, is my favorite sound as we finally consummate our marriage. As I fall apart underneath Benny and he comes inside me, Carla's warning corrupts my high.

"And whatever you do, don't fall in love with your husband. He'll rip your heart into pieces."

But I think it's already too late.

I'm falling for my husband.

CHAPTER TWENTY

BENNY

Tonight wasn't just sex with a woman.

It was sex with *my wife*.

A wife I hadn't wanted.

Now, it's the one I don't want to lose.

My mouth waters as I think about what I discovered.

I'm the first man to have her.

Damn, what a high that gave me.

I retreat to the bathroom, grab a warm washcloth, and clean her after we finish. Seeing her arousal mixed with her blood gives me the urge to fuck her again … and to keep fucking her until she knows who she belongs to.

I've never had this feeling with anyone else. It's like this animal inside me has been released, and all he wants to do is mark her so everyone knows she's mine.

I took her hand in marriage.

Her innocence.

And soon, I'll take that pesky, stubborn heart of hers.

Everything of Neomi's will be mine.

When I join her in bed, she curls up to my side, grabs the remote, and chooses a show. The only TV I usually watch is the news to keep up with what's happening in the city.

She selects a show.

I pay little attention to the screen.

There's too much on my mind.

The first: finding out who shot at us tonight.

Someone wants Neomi, or me, or both of us dead.

I need to figure out who that person is and put a bullet between their eyes.

Eh, I'll probably not use a gun.

Torture is the best choice for someone who thinks they can hurt what's mine.

But instead of doing that, I stay with my wife in bed and neglect those responsibilities.

Wait. Fuck that.

Neomi is my responsibility.

I want her to feel safe and loved.

I have to keep us protected. I promised my wife that I wouldn't leave her alone in this piece-of-shit world, and I intend to keep it.

She gave me something she had sworn she never would.

Me not leaving her tonight doesn't compensate for even half of that.

I wait until she's snoring in my arms and the remote drops from her hand before I slip out of bed. I tuck her in, throw on some sweats, empty my pants pockets from earlier, and walk downstairs. I peek through the front window curtain to find Luca's Suburban running in the driveway.

Luca rolls down his window when I step outside and head toward him. His expression confirms he knows he fucked up tonight. And as much as I'm not a man who allows excuses, Neomi put him in a challenging situation. It's not like he could've forced them to sit downstairs with him. But he should've checked on her, watched the cameras, and found it odd that only one sister was hanging out with him.

Fuck, I hope he and Isabella kept their hands to themselves.

The last thing I need is Severino breathing down my neck because my cousin got too friendly with his youngest daughter.

I hold up my hand when he starts to explain himself. "We'll discuss that tomorrow."

I'm being lenient with him.

A rarity for me.

It's as if Neomi's pussy has calmed me.

I hold up the wallet I snatched from the dead driver, open it, and pluck out the ID. "This is the man who was driving the car tonight. Look familiar?"

Luca leans in to look at the ID before shaking his head. "Nah. The name doesn't ring a bell either."

I snap a quick photo of the ID and text it to Raul. He's one of the best hackers in the country. He'll have every detail on the dead disgrace of a man by the time I wake up.

"See if you can get any information and report back to me in the morning," I tell Luca. "The more info I have, the faster I can get rid of this problem."

He nods.

I walk back inside and return to bed with my wife.

I'm not leaving her tonight.

I'll deal with the chaos tomorrow.

CHAPTER TWENTY-ONE

NEOMI

I wake up feeling at peace.

I got a good night's rest for the first time in a long time.

Weird that it's also the morning after I was involved in a high-speed chase and shot at. Oh, and I also killed two men.

My throat tightens at the reminder.

The peace is fading.

I'm no murderer.

It was self-defense.

It was either them or us.

I chose us.

Chose to live.

But that doesn't stop guilt from swarming my soul and biting into my flesh.

They were bad men who would've killed more people, is how I attempt to reassure myself that I'm not a terrible human.

Stretching out in bed, I hear Benny's voice downstairs. His words aren't clear enough for me to make out though.

My body is sore, but it's a comforting ache.

A memory of what happened last night.

What I gave my husband.

All our arguing and fake hating had been nothing but foreplay.

I slide out of bed, stroll to the bathroom, and turn on the shower. While waiting for it to warm, I stare at my reflection in the mirror. My cheeks blush as I remember all the ways he touched me.

I begged Benny to fuck me.

Broke the promise to myself.

But surprisingly, my dignity is fully intact.

He had been right.

I begged. Pleaded. I wanted him so desperately that I would've done anything he asked.

At least he didn't force me onto my knees … yet.

I'm sure his filthy mouth and touch have that planned for us sometime.

I didn't want Benny to know I was a virgin.

I knew he wasn't one, so keeping my virtue a secret gave me a sense of satisfaction. I wanted him to assume I'd also been up to no good before our marriage.

I've had opportunities to lose my virginity, but my conscience wouldn't allow it. If someone found out I had slept with another man while engaged to Benny, there'd have been hell to pay. And I wouldn't have been the one paying for that hell. It'd have been the man. So, I steered clear of dating and sleeping around.

I step into the shower and sigh as water eases down my sore body. I frown, hating that I'm erasing where Benny was. I jump when someone pulls the shower curtain back but relax at seeing a naked Benny.

My husband is gorgeous.

He called me breathtaking, but he has no idea he shares that attribute.

His muscles flex as he joins me in the shower.

I cross my arms and cover myself as I scoot over to allow him room.

My insecurity is a surprise.

This man had his tongue in my vagina last night.

He licked my hymen blood.

Now, I'm suddenly Miss Don't Look at My Chest?

It's nerves. I don't know what version of Benny I'll get this morning.

Was I just a fuck to him?

Or was it more to him too?

Our adrenaline had been up last night.

We'd nearly died together.

Goose bumps cover his chest since he's allowing me most of the water. The shower is small, our bodies spanning nearly every inch, and the water pressure is lacking.

Benny wraps his strong arms around my waist and inches closer, careful not to drag me away from the water.

"Good morning," he says, kissing the top of my head.

"Morning." I press my face into his chilly chest.

Being flush against his skin wraps me into a sense of security. I relax … until he lowers his hand between my legs. I wince as every muscle in my body tenses.

Benny freezes.

"I'm sore," I whimper, my shoulders hunching forward.

My words dawn on him.

"I'm sorry, baby." He grabs my washcloth from the shelf and runs it under the warm water.

A long ease of tension releases from my body when he gently presses the washcloth against my mound.

"Does this help?"

I nod, at a loss for words.

Another version of Benny Marchetti.

He's a man of many surprises.

He keeps the washcloth there for a minute, giving my body some relief. I lose the warmth when he shuffles back a few steps. He presses his lips to mine, slipping a little tongue in, but it doesn't linger long. His attention turns to my washcloth, and he lathers it with soap. His hands are soft and gentle as he washes my body.

He doesn't complain about the lack of water on his body.

About how cold he truly has to be.

His movements are slow, and he asks if I'm sore when he touches certain places on my body where he was a little rough last night.

This isn't about sex.

It's my husband taking care of me.

When he finishes washing me, I do the same with him, and he finally agrees to steal some of my hot water. I haven't had the chance to familiarize myself with Benny's body, as he has with mine. I scrape my nails along his skin and gather up the courage to slip my hand between his legs and teasingly stroke his hard cock.

It's been standing at attention since he joined me in the shower.

Poking my body as he washed me.

It jerks at my touch.

"My naughty little wife," Benny says, biting into his lip.

He doesn't make a move.

I get to make the rules this time.

Our shower turns playful.

Two people exploring each other's body.

I stroke his erection until he grunts out his release and comes in my hand. I play with his cum between my fingers and frown as it washes off my hand down the drain. A strange part of me wishes I'd scrubbed it into my skin, like he did with the soap.

When it's his turn, he pushes me against the wall, sucks on my nipples, and plays with my clit until I'm moaning his name.

He's gentle with me.

Focused.

And checks on me with every touch he makes.

The two sides of my husband couldn't be more opposite, but I love each one in its own way.

We don't leave the shower until the water turns cold. He dries me with the towel before himself, and I step into a black cotton jumpsuit as he towels off.

"We have a meeting today," he tells me while I run a brush through my hair. "In an hour."

I pause mid-stroke. "What kind of meeting?"

"It's a surprise." He winds up his towel and playfully smacks me on the ass.

"As someone who grew up in the Mafia and got shot at last night, surprises aren't my favorite."

"I'm not taking you to a back alley to off you. I promise."

"It wasn't what I was thinking, but now, that's exactly where my brain is."

He kisses me. "Tell it to go somewhere else then."

Once we dress, I make breakfast.

Domestic wife over here.

But in the back of my mind, there's a nagging, saying, *This is too good to be true.*

"Love runs in the opposite direction of me, Neomi. It'd be a waste of my valuable time to even look for it."

I'd be a fool to believe otherwise.

I look at Benny from the passenger seat on our ride to this mystery meeting. "Why do you always drive?"

We're in a new, shiny Escalade. This morning, a man towed the bullet-ridden Range Rover, and two of Benny's men dropped off our new SUV.

"Do you prefer we try another form of transportation for a destination fifteen miles away, where you can't take a train?" Benny replies.

I slap his arm. "That's not what I meant. Almost every boss I know has a driver. But you don't."

"I'm not a boss."

"You're *next in line*. Tommaso has a driver."

A brief silence passes before he answers, "I don't like others in control of where I go."

"So, it's a control thing?"

"That, among other things."

"What are the other things?"

"Natalia was kidnapped by a man loyal to my father for decades." His skin bunches around his eyes. "I'll never put my life in someone's hands unless it's my father or Luca. And I doubt either would want to take the job of my chauffeur."

I don't know the entire story of Natalia's kidnapping, but sorrow floods me. I was terrified of being *almost* kidnapped. I can't imagine what it'd feel like if it actually happened.

Natalia's kidnapping led our fathers to set our wedding date. Cristian wanted the Cavallaros on his side. The deal was similar to what they'd made when Cristian wanted revenge for Benita's murder—my father's loyalty and connections.

Benny turns on the road leading to the mansion and brakes at the gate. He makes small talk with two guards before the gate opens, and we drive through. Today is the first time I get a good look at the mansion. My other visits were in the evening. The first was when I was stressed about marrying Benny, and the second when I was covered in blood, post-kidnapping.

The mansion is almost half castle, half cathedral, and I don't think any New York architecture can compete with its uniqueness. It belongs in medieval times—during the Romanesque era. You hardly pay attention to the immaculate landscaping since the towering home holds all your awareness with its stone walls and high arches.

Instead of driving toward the circular drive, Benny makes a quick right onto a small private road hidden between two rows of trees. He parks behind a black Mercedes on the side of the road. The Mercedes's doors open, and a man and woman step out.

Curiosity trickles through me as we exit the car. The man

rubs a chubby hand through his graying hair and chews on a toothpick while we walk toward them. The woman straightens the collar on the blazer of her pantsuit, and her brown hair is in a low bun at the base of her neck.

"This is Giles, the architect who built my father's home, and Dorinda, an interior designer," Benny introduces. "We are building our dream home here. You tell them what you want, and they'll create it."

"You're building a house for me?"

Benny shakes his head. "I have too much business to do to build you a home." He signals back and forth between Dorinda and Giles. "I'm paying these two to do it for me."

Even though it might appear rude, I turn my back to the two and lower my voice while smiling at Benny. "Is this your way of saying you like your wife?"

"This is my way of saying I want my wife to be the happiest woman on earth, and if a new home makes her happy, I'll build her a new home."

We're interrupted by Benny's phone ringing.

He fishes his phone from his pocket, checks the caller ID, and answers. "Yeah?" He repeatedly nods, listening to the person on the other line, and ends the call.

"That was Raul," he tells me. "He found something in my office at Seven Seconds. I'll be back soon."

My pulse picks up. "What did he find in your office?"

"I have no idea."

Uh-oh.

Maybe I didn't choose the best hiding spot.

Benny drives me to the mansion, where Dorinda and Giles meet me in the dining room. I spend the next two hours answering questions about what I want in a new home. I flip through

Dorinda's portfolio, and they request I create a Pinterest board for my ideas.

When we finish, I walk them out and say goodbye, and as if the world hates me, I run into Gretchen.

Her blue eyes widen in shock.

My gut twists.

"I think it's time we chat," I tell her.

Chatting with a woman who's slept with my husband is the last thing on my want list, but it needs to happen. I can't be like my mother and turn a blind eye to other women.

"Uh ..." She stares at me in reluctance, like I'm holding a gun to her head and asking for her ATM pin number. "What?"

"Look." I raise my hand. "I understand our situation. You and your mother work here. I assume you need this job, and given who you work for, it'd be hard to find work elsewhere."

The Marchettis have more help than my parents. I grew up with landscapers and a cleaning crew who visited our home once a week, but that's it. There were no cooks or in-house help. From what I've heard, it's hard for employees to transfer from family to family—unless their new boss intends to drag information from them.

"We do," she says, rapidly blinking. "My mother has worked for Cristian for decades. It's all she knows."

Gretchen is a pretty little thing, so I'm not surprised she caught Benny's attention. Blonde, perky breasts, and even in her housekeeper attire, you can make out her slim figure.

"I don't want either of you unemployed," I continue, "but you need to understand how disrespectful your behavior was—whether you knew me or not. I could kill you, like Benny did Alden."

Gretchen scrambles back a step.

"*But* I'm *a tad bit* calmer than my husband."

She retreats another step and flinches harder when I say *husband* than she did when I mentioned killing her even though rubbing it in her face hadn't been my intention.

She loves Benny. It's written all over her face.

"Benny told me your marriage would be fake," she says.

"Even so, it's against girl code." I offer my hand, and she shakes it. "Let's make an agreement. You stay away from my husband. If he attempts to come on to you, tell me. If he so much as asks you to even glance at his dick, you let me know." I blow out a long breath. "I'm trying my best here, Gretchen, but it's awkward."

She's lucky I'm not chasing her outside with a damn butcher knife, like I've witnessed my mother do.

Gretchen shifts from one foot to the other in her white Nikes when we drop our hands. "Friends?"

"We're not friends. I know everyone has a past. Your past was fucking my husband, which had better stay in the past."

She slowly nods.

"Not friends, but also not sleeping with the same man."

Gigi and Natalia rush into the foyer, as if the mansion were on fire.

Gigi skirts to a stop. "I heard you two were together." Her gaze travels between Gretchen and me. "But it appears all is well."

"Do all you people think I'm crazy?" I ask.

"We absolutely do," Natalia replies.

CHAPTER TWENTY-TWO

BENNY

I still feel Neomi's scratches on my back as I walk into Seven Seconds. My dick stirs at the reminder of what she gave me ... how it felt when I slid inside her needy pussy. I want to rush to the mansion, take her home, and spend all day pleasuring her sexy body.

I want to touch my unwanted wife every second of every damn day.

Raul smirks and runs a hand over his mustache when I walk into the club's security room, where he and two other men are. The club hasn't opened for the night, so little action is happening.

I jerk my head toward the hallway. Raul follows me into my office. His voice was full of concern when he called and said they'd found something in my office. But now, he's chill as fuck.

I circle my desk and collapse into the chair. "What'd you find?"

My employees and I regularly check my office for bugs, cameras, and items that don't belong. They debugged it after I left with Neomi.

Raul slips something from his pocket and places it on the desk.

I lean forward and pick up what appears to be a small recording device. Playing with it in my hand, I wait for Raul to provide answers.

"We found it on the bookshelf." He points in that direction. "It was placed last night, so there's hardly any footage on it."

Warning bells ring in my ears.

"Did you watch the footage?" I snap, tightening my lips.

He bows his head and slowly nods.

I slam my hand onto the desk, hoping to God they didn't witness me almost taking my wife in here. "Dammit, Raul. You don't watch footage until I instruct you to, and I most definitely did not instruct you to watch shit."

"I'm sorry, boss." Raul clears his throat. "After what happened with the shooting and whatnot, I thought it might give us intel." He scrubs his hand over his mouth, and I see a hint of a smile.

Since when do my men smile?

"There's nothing on the footage but the culprit revealing themself," he continues. "A thumb drive is connected to the side. It seems they forgot to remove that."

"Amateur," I say with a huff.

"I figured you'd want to watch it. It's very ... interesting."

I nod and wave him out of my office. When he leaves, I insert the thumb drive into my computer and relax in my chair, waiting for the show. I play with a pen in my hand as the video starts. And then I understand Raul's smile.

I can't stop myself from doing the same.

I watch as my little wife plants the camera. She steps back, proud of herself, and inspects her pitiful spy work.

"This goddamn woman." I shake my head and turn off the screen before tucking the thumb drive into my pocket.

"Boss!" Raul calls out, chasing me after I leave my office and head for the door. "I also have info on the ID you sent me."

"Don't you think you should've told me that first?" I rub my forehead.

He shoots me an apologetic smile. "The guy was Laurence Hodgkins."

"Never heard the name before."

"He's married to Aria Lombardi."

"Ah. Now, that makes sense."

The Lombardis swore war on my family, and now, they're making good on their promise. Stupid cunts. I want to gut every one of them for putting Neomi in harm's way.

I slap Raul on the back, give a silent thanks, and leave the club. I slam the Escalade door and grab my phone to tell my father every man with the Lombardi name—or who's married to one—needs to die. But my phone rings before I hit his name.

Tommaso's name flashes across the screen.

I debate on answering since I don't have time for his bullshit.

There's a bitter tang in my mouth when I do.

"Benny, we need to talk, man," Tommaso says, his voice rambling at high speed, as if he snorted six lines of coke.

"What do you want, Tommaso?" I ask, sounding bored.

Here I thought, the biggest pain in my marriage would be my sneaky little wife. It turns out, her brother is more of a headache.

"Come to my place." His tone reeks of desperation. "I can't talk about it over the phone."

"I'll give you five minutes of my time." I end the call.

I don't have patience for stupidity.

Which means I have no patience for Tommaso.

I step into his townhome without knocking, and he jumps from the couch at the sound of the door clicking shut. For someone scared for their life, he wasn't smart enough to lock his front door.

His eyes are bloodshot, and his clothes are wrinkled. Dark circles swoop under his eyes. My dude has seen better days.

The townhome is a wreck, but not much different from the last time I was here. Alcohol and drugs litter the table. All it's missing is a woman peeking around the corner. But Tommaso lacks the funds to pay for pussy, so that makes sense.

"They're killing everyone, man," Tommaso croaks, manically pacing in front of me. "My best friend. My coke dealer. And now, my driver."

"I have a question, Tommaso." I rest my back against his wall and cross my ankles. "Why are they killing everyone *but you*? You're the one in debt to them."

Tommaso stalls. "I kind of ..." He scratches his head and slumps on the couch. "They took out loans for me, and I promised to pay them back, so they wouldn't be in trouble with Sammie. But I couldn't!" His voice quickens. "So, I told them to figure it out themselves."

I can't stop from lunging toward him and ramming my fist into his face. I snatch his collar, drag him off the couch, and grip his shirt to slam him into the wall.

"Those people died because of you," I snarl, shoving my arm against his neck and pinning him to the wall. "Go turn yourself into Sammie and let him take care of you like the coward you are."

My blood boils.

Tommaso knew what he was doing when he asked his men to take out loans.

As the son of the don, they couldn't say no. There would've been repercussions. Tommaso led them straight into their graves because he's a piece of shit. Men like him need to be off the streets because they're toxic to this world.

Tommaso gasps for breath as I shove my arm deeper into his windpipe. It could be so easy to kill him here and blame it on someone else. No one would know it was me, and it'd save a lot of people the trouble. His face grows red, his eyes watering, as I contemplate my next move—not caring I'm already choking him to death.

Tommaso's body twitches, and he fights to push me off him. Just as I'm ready to finish the job, Neomi enters my thoughts.

I can't hurt her like that.

I frown while releasing Tommaso and step back.

He collapses to his knees like a rumpled shirt, circles his hand around his throat, and wheezes for breaths.

"Just loan me the money, man," he pleads, staying on his knees and staring up at me. "*Please*, Benny." He drops his shoulders and ducks his chin in. "Don't do it for me. Do it for my sister."

I kick him in the face for mentioning her.

For using her as a manipulative tool for his benefit.

He falls against the wall, and blood pours from his face.

"I'm not giving you a million dollars, especially after seeing this." I gesture toward the drugs and alcohol. "Sell a fucking kidney if you have to." I knock on the wall. "Good luck. You're going to need it."

"What about half?" he yells to my back. "Sammie said he'll take half a million right now until I can get the rest to him."

I don't turn to look at him. "No."

He still struggles to breathe. "They might not go after Neomi because she's married to you, but they'll go after my sisters. Neomi will never forgive you if she finds out you could've stopped it."

I turn on my heel, charge in his direction, and wrench his shirt in my fist. My pulse skyrockets.

"I'll give you five hundred grand." I stare at him in repulsion, spit flying with my words while I work my jaw. "Tell him you'll have it tonight."

He sags against the wall when I release him and rubs at his throat. "Thank you, Benny."

"I'm not doing this for you."

I turn around and leave, slamming the door shut behind me.

Now, I have something to return to my wife.

CHAPTER TWENTY-THREE

NEOMI

With everyone gone, the mansion is boring. Natalia left with Cristian for a doctor's appointment.

Gigi went to her aunt Helena's bakery to help since they're short-staffed.

I briefly consider inviting my sisters over, but I'm unsure what Monster Marchetti's rules are toward guests.

I decide to pass the time by searching Benny's room. Not that I find much—condoms, a few weapons, and a safe in the corner of his closet, hidden by a faux bookcase. I attempt to crack the safe's code four times before accepting defeat. It's not that I want to rob Benny. I'm just nosy.

Cristian and Natalia stroll into the mansion when I return downstairs. Well, Cristian strolls. Natalia waddles. She's wearing an oversize black sweater, showing off her baby bump, and leggings.

They're staring at a piece of paper in Natalia's hand.

"I can't believe he's *that* big," Natalia says in a chirpy voice laced with excitement. She rubs her stomach while holding the paper in the air.

Cristian plants a kiss on her head. "We're getting closer,

sweetheart." He lowers himself to where he's eye-level with her belly and kisses there next.

My chest squeezes, and I can't stop myself from smiling.

The rumors aren't true.

Monster Marchetti does have a sliver of a heart.

At least for his wife and children.

Anyone else, I'm sure he'd slit their throat in a heartbeat.

That means there's hope the prince does too.

Benny's cold blood can warm when he's around those he loves.

"Oh, hey, Neomi," Natalia says when she notices me.

I wave, feeling like I've witnessed a private moment between them.

Cristian slowly rises to his feet. "I'll be in my office if you need me." He kisses her and then nods at me as he passes, clad in his classic black suit. He enters the room I banged on when I was looking for Benny after our wedding.

"We have a new photo of baby Marchetti." Natalia waves the paper and is practically dancing in place. "Want to see?"

I smile and walk toward her.

Natalia's tan face glows as she shows me the ultrasound photo like it's her most prized possession.

"There's my future brother-in-law," I say playfully. I tap the photo, and as if speaking to him, I say, "I hope you're being easy on your mommy in there."

She blows a breath upward. "Oh, he loves blessing me with morning sickness and heartburn. Sometimes, I wonder if he's my son since he gets so temperamental after I eat pizza."

I laugh and follow her into the living room. The room matches the rest of the home with its deep burgundy walls and velvet curtains. Beautiful artwork hangs along the walls, and I stop at a particular piece hanging over the stone fireplace with gorgeous, ornate designs carved into it.

I admire the artwork that doesn't fit with the other decor. It's bright yellow with hints of pink.

"Funny story about this piece," Natalia says, stopping at my side. "I worked at an art gallery, and Cristian purchased this so I'd *meet my sales of the day* and have lunch with him." She laughs and shakes her head at the memory. "He didn't even look at it before buying. I thought it'd be cute to hang it in here—a nice little reminder of how far we've come."

Natalia radiates with love.

No one ever expected Cristian Marchetti to remarry. Then, out of nowhere, he exchanged *I do*s with Natalia. According to the gossip, it was a forced marriage, but their love grew roots that connected them, and now, they're happy.

"Aw, that's sweet," I say.

"Don't let Cristian hear you say that. It's a secret we keep here."

I smile at her. "Your secret is safe with me."

Not that it's much of a secret.

Cristian had no problem going to war for Natalia. Undoubtedly, he has a soft spot in his heart for her.

Natalia cradles her belly as she plops onto the leather sectional, and I sit on the other end. It takes her a moment to make herself comfortable.

I wonder if I'll get that too—to be a mother.

Will Benny and I have children?

Does he want children?

I do, but I don't want to bring them into an unhappy home … a bad environment.

"How's married life?" Natalia asks, breaking into my thoughts.

"It's, uh … interesting."

She nods, understanding my answer. "Benny can be a little …" This time, it's her looking for the right word.

I find it for her. "Overbearing?"

"Yes, but if he cares about you, he'll do anything to keep you safe." She shrugs. "He's a Marchetti."

He's a Marchetti.

She says it as if it explains so much.

That they're their own species.

"Trust me, Benny cares about you." Natalia runs her hand through her long black hair. "These men just display their emotions differently."

"Yes, I figured that out when he showed his jealousy by killing a man in front of me."

"Babe, I wasn't even brought up in this life, and I knew that wouldn't end well."

I nod in agreement.

"He learned his lesson."

"Do you really think so?"

"I *know* so. Cristian was furious, and he vented to me. Benny only makes a mistake once. He won't touch Gretchen again."

"How can you be so sure?"

"Benny keeps his word."

Our conversation is interrupted when the front door opens, and Benny yells my name.

Natalia laughs. "His ears must've been ringing."

"In here!" I shout.

Benny silently strolls into the living room, his hands shoved in his pockets, and my mouth waters at the sight of him.

He stands at the coffee table, fishes something from his pocket, and holds it up.

I stare at the camera, pretending to be confused, and refuse to make eye contact with him. "What's that?"

Benny holds it flat on his hand and moves closer to give me a better look. "*Someone* stashed this in my office."

I press my hand on my chest and gasp. "You'd better go find who did it."

"I'm looking at her."

Natalia snorts, and Benny shoots her a quick glance.

She covers her mouth, as if holding in laughter and pulls herself up from the couch. "I need to go tell your father about this. You two have fun." She pats Benny's shoulder as she passes him. "By the way, your brother is the size of a plum." She releases the laughter she was masking as she exits the room.

Shit.

I thought I'd found a decent hiding spot, but I should've known Benny had his office checked regularly. My father has our home swept every two weeks for planted devices by three different people, in case one is a rat.

My father has a box full of those hidden cameras in our garage, ready for use whenever needed.

Benny theatrically plays with the camera in his hand. "Let's go upstairs and chat."

"Hard pass. I just made myself comfortable." I make a show of stretching out. "I'd suggest you spend your time looking for whoever is planting devices in your office."

He stuffs the camera in his back pocket, and I expect him to leave the room.

I'm so wrong. I gasp, not having a second to put up a fight when Benny hauls me off the couch and throws me over his shoulder.

"What the hell?" I shriek, slapping his back. "Put me down, Benito Marchetti."

"Oh, she's back to Benito." He smacks my ass and carries me up the stairs. When we're out of earshot from others, he lowers his voice. "I'm going to make you scream it when I'm fucking you."

"Pfft, yeah, right." I yelp when he slaps my ass again—this time harder.

The sting radiates down my legs as he hauls me into his bedroom. I slam my hand over my mouth to mask my half moan, half laugh.

I said *yeah, right*, but given my latest history with Benny, when I tell him I won't do something, he seems to want to drag it out of me more.

He drops me onto my feet, pushing me to the center of his

bedroom, and slams the door shut.

Does he think he'll fuck me here?

In his father's home?

My heart pumps so hard that I can hear it in my ears.

Although I'm not sure if that's happening out of fear or excitement.

Benny locks the door and casually strolls toward me. He retrieves the camera from his pocket and tosses it back and forth between his hands.

I frown. "I should've known you'd find it."

He stops the tossing when he reaches me. "Then, why'd you do it?"

"To keep an eye on you."

"To keep an eye on me sitting at a desk and working?"

"To make sure my husband didn't fuck a woman in his office and then come home, thinking he could do the same to me."

I planted the camera *before* we had sex for the first time, but maybe deep down, I knew we'd eventually consummate our marriage. No matter how much I lied to myself.

My face reddens as I continue, "I've never been a fan of sharing. Ask my sisters."

He's so close that I can practically taste his peppermint breath.

"Why'd you think I'd be touching other women in my office?"

I make an *are you serious* expression. "Your history in the billiards room can be exhibit A."

"Would you be jealous?" He carries amusement in his tone.

"I think any wife would be jealous of another woman touching her husband."

He circles me like a shark does its prey. "What if the wife claims she doesn't like him?"

I scoff. "I think we both know that when I say those words, they're becoming more of a lie each time."

Benny freezes.

My honesty shocks us both.

I wasn't supposed to say that.

I'm internally screaming at myself for it.

He stares at me in gratification, as if I did him the favor of a lifetime.

I swallow and am frozen in place while waiting for his next move.

He wiggles the camera in the air. "Who else has access to this?"

"No one. The only access is that thumb drive. It saves everything on it."

He strolls to the dresser, shoves away cologne bottles, and settles the camera in its place. I lose a breath when he creates a show of pointing the camera toward me.

"Since you're such a fan of recording"—he rests his back against the dresser next to the camera and crosses his arms—"strip for me."

I clear my throat. "Excuse me?"

"I said, *strip for me.*" He uncrosses his arms to rub his chin as the words leave his mouth and then recrosses them. "Instead of watching me with another woman, which you assumed you would, you'll get quite the show from us instead."

I stifle a breath. "Hard pass on being a victim to revenge porn."

He flinches. "Like I'd ever allow anyone else to see what's mine."

The room closes in as he removes the thumb drive from the side of the camera.

"You and I will be the only people to have access to this." He plays with it between his fingers while clicking his tongue against the roof of his mouth. "Now, I want to punish you for being sneaky. The first step of your atonement is to strip for your husband." He licks his top, then bottom lip while sliding the thumb drive back into the camera.

There's no joking on his face.

Or in his voice.

My brain spins.

"Now, Neomi." He snaps his fingers. "Or I will hold you down, slip this camera inside your pussy, and provide myself with an even better view."

My skin warms so hot that I'm waiting for it to burn off.

Benny has lost his marbles.

He raises his brow in question.

I choose to strip.

The room is quiet, except for our rapid breathing, as I drag my sweater over my head and unclasp my bra. My movements aren't slow. I want some say in this too. Benny will not make all the rules. I smirk while tossing my sweater in his direction. My target is the camera, but he catches it before it hits the recording device.

"Do that with your panties next," he says in a raspy voice.

He drops the sweater and palms his cock over his pants. I notice the outline of an erection swelling underneath the fabric.

I kick off my boots, slide out of my jeans, and slip off my thong. The loud hiss that leaves him reverberates through the room when I wad the panties up in my hand and hold them up. For a moment, I contemplate if I should follow his orders.

Benny slowly shakes his head like he can read my mind. "Don't test me, Neomi."

When I hurl it toward him, he catches the thong with one hand while keeping the other over his dick.

Shock flickers through me when he shoves the panties against his face and groans.

It's carnal.

Dirty.

So damn erotic.

I want to charge toward him, push him on the ground, and ride his cock.

But I don't because as much as I want him inside me, what he's doing with my thong entrances me. He curls his tongue around my thong, and I almost die when he draws it into his mouth, sucking the fabric between his lips.

What do I taste like?

Good? Bland?

When he shoved my panties into my mouth in his office, I made it my mission not to taste myself. It seemed too lewd. But Benny kissed me after eating me out last night. I found it hot but didn't taste anything significant.

But Benny acts like a man enjoying the best meal of his life while he sucks on my thong.

Now fully naked, I wait for his next order.

"Sit on the edge of the bed and touch yourself," he demands. "Play with your swollen clit that I sucked on last night." He groans, his own words turning him on. "Remember how good my mouth felt on you, my sweet wife?"

His words are like ecstasy to me.

I gape at him. "You want me to … *in front of you?*"

"In front of me." He shoves my panties into his pocket and taps his knuckles against the camera. "Show that pretty pussy to the camera and give me the view of a lifetime."

His request is risky.

Benny could blackmail me with it.

Someone could find it and put the video online.

But my hardly functioning brain isn't considering rationality at this point.

I'm more worried about how well I can pleasure myself with him watching.

Will it be awkward?

It'll definitely be awkward.

I've never had an audience. My masturbation has always been in the privacy of my bed with my hand hidden beneath my blanket as I made myself come.

Benny loosens his cuff links and spreads his legs. He makes a show of making himself comfortable while waiting for *my show.*

"I want to watch you fuck yourself with your fingers." He

throws his head back. "Do that, and I will fuck your pussy with every inch of my cock while you writhe underneath me in pleasure."

My brain might be half functioning, but it apparently understands the assignment. I run his order through my mind—ensuring I have it right—and lower myself to the edge of the bed. My legs tremble as I part them wide.

"Already so wet," Benny says, watching me. "Pull your ass up, baby. Give me a better view."

My stomach clenches like I'm doing squats as I lift my ass.

"Your heels on the bed."

My feet slip off the bed once as I maneuver myself.

"Now, show me how you touch yourself, Neomi."

I delve my hand between my legs and run two fingers through my slit. Slight embarrassment from being so on display creeps through me, but my need for him outweighs any shame.

He grips the edge of the dresser, his knuckles white as I moan his name and tease my slit. *Tease him.*

The more he's turned on, the faster he'll take over the job of pleasuring me.

"I won't help you come yet. That is your punishment for being sneaky and assuming you could outsmart me."

The sound of him unbuckling his belt mixes with my moans.

"Thrust two fingers inside yourself." He unzips his pants but doesn't lower them. "Slowly, so when I rewatch, I can take my time jerking myself."

He watches me as I plunge two fingers inside myself.

Thrusting them in and out.

And I gyrate my hips, like I did with Benny last night.

"Play with your clit."

I probably look inexperienced, but Benny doesn't complain.

Nor does he appear bored.

His gaze is glued on me—moving from my parted thighs to my bouncing bare breasts and my face. He guides me on what to do, and I huff out breaths while complying.

The ache between my legs grows so intense that I slide against his comforter, needing more friction.

"Fuuuck," he groans. "Yes, baby. Rub your pussy against my blanket like you would my face. I want your sweat in this bed. Your smell. Your pussy juices. I want all of it on every piece of furniture I own, on every inch of my fucking skin. I want you smeared everywhere, Neomi."

As if that one simple shift sets him off, he hurriedly unbuttons his shirt, allowing it to slip off his arms. The sight of his bare chest, his nipples hardening, causes me to hump his bed faster. He roughly shoves his pants down, releasing his thick cock, and I watch him as intensely as he stares at me.

He jerks himself off.

His breathing labored.

Curse words and my name fall from his lips like sin.

I can't take it anymore.

I'm crashing.

Hitting my brink.

As much as I wanted to wait for Benny to finally fuck me, I can't.

I arch my back, thrusting my chest forward, and run my hand along my stomach as pleasure rips through me.

I come on Benny's blanket.

Soaking it with my release and smearing it, like he ordered.

I've never seen someone remove their shoes and socks so fast. He throws them across the room. One slams into a mirror, and I'm shocked it doesn't shatter.

He grabs the camera and darts toward me. As he sets the camera on the nightstand, he grabs my ankles and yanks me to the edge of the bed. My eyes widen, and my mouth opens when he settles his thighs on each side of my face. His cock is *right there*.

He rubs it over my face, like I rubbed my pussy against his bed. The bottom of his shaft drags over my lips, nose, and cheeks, nearly smothering me. I hold out my tongue, licking what I can of his length and balls, as he punishes my face for my sneaky behavior.

He groans, slamming one hand on the bed next to my face and the other to my chest, holding me in place.

I thought him watching me was erotic.

But this Benny is—*God*—so raw.

So fucking hot.

"You want this big cock inside you?" he asks, rotating his hips, like he wants me to feel his cock on every inch of my face. "Stretching you?"

The position we're in is awkward, and if he wasn't holding my chest down, I'd slip off the bed. To help him keep me up, I lower my heels to the floor while relishing his sensitive skin along mine.

"Is your pussy still too sore for me?" he pants harshly. "I saw how wet it was. I know I could slide inside so easily."

He pulls back, releases me, and lowers his gaze to meet mine. "If it is too sore, can I still have it? Will you take this cock like a good girl even if it stings?"

I run a hand over where his dick was.

"Answer my question." He scoops pre-cum off the tip of his dick and smothers it across my mouth. "Answer it with my cum on your lips. Taste it with your every word."

The expression on Benny's face is the opposite of how he looked last night.

This is the merciless Benny.

The man who will fuck me like he violently kills on the streets.

My insides spark at the excitement of getting such a side of him.

"Please." I lick his cum from my lips.

He lowers his length to my clit, nudging it with the head, and I slam my eyes shut.

"I was gentle last night, but sometimes, even girls who beg for my cock so good don't get gentle." He flips me onto my stomach and drags my knees up so my ass is in the air. "Sometimes, when they get in trouble, they're spanked and fucked hard with no mercy."

He plunges inside me and makes good on his words—where he told me I wouldn't get his mouth or fingers.

He fucks me wildly.

Digs his nails into my waist.

I'm forced farther up the bed with every untamed thrust.

"Put your face down. In the comforter," he says, driving into me. "Smell the evidence you left of your pussy there."

When I don't move fast enough, he grips the back of my head and does it for me. My breathing is limited, and the blanket sticks to my skin.

"That's what I smell when my head is between your legs." He inhales deeply and grunts. His balls smack into my ass.

"More," I say when he loosens his hold and allows me to turn my head. "Give me more, Benny." I dig my nails into the blanket and glance back at him, pleasure swarming every inch of my face.

"Turn your head. Look at the camera while you beg for more of my cock." He loosens his hold on my head, allowing me to do so.

I stare straight into the lens. "Fuck me harder, Benny."

He gives me one single plunge. "Say please."

"Please."

"Look at that, my wife who said she'd never beg is now making it part of her regular vocabulary." He smacks my ass. "Just like she said I'd also never spank her."

He gives me more.

Gives me everything.

Makes me feel like a wife whose husband is wild for her.

Out-of-control lust for intimacy with her.

No barriers or confliction between us.

Benny collects my hair in his hand. "I'm giving you sixty seconds to come on this hard cock, or I'm pulling out of you and making you go about the rest of your day without being filled with my cum."

I stare back at him in challenge. "It's *your* job to make me come, Benny. Don't be an inadequate husband."

My words set him on fire.

He pounds into me, as if using my body to move mountains.

Tells me what a good girl I am.

How good it feels inside me.

He counts down the seconds.

It doesn't take sixty.

It takes five.

My knees collapse on the bed, my body losing all power of itself, but Benny hoists me back up. The wild fucking doesn't stop until he's gripping one ass cheek in his hand, moaning my name, and filling me with his cum.

I glance in Benny's en suite bathroom mirror and fuss with my hair. "I can't believe you didn't tell me we were having dinner with your family before screwing my brains out here."

After we pulled our sticky bodies away from each other, Benny suggested we shower. I declined since I didn't want my hair to get wet. He helped clean me with a washcloth—*no judging. I'll shower as soon as I get home*—before he showered.

But now that I'm looking at myself, I realize I made the wrong choice.

I should've also stopped and considered the disrespect of sleeping with Benny in his father's home—even if Benny is a guy. I don't want Cristian to be unhappy about it.

Though I'm probably not the first woman Benny has screwed here.

I cringe at the thought.

"You look beautiful. I love your *just fucked* look the best,"

Benny says, coming up behind me while wearing only a taupe towel tied around his waist.

Water drips from the tips of his hair while I run my hand through a knot in mine.

"Concetta Cavallaro would not approve of this look or behavior," I mutter.

In fact, my mother would have a coronary.

He circles an arm around my waist, and the smell of fresh soap invades our air. "But Benny Marchetti does."

I shudder when he gently kisses my cheek before lowering his hand between my legs over my jeans. As a natural reaction, I wince.

"Did I make you sorer?" he asks with concern.

I smile at his reflection and shake my head. "No."

"You lying?"

"Absolutely not."

He rests his chin in the crook of my neck and blows out a long breath. "I should've waited before taking you so rough. It was only your second time—"

I speak over him. "I liked it."

As a virgin, I never knew what I'd like during sex.

I've watched a variety of porn—romantic couples, BDSM, even girl-on-girl—while discovering what turned me on.

But you can watch tons of porn and still not know what your body physically likes.

My body likes when Benny worships it.

It also likes when he abuses it—*so long as* I'm okay with it.

I trust Benny enough to know he'll stop if I'm not comfortable.

Benny squeezes my waist. "You let me know if I'm ever too rough."

"I like you rough."

"Let. Me. Know."

He retreats to the bedroom while my complaining moves from the rat's nest on my head to my smeared makeup.

When Benny returns to the bathroom, the camera is in his hand.

He removes the thumb drive and plays with it between his fingers. "This might be my new best friend."

I stare at him pointedly. "Burn it."

"I can't wait to watch it. Can't wait *for us* to watch it."

My lips twitch into a smile.

I want to try every fantasy with my husband.

"Neomi, I appreciate you not killing my employee today," Cristian says from the head of the dining table when Benny and I sit for dinner.

My stomach rumbles at the smell of whatever is cooking in the kitchen, and my eyes widen at Cristian's comment.

"I have cameras on every inch of this place," he adds.

I'm certain the Marchettis have a death penalty rule for snitches, but here's Cristian, ratting on me, as if he'd been offered a pretty plea deal.

My husband keeps secrets from me.

I planned to keep my conversation with his mistress one of mine.

But of course, nothing can stay hidden when it comes to the Marchettis.

"Cameras everywhere, *except* for the bedrooms and bathrooms," Gigi points out, smiling at me. "Those are camera-free, for obvious reasons."

My cheeks turn as red as the wine in my glass when Benny winks at me and squeezes my thigh. His bedroom wasn't camera-free around an hour ago.

I snatch the glass, needing something to hold on to, and smile at Cristian. "I figured you'd hate me if I was the cause of another dead body in your beautiful home."

Technically, Alden's dead body was Benny's doing.

I hadn't forced him to pull the trigger.

I might've nudged him a bit, but he could've restrained himself.

My intent wasn't to hurt Gretchen during our chat. Hell, I hadn't even planned to speak with her until she appeared in my view again. Us running into each other was a sign we needed to talk. As much as I want to be a jealous bitch and have Gretchen fired, I won't.

Unless she decides to drop to her knees in front of my husband again.

"I appreciate it," Cristian replies, his tone as dry as the paint on the walls.

"What are you talking about?" Benny asks, his gaze wandering to me.

"Neomi and Gretchen hung out today," Gigi answers for me, perking up in her chair and eagerly swirling her wine in her glass. "Quality girl time."

Gigi likes to stir up shit.

She's definitely a Marchetti.

Natalia covers her mouth and laughs.

All eyes are on Benny, waiting for his reaction.

"Everything good then?" Benny asks, and a slight yawn leaves him with the last word.

"Considering they are both breathing, I believe so," Cristian says, straightening his white cloth napkin onto his lap.

Benny gives no reaction to Gretchen and me speaking. You'd think we were old friends.

The door swings open, and two servers step through with plates in their hands. All Gretchen conversation ceases as they deliver the rib eye with pesto pasta and Caesar salad.

We make small talk while eating.

I don't say much. I just watch.

I focus on Cristian and Natalia interacting.

Just like in the foyer, he speaks and stares at her as if she owns his world.

They call him Monster Marchetti, but there's a light when she's with him.

I want the same with Benny.

And just maybe ... I might get it.

"Are you upset I spoke with Gretchen?" I ask Benny on our drive home.

He hasn't shown one sign he's angry.

In fact, he's acted the opposite.

Squeezing my thigh under the dinner table.

Giving me half his chocolate cake after I devoured mine.

Complimenting my cooking skills to his family.

My question is from my insecurity ... and curiosity.

Benny clicks the turn signal and cuts a right at a stop sign. "Why would I be mad?"

I smooth a hand down my hair. "Because she used to be your ..."

"My what?"

"I don't know." I stiffen my spine and sit straighter in my seat. "Why don't you answer for me?"

Before our engagement party, I didn't monitor Benny's doings, as he did with me. I was confident he was up to no good, so I had no purpose to seek reasons to hate him further.

I wouldn't be as bothered if Gretchen were a random woman with no affiliation to his family. But this is different. They'll see each other regularly, and when we spoke, I could tell Benny meant something to her. She wasn't a stray he'd picked up at our engagement party, like Alden had been with me.

They have history.

Familiarity.

Something I don't have with my husband.

"Gretchen and I regularly had sex," he answers. "She was convenient."

I scrunch up my face. "Calling someone convenient regarding sex sounds gross. How many *conveniences* did you have? One on every corner, like a 7-Eleven?"

"I'm picky about who I sleep with, so *no*. For the past six months, *prior to our marriage*, Gretchen was the only woman I slept with."

"Did you ..." I play with my hands in my lap. "*Do you* care about her?"

Exclusively sleeping with someone for six months isn't a fling.

It's pretty much dating, even if Benny wants to deny it. There might've been a lack of romance and roses, but emotions are bound to form over that length of time.

My heart flip-flops in my chest.

I haven't been Benny's wife for even a week, I have only slept with him twice, and I'm scared of losing what we're building. I can't imagine having him for six months and then him walking away with someone else.

Benny scratches his head. "I don't want any ill will to happen to Gretchen, but if you're referring to me loving her, the answer is no."

"If you didn't have to marry me, would you be in a relationship with her?"

"No."

I dig my nails into the leather center console and huff. "Of course, you're going to say that."

"All I have for you is the truth. If I hadn't been forced to marry you, I'd be single. A relationship—*love*—was the last thing on my mind."

"What about now?" I whisper into the darkness of the car.

"Now, it seems I can't take my mind off you."

"Is that a good thing?"

"Yes, baby. It's a *very* good thing."

CHAPTER TWENTY-FOUR

BENNY

Luca stares at me as if I've lost my mind. "I know he's your brother-in-law, but we regularly deal with men like him, Benny. You'll never get your money back, and you'll be out half a mil."

I'm aware Tommaso won't pay me back. I'll be lucky if I get a couple of hundred dollars before he raises another debt with someone else. I'm no fan of handing out loans. I acquire my income from club profits, racketeering, and extortion, among other illegal activities.

Men don't like to owe me anything, but it'll be different with Tommaso. After my lack of killing him at his townhome for his sister, I'll be at the bottom of the payback list. But I can only be so understanding until he crosses enough lines where I can't control myself.

I won't kill him over money.

I can easily make more money.

He'll die if my wife is put in harm's way again.

"I'm not doing it for that fucker," I reply, running my hands through my hair. "I'm doing it for my wife. I can replace the money, but I can't replace her." Or her heart if one of her sisters dies.

"Holy shit." Luca's eyes widen, and a shit-eating grin takes over his face.

I wave my hand dismissively. "She's my wife, you idiot."

He continues to smirk.

"Shut up and make sure nothing happens to her." I toss him the keys to the front door. "I'll be back in a few hours. If she sneaks out, you're sleeping outside in the cold until at least one of your fingers gets frostbite and falls off."

"Having you as a cousin is so fun," he mutters, twirling the keys around his finger.

I flip him off, slap the hood of the Escalade before slipping inside, and drive to the club.

After I recorded the best porn ever with my wife, we came home. She yawned a good twenty-five times on the drive. When I told her I had a few problems to take care of, I was surprised she hadn't argued and thrown out a reason about not trusting me. Instead, she said she would watch *Buffy* and then probably crash before making it through an episode.

My throat turns dry at the thought of her not trusting me.

It's my fault.

I regret what I did at our engagement party.

Deep down, I worry she'll always see me as that guy.

We had no loyalty toward each other. Neomi swore we'd never be anything but married strangers. But now, the thought of touching another woman makes my skin crawl.

I need to convince Neomi of that.

I call Tommaso, but it goes to voicemail. We texted earlier. I instructed him to tell Sammie he'd have half the money but not tell him—*or* anyone else—where he was getting it. Traveling with such a large amount of money in cash is dangerous. He replied that Sammie said to call him as soon as he had the money, and he'd be there.

My first stop is the club. I swerve into my designated parking space, nod to the guard at the door, and head straight for my office. Locking the door behind me, I key the password into the hidden keypad on the bookshelf. The front of the book-case swings open, revealing a secret door, and I input another password before entering the safe room. Four floor-to-ceiling safes line the long wall. The other wall holds shelves of weapons, and file cabinets are on the other. This room is the FBI's wet dream.

I grab a black duffel bag from the floor, open the safe, and pack the cash inside the bag. It takes two bags to fit all the money. Even though I try to appear as discreet as possible, anyone walking out of a club with two large bags looks suspect. When I return to the Escalade, I shove the bags underneath the passenger seat and call Tommaso again.

No answer.

The fuck?

With his earlier desperation, I figured he'd be waiting by the phone for my call. Annoyance hits me as I drive to his town-home. If he's partying, assuming he's off the hook now that I'm helping him, I'm going back on my word.

It'll be the first time I ever do, but it's worth breaking my streak for Tommaso.

I spot his red BMW parked in its usual space and park behind it. I leave the duffel bags in the car, lock it, and curse his name as I walk up the porch steps.

"Tommaso," I say, banging on the door.

No answer.

I wiggle the doorknob to find it unlocked.

"Tommaso," I yell again before opening the door and entering.

I ease my gun from my pocket when I spot blood on the white tiles. The only noise is a news reporter on the TV, rattling off the city's rise in crime stats.

I peek around the corner and find Tommaso in the living room. He's on the couch with a gunshot between his lifeless eyes, and his hands are tied behind his back. There's no evidence of anything stolen to sell and get some of their money back.

Tommaso's townhome is full of shit they could have pawned for a pretty penny.

"Fuck," I hiss, walking over to him.

Even though I know what dead looks like, I check his pulse.

Dead.

Whoever pulled the trigger sure helped me out.

I grab my phone and call Severino.

He answers on the third ring.

"It's Benny," I say. "You need to come to Tommaso's now."

"What's going on?" Severino snaps. "Let me speak with my son."

"I'm afraid that's not possible."

"I'm on my way." He ends the call, but from his tone, he knows.

Severino understands he's about to see his son's dead body.

And now, I have to tell my wife her brother is dead.

CHAPTER TWENTY-FIVE

NEOMI

"Wake up, baby."

I slowly open one eye and then the other at the sound of Benny's voice.

The lamp on the nightstand shines in the darkness, creating my only source of light. Benny sits on the edge of the bed next to me. The bed indents at his weight, and he stares down at me.

He's still wearing the clothes he had on when we left earlier. I relax, cuddling into his touch, and he runs a chilly hand along my cheek.

But that relaxation dissipates when he fails to meet my eyes. His shoulders hunch forward, and a vein stands out in his neck.

Dread swallows my stomach.

I've accompanied my mother on too many visits to homes where she broke the news that one of their loved ones had passed. My father preferred us to tell them. It showed compassion for the people who'd put their lives on the line for our family.

I sit up and scoot back until my back is against the headboard, shoving bedhead hair from my face.

"Benny"—my voice cracks—"what is it?"

I'm met with silence.

I shove his shoulder. "Benny!"

His face is tense. "Your brother is dead."

There's a lack of compassion there.

Not purposely, but I understand it.

My stomach clenches so tight that I'm worried it'll never loosen.

"You're lying!" I scream, shoving his shoulder again but with more force this time.

His Adam's apple bobs as he stares at me with a grave face. "He's gone, baby. He was murdered."

My lower lip trembles, sorrow trickling through my veins, and I spring out of bed. I scramble around the room, appearing lost while also on a mission. My brain is scattered, so many emotions slicing through me, and the only one I can keep up with is, *I need to get out of here.*

"I need to go see my parents," I say, finally able to form words. "My sisters." I shove open the closet door and attempt to tear a shirt down. Clothing falls, and hangers bend during my struggle.

It's like I have no control over my motor functions.

My body locks up when Benny's arms wrap around me from behind.

"Relax, baby," he says, his voice the softest I've ever heard.

I gulp, my insides shaking. "Let me go, Benny."

He doesn't listen.

I squirm, attempting to escape, but he doesn't loosen his hold.

I kick at his shins.

Elbow his stomach.

The longer he holds me, the harder I fight.

"*Please,* calm down." He whips me around to face him while maintaining his grip. "It's late. I can't let you leave right now. We'll go to your parents' in the morning."

"No!" I scream, turning my head away from him and kneading my knuckles into his chest. "Let me go!"

He grabs my chin, forcing me to stare at him while I struggle. My eyes grow wet, and tears threaten their appearance.

I have to get out of here.

And finally, because I don't know any other way to convince him to let me go, I grit out the words, "Please let me go, Benny. I don't want you to see me like this."

I don't cry in front of people.

I'm the only witness to my sadness.

My father taught us that early.

We display anger and happiness. Nothing more.

If we wanted to cry, we had to leave the room and couldn't return until every trace of a tear was gone. I want to be strong and go to my family, but first, I need to be alone to release my pain. I want to shove myself in a room alone and cry until another tear cannot come.

Benny doesn't allow that.

He only holds me tighter.

"Let it out, baby," he says, dragging me into his chest and massaging my back. "Fall apart in my arms, so I can put you back together."

With my face shoved in his shirt, I shake my head but stop fighting.

It's useless.

He won't allow me to hide.

Even if I were to escape his arms, he'd kick down the door to hold me.

To comfort me.

Benny's voice turns scratchy, as if my pain is bleeding into him. "Let me be your husband—*your real husband*—and hold you while you fall apart."

Just like I lose the strength to fight Benny, I lose the power to hold in my tears. All my control splinters, crashing at our feet, and a screeching sob leaves me. My body relaxes into his, nearly collapsing into his arms, as I give him my pain.

He breathes it in.

Inhaling it.

He presses his lips to my hair.

Caresses my back.

Makes me feel like I have someone—that he gives a damn.

We stand there for what seems like hours.

How did this happen?

Who killed my brother?

Benny's shirt is soaked with my tears and snot when I finally pull away. I stare at the ground, my heart shattering, and he keeps his arm around my shoulders while guiding me back to bed.

He makes sure I'm settled before walking to the bathroom and returning with tissue. Instead of handing them over, he wipes my face, even collecting the snot.

"I need to call my parents." My throat is hoarse.

Just thinking of the pain they're going through causes another round of tears. My stomach churns.

What did Tommaso do?

How can he be gone?

We always said his behavior would lead him to an early grave, but I didn't believe it'd happen so young.

"Your father is breaking the news to them," he says, smoothing his thumb over my cheek. "It's late. I told him we'd go there in the morning."

My eyes are heavy, and I struggle to keep them open as I nod.

When he pulls away, I dig my nails into his shirt. "Please don't leave me."

"I'm right here, baby," he says, pressing a kiss on my lips. "I'll be right here all night."

He wraps me in his arms.

Tonight, my husband will hold me while I break down.

Tomorrow, I will ask him to kill for me.

My brother is dead.

I'll never hear Tommaso crack a stupid joke or attempt to boss me around again. My parents lost their only son. The heir to the Cavallaro family throne is gone.

Will our family cease to exist when my father is gone?

Or will he appoint someone else to take over?

For generations, they passed down control of the family from father to son. That legacy can no longer persevere.

One small change, and everything collapses.

My head throbs, and I feel like I didn't get a wink of sleep as I roll over in bed to find Benny beside me. He's still in his clothes from last night. His messy black hair and tired eyes confirm he got less sleep than I did.

He drops his phone in his lap. "You're awake."

My throat is dry. "I'm awake."

There's no doubt this is different for us.

Slightly awkward.

I shut my eyes, and flashbacks of how he comforted me last night sweep through me. My crying didn't last long after he tucked me into bed. As silence circled us, Benny stayed with me, not leaving my side. I cursed my brother with sadness and anger, and Benny comforted me.

"How are you feeling?" he asks.

I rise and sit next to him. "Like my entire world is falling apart." I run my fingers along the blanket, ripping at a snagged thread. "Will you promise me something?"

"What did I tell you about my promises?"

I slowly drag my gaze to his and meet his eyes. His are soft and curious to my dull ones.

"You don't make promises you can't keep," I whisper.

He slowly nods.

I clear my throat to make it as clear and alert as possible. "I want you to kill the man who murdered my brother."

Benny frowns and scrubs a hand over his tired face.

"It was the loan shark, right?"

His brow furrows, a slight wrinkle forming on his forehead. "At first, it's what I thought. But shit isn't adding up."

"What isn't adding up?"

He blinks, as if his mind has been attempting to solve this question all night. "I told Tommaso I'd pay a portion of his debt to get Sammie off his back, and according to Tommaso's texts, Sammie agreed. He planned to pick up the money after I dropped it off."

I scoot in closer to him and rest my head along his shoulder. "Is that where you went last night?"

"Yes, but it makes no sense for Sammie to kill him when he knew a half-million dollars was coming."

"A half-million dollars?" I shriek, jerking away to gape at him. "Are you nuts?"

Benny shakes his head, a slight smirk on his lips at my reaction. "Not nuts, baby. Just a man protecting his wife." He drags me back to him, lifts his arm, and tucks me into him.

"Whoever it is, I want them dead." I hate how much anger is in my voice, but I can't help it.

"Then, I will kill them for you."

You know what's more heartbreaking than losing someone you love?

Watching someone you love absolutely break from that loss.

My family will never recover from this.

My parents lost their only son. Their first child.

My mother refuses to leave her bedroom.

My father refuses to stay home.

My sisters are lost.

They all deal with their pain in different ways.

I feel almost selfish for having Benny—for having someone unbroken to lean on during this time.

I've been at my parents' from sunup to sundown for the past

week. I spend time with my sisters, tend to my mother, and assist with any arrangements for Tommaso. Benny works and then returns to my parents' around dinner. We eat with my sisters, or Benny and I go home and have dinner. He hasn't spent one night away from me, not even staying late at the club.

It's like I have a true marriage.

A real husband and partner.

It's midday, and I'm helping Bria and Isabella with lunch when my father pokes his head into the kitchen.

"Neomi, can we talk in my office?" he asks.

I drop my knife on the cutting board. "Of course."

He doesn't wait for me to wash my hands and is already seated behind his desk when I enter his office. I gulp while sitting, remembering the last time I was here. It was the night of my engagement party, when he scolded me for my behavior.

That all seems like it happened so long ago.

I shut my eyes and remember how Tommaso was pushy about me behaving with Benny. I should've put two and two together then.

For years, Tommaso had talked shit about Benny and didn't support our marriage, but suddenly, he had a change of heart. I thought my father's influence had changed his mind, but he did it for his survival—further proving every man is for himself.

That also proves people aren't as indestructible as they believe.

Tommaso had the Cavallaro name and Benny as his brother-in-law, and he still couldn't stay alive.

No matter who you know or where you come from, your actions will always carry more weight. You can have the brightest future ahead, but one wrong move can destroy it all.

My father grabs a handkerchief from his desk and wipes his clammy forehead. "Hi, honey."

"Hi, Daddy," I reply softly.

The tension is heavy.

My father stares at me, his face a mixture of anguish and

sternness. "If something happens to me, you must stay strong for this family." He holds his fist to his mouth and clears his throat to erase the emotion cutting through. "Your mother and sisters will need you."

"Why would you say that?" I harshly squint at him and wish I could raise my voice. "You're not going anywhere for a long time."

He sighs and slumps his shoulders. "The Cavallaro name will die with me."

"No, it won't." My voice breaks. "Don't say that."

My father—the boss of a Mafia empire—stares at me in pain.

Devastation.

No amount of money or power can fix heartache.

He plans to kill whoever killed Tommaso. I can see it in his eyes.

I want to tell him Benny has it covered, but I don't.

He wouldn't allow that since he wants it himself.

"You must designate a new underboss to replace you when you can no longer lead." I wince, my stomach twisting with despair. "A cousin. A family member. Someone you trust."

He nods.

"Daddy, I'm serious."

He nods again, this time slower.

I can't tell if he's considering my advice or not.

For him to even sit here and listen to it is something he wouldn't have done before.

The glass of amber liquid shakes when he slams his hand onto his desk. His despair veering into anger. "How could your brother be so stupid?"

Tears prick at my eyes. "Tommaso was a good man. He just made a few reckless decisions."

"Reckless decisions that put him in his grave." He settles his heavy gaze on me. "Promise me you'll be there for your mother and sisters and take care of this family."

I'm quiet.

He smacks his desk again, forcing the words out of my mouth.

"I promise," I whisper.

We live in a rough world.

It's a high when you're winning, but an overdose when you're not.

And right now, the Cavallaros aren't winning.

We're dying.

CHAPTER TWENTY-SIX

BENNY

"Sammie will be added to my Dumbest Motherfuckers list if he killed Tommaso." My father flicks a Zippo lighter while sitting behind his desk. "You don't kill the man before collecting the cash. Whoever does such an atrocity should get a bullet through their brain because we don't need someone so stupid on this planet."

I make myself comfortable in the chair across from him. "Tommaso didn't die over a debt. It was personal."

"Have you paid Sammie a visit?"

"Not yet. He refuses to meet with me, and Raul hasn't tracked his location yet. He's in a safe house somewhere."

He shuts the lighter and tosses it onto his desk. "Do you plan to kill him?"

"Neomi wants me to, but I don't want to kill the wrong man."

I kill for purpose. Not pleasure.

"Killing the wrong man happens sometimes," my father says, as if he were giving me a pep talk after losing a baseball game. "If it happens, learn from your mistakes and move on."

"Yes, but killing anyone can create blowback. Someone they

love will want revenge, and the fewer *someones* I have on my hands, the better."

"Spoken like a true boss." He leans back in his chair, and I become eye-level with the large family portrait hanging behind his desk. "Tommaso would've been murdered eventually. He was playing reckless games with dangerous men."

I nod in agreement.

It's why I didn't kill him that first day in his townhome.

I knew someone else would do the job for me, and his blood wouldn't be on my hands.

I cross my legs. "Speaking of dangerous men, any info on the Lombardi situation?"

He sighs and kicks his feet onto his desk. "Vincent Lombardi won't take my calls."

"Did you try a burner?"

He glares at my questioning him. "Yes."

"Dodging calls screams guilt." I scratch my forehead.

"It does, but even when I've been on bad terms with Vincent, he's always answered my calls."

"Do you think it was him who interrupted our wedding?"

"Him or someone who works for him."

"Raul is tracking their men. We've killed two more so far."

Lombardi will want to kill us just for that.

He nods. "In the meantime, lie low."

I crack my knuckles and move my neck from side to side, releasing tension. "I can't lie low until I've killed a man for my wife."

"Happy wife, happy life." He drops his feet from his desk. "Kill the man and then bring her flowers."

"When did you get so romantic?"

"I'm not romantic." He taps the side of his head. "I'm smart."

When I walk into Paradise Gentlemen's Club, the smell of cheap cologne and smoke whacks me in the face. The clock hasn't struck noon, but a few men are sitting alone at tables with their eyes on the woman dancing naked onstage.

"Hey, at least the scenery is nice on the job today," Luca comments as we stroll toward the back of the club.

The bouncer, a man with a bulging stomach, whose attention was on his phone, didn't even stop us at the door. Unfortunately, that luck doesn't follow me when I reach the door leading to the back hallway. I bribed a stripper and her drug addict boyfriend to provide me with the club's layout after Raul informed me Sammie was a silent partner here.

Silent partner, my ass.

According to my sources, Sammie spends nearly all his free time here.

"Hey, man—" the guy guarding the door yells, but his words are cut off by me slamming my fist in his face. He teeters back before collapsing against the wall and groaning.

I kick his foot away that was blocking the door and walk into Sammie's office. Surprised, he pushes a pigtailed, naked blonde off his lap. She falls to her knees, and he straightens his tie to gain his composure.

"Excuse us," he tells her, smacking her ass when she stands.

She nods, her gaze shooting from Luca to me. As she passes Luca, she runs her hand down his chest and arm. She tries the same with me, but I step around her and shake my head.

She has no idea the chaos she'd cause if I went home to my wife with even a hint of smelling like another woman. Sammie would have an even bigger problem because she'd kill him and burn down the club.

"Are you here to pay your brother-in-law's debt?" he asks, running a hand down his wrinkled shirt.

I grind my teeth, wanting to kill him for that question alone, and draw my Glock from my pocket.

He rolls back in his chair. "Benny, I didn't kill Tommaso."

I click the gun's safety and point it at him, not in the mood for games.

"Whoa." Sammie holds up his hands, surrendering, and violently shakes his head. "Why would I throw away the opportunity to be paid back? *But*, from what I recall, Tommaso said you were paying a portion of his debt."

"Calm your money-hungry dick down. You're not getting a penny from me." I shake my head. "As far as your interest in killing the men who took your opportunity of repayment, give me their names, and I'll do it for you."

He raises his brows and shows off a chipped-tooth smile. "As you are a man with a price for everything, so am I."

"God, I don't have time for this shit." I circle the desk, jerk him out of the chair, and throw him on the floor where he pushed the stripper. Anger surges through me as I shove the heel of my Italian loafer into his neck. "The price is allowing you to still breathe."

"A dead man can't give you answers," he gasps around my foot.

"Good point." I dig my foot into his windpipe before bending to one knee and pointing the gun at his dick. "I'll start this game by shooting random parts of your body until you sputter out names I want."

"All right!" His chubby face is red as he pants for breaths.

I step back but keep my gun pointed at his waist.

He writhes on the cheap linoleum floor, like a turtle who turned on its shell and can't roll over.

"Names, Sammie." I snap my fingers and kick him in the face. "And I'd better get them quick."

"Brian and Mikey Kaminski," he grunts, drool running from his mouth. "They're brothers. They live off Lyndhurst. The only yellow house on the street. Their men are also the ones who arrived, uninvited, to your wedding."

I tap his head with the toe of my shoe as blood drips from his nose. "Thanks, Sammie. Always a pleasure."

We leave without helping Sammie up.

Let him lie there for a while.

Think of his bad life decisions.

The car ride to Lyndhurst is only five minutes.

"You know, Severino wants to be the one to do this," Luca tells me when I park down the road from the yellow house. "He'll be pissed you took the power of killing his son's murderer away from him."

I work my jaw, studying the home. "Don't care."

Luca speaks the truth. Severino has expressed the same concerns. He asked me to bring him any information regarding Tommaso's death. And since we're allies and he's my father-in-law, doing so sounds simple. It'd also save me the headache.

I told him I'd do that, but I never promised I wouldn't do what I wanted first.

I promised my wife I'd kill her brother's murderer, and I will make good on that. If another man was with the murderer—which Sammie made it seem like—then Severino can have him. But whoever put that life-ending bullet in Tommaso's head will deal with me.

I don't care if Severino believes he has more of a right to kill Tommaso's killer. To which he does, honestly. But I'm not a righteous man. Nor do I regard if another man deserves something more than I do.

If I want it, I'll take it.

And I want to keep my word to my wife.

The yellow home resembles a cottage with its white shutters and cozy landscaping. Either Sammie lied or the two idiots live with their grandmother. A duck statue on the front porch, dressed in a bright yellow raincoat and hat, holds a sign saying, *It's Fall, Y'all.*

I duck my head to twist the silencer onto my gun and open the door.

Luca does the same beside me.

A rush of leaves spills over my windshield as I tuck my gun into my pants and step out of the sedan. It's one of our random cars with fake plates and the VIN scratched off.

A woman walking her rat-looking dog passes us. She takes one glance at us, hoists her dog into her arms, and hurries into her house.

This isn't about revenge for Tommaso.

Fuck Tommaso.

It's revenge for the person who hurt my wife.

I don't cherish men's lives.

But I cherish my wife's heart.

And no motherfucker is allowed to harm it.

I pay attention to my surroundings as Luca and I walk toward the house. Parked in the driveway is a minivan and a rusted Chevy Caprice. The lights are off, and the inside is quiet. I peek into a window, seeing nothing but flower-patterned furniture and junk decor I could find at any garage sale.

"Pretty sure this is a grandma's house," Luca says. "If Sammie was fucking with us, I'm going to cut his hand off for wasting our time."

Yelling from the unattached garage catches our attention. I grip my gun as I creep along the side of the garage, and through the window, I see two men on a ratty couch, playing video games.

I wiggle the door handle. It's unlocked.

What a polite invitation for me.

I let Luca and myself in.

The men's gaze darts to us.

One dives off the couch and straightens himself on the floor.

The other stares at us, as if he were frozen.

The TV makes an annoying sound and tells them they lost their round.

I shut the door behind me.

Luca points his gun toward the guy on the couch while I aim mine at the floor.

"You, moron on the floor," I say. "Get your ass on the couch."

I wait for his reaction.

There are many reasons he went to the ground.

To hide.

Or to grab a weapon.

His movements are slow and careful as he crawls back up to the couch and sits where he was before. His hands are empty. Turns out, he's as big of an idiot as I guessed when I looked into the window and saw two grown-ass men playing a video game in their grandmother's garage.

Luca stands behind the couch.

I stand in front of them and cross my arms.

They're twin brothers.

My guess is, they're around Tommaso's age.

The one who stayed on the couch is biting his nails.

The other is nearly shaking.

I slip my hands into my pockets. "All right, this place smells like a dirty gym bag, so I'd prefer to figure this out rather quickly." I motion between the two of them. "Which one of you killed Tommaso Cavallaro?"

Sometimes, I enjoy playing games with my victims.

I want to get it over with right now so I can leave.

I blow out an exaggerated breath. "One of you had better talk, or I'm going to eeny, meeny, miny, moe which twin's head I should blow off."

Neither of them cracks.

I raise my gun to the head of the one on the right.

That sure gives me a response.

"He slept with his girlfriend, man," the guy with the gun pointed at his head stammers, jerking his head toward his brother.

I've never had a man break so easily.

"Shut your fucking mouth, Mikey," the other guy—who I can now assume is Brian—yells at his brother.

"What?" Mikey asks Brian. "They're here. We're busted." He snarls at his brother, "I told you not to fuck with the Marchettis, and now, look where we are!"

"Tommaso wasn't a Marchetti," Brian hisses. "He deserved to die."

I can't help but laugh. "You killed him because he'd slept with your girlfriend?"

A glare smears across Brian's face. "He slept with my girlfriend, and then when I told him I would kill him for that, he slept with our mother!"

Brian clenches his fist, and I wonder if he'll try to fight me. But he remains in place. His hate is toward Tommaso. Not me.

I mean, he should hate me.

I'm going to kill him.

He just doesn't know it yet.

"I had no choice but to kill him, Benny." He straightens his shoulders. "Tommaso didn't even like you. He talked *mad shit* about you, bro."

Mikey eagerly nods. "Tommaso said the Marchettis were weak and you'd never make a good boss. He said as soon as he took over, he was ending you."

I don't even bother taking the bait from these motherfuckers.

Their opinions mean nothing to me.

"He was an asshole, wasn't he?" I say, lightening the tone of my voice. "Honestly, I don't even care he's dead."

Brian's shoulders ease.

Mikey stops his nail-biting.

I sit on the chair beside them, draping an arm along the back. "So, which one of you pulled the trigger? Killed the stupid bastard?"

They exchange nervous glances.

"Look, how about this?" I lean forward and twirl my gun around my fingers. "I'll only kill one of you. That'll make it easier for your family."

Brian attempts to jump off the couch, but Luca shoves him back down.

"Which one of you pulled the trigger?"

Mikey points at Brian. "It was him!" His voice turns panicked. "I was just along for the ride, in case he needed backup."

Brian attempts to lunge toward Mikey, but Luca keeps him pinned down.

I raise my gun and pull the trigger, and Brian's head jerks back at the impact of the bullet hitting him between the eyes— the same place he shot Tommaso.

Mikey screams, but Luca slams his hand over his mouth.

Blood is splattered over the couch, the walls, and a picture of them with their grandmother on the end table.

"A warning would've been nice," Luca says, angling his gaze toward the blood on his black shirt.

"I told you I wouldn't hurt you, Mikey. So, behave and shut up," I say, standing before shifting my gaze to Luca. "Keep him there. I'll get the car and pull it into the back alley."

Luca checks his watch with his free hand and nods.

I leave the garage, return to the car, and park behind the garage. Lucky for me, the alley provides easy access for us to handle the situation without carrying a body down the street. I pop the trunk and grab what I need to get rid of Brian's body and hold Mikey.

Luca still has Mikey restrained as I step inside the garage.

I toss Luca the tape, and he catches it with one hand.

"Tape his mouth," I instruct before placing the rope on the table.

Luca nods, uses his teeth to rip the tape, and then smacks it over Mikey's mouth.

Mikey's skin glistens with sweat, and his body trembles so hard that his teeth are chattering.

I kneel so we're at eye-level and tap Mikey's leg. "Now, I know I said I wouldn't hurt you, which is true. But let's go meet someone who will."

I rise and pat the top of his damp hair, and Luca helps me tie Mikey's hands and feet.

Mikey's head thrashes from side to side when we hurl him in the trunk. His eyes are wide and tortured when we drop his brother's dead body next to him.

"Enjoy some brotherly bonding, Mikey," I say, slamming the trunk shut.

Mikey's annoying ass bangs on the trunk as I drive to Severino's.

Can't motherfuckers have some manners when in another man's car?

A few moments ago, I called Severino, said I had a gift for him and to meet me at his house.

Neomi isn't at her parents' today. She invited her sisters over to spend the day at our home to get a change of scenery. Three guards are there, watching the house, and I made her swear they wouldn't try any sneaky shit.

I instruct Severino to open the garage door when we arrive. When the door shuts behind us, I pop the trunk.

Severino whistles as he stands over Mikey's and Brian's bodies.

Mikey is still putting up a fight—jerking his body, rolling, and crying out whenever he accidentally touches Brian.

"Meet Mikey and Brian." I motion toward them like I'm a game-show host. "The men responsible for your son's death."

Severino's face lights up, and he scrubs his hands together like he's about to devour the juiciest steak he's ever seen.

He glances at me. "You certain this is them?"

I nod. "They're brothers." My shoes squeak against the epoxy floor as I shift from one foot to the other.

"One of them is dead already." Severino raises a brow.

"He got a little cocky." I grab Mikey and drag him out of the car.

He collapses onto the floor at my feet.

"I saved you the one who matters," I add.

Severino strokes his chin with satisfaction.

I chose my wording carefully, wanting to give Severino the impression Mikey was the one who killed Tommaso. He was involved, so that's all that matters.

He can take the credit.

I don't need public applause for anything I do.

I did it for one reason—my wife.

Mikey shimmies along the floor, as if he can escape, so I kick him.

"Do you want me to wait around and dispose of the bodies?" I ask, grabbing Mikey and Brian's wallets from their pockets and plucking out their IDs.

Severino gives Mikey another kick when I'm finished. "No, I got this." He claps me on the back. "I appreciate you bringing them to me."

"Luca, you stay and help," I instruct.

Luca nods.

Even if I'm handing the bodies to Severino, I still need all my bases covered, which includes ensuring the bodies disappear after they finish. No body, no case. I don't doubt Severino's skills since he's one of the best in the game, but there's no such thing as being too careful.

"Is Neomi's car here?" I ask Severino.

He nods. "The Range Rover on the very end. Keys are in it."

"Thanks." I salute them. "You boys have fun."

Neomi has complained she wants her car, but I told her it wasn't necessary when she couldn't drive anywhere solo.

I'll have two surprises for her this evening.

It's ten at night when I get home.

After leaving Severino's, I made two pit stops.

The first was to the club to handle business.

The second was to the mansion to inform my father of the Mikey and Brian situation. It wasn't an appropriate phone conversation.

I pull up the drive to the house. If you'd told me a year ago that Neomi and I would be living in my grandparents' home, I'd have laughed in your face. I knew it wasn't my style when we moved into the brick raised-ranch home, but now, I've felt nothing but comfort.

I tell the outside guards they can retire for the night and twirl Neomi's keys between my fingers while strolling up the stone walkway into the house.

I shut off the alarm and hear the TV playing in the bedroom. I kick off my shoes, and Romeo meets me in the foyer. I sent him a heads-up text that I was on my way home so he wouldn't be worried when the alarm set off.

I thank him for watching them, we say goodbye, and I stroll into the living room when he leaves. Neomi, Bria, and Isabella are on the couch, snuggled together and sleeping. *Buffy the Vampire Slayer* plays on the TV.

I'm surprised the alarm didn't wake them.

I quietly walk to the couch and carefully lift a snoring Neomi. The blanket on them slips to the ground. Neomi yawns, falling into me, and I wrap her arms around my neck to keep her balanced. Her sock-covered feet slip against the wood floor as I toss the blanket over her sisters. The guest room is ready if they wake up in the middle of the night.

I half carry, half guide Neomi up the stairs. She blinks, and with every step, she wakes up more. When we enter the bedroom, I help her sit on the edge of the bed.

She rubs her eyes while wearing a puppy-patterned pajama set.

"Hey, you," she says with a long yawn.

"Hey, baby." I smack a kiss on her forehead while loosening my cuff links. "Did you have fun tonight?"

She chews into her lower lip. "As much fun as we could have, I guess."

I drop the cuff links onto the dresser and dig in my pockets to drag out the ID cards I took. I'll burn them later.

When I hand the IDs to her, she plays with them in her hand while staring at me with strained eyes.

"Those are the men who killed your brother," I explain.

She holds up the cards. "They were Tommaso's friends."

"Until he slept with Brian's girlfriend." I unbutton my shirt. "And then their mother, apparently."

"Ew." She scrunches up that cute nose of hers and drops the IDs on the bed.

"Brian and Mikey worked for Sammie at one point."

"Are they the ones who tried to kidnap me at the wedding?"

"According to your father, per Mikey, their plan was to get ransom money for you. Like your brother, they had their addictions. They saw it as fast cash and revenge on your brother. But your brother believed Sammie was behind it … until he learned the truth. When he did, he threatened to rat them out to me for the attempted kidnap on you. That added more fuel to their fire, so they killed him."

I gathered this information from Luca. He had met me at the mansion after he finished helping Severino. Severino hadn't extended the quick-death courtesy to Mikey, as I had with Brian. From Luca's report, he helped Severino dump Brian's body in the

Hudson, but Severino said he wanted to spend more time with Mikey before allowing him to meet his maker. Luca said Severino cut out Mikey's tongue.

"Where are Brian and Mikey now?"

I shrug out of my shirt. "I killed Brian. Your father has Mikey."

"Did Brian or Mikey pull the trigger?"

"Brian, but as far as your father is concerned, Mikey killed him. I think we'll agree we're on the same page with that?"

She nods. "Absolutely."

I lower myself onto the bed beside her, and she crawls into my lap, looping her arms around my neck. My dick instantly hardens when she presses herself into my crotch.

"Thank you, Benny."

"You don't have to thank me." I brush wisps of hair from her eyes before cupping her waist. "I'll kill anyone for you."

She cracks a smile. "Is it weird I find that romantic?"

"Not at all, baby."

We lock eyes.

Mine are intense.

Hers are dazed.

A breath leaves me when she lowers her mouth to mine. She runs her tongue along the seam of my lips before slipping it between them. Our kiss is needy but slow.

Just as I'm about to grind her hips on me, she beats me to it. Our eye contact shatters, and she throws her head back while rolling her hips forward.

My cock swells with need for her as my breathing labors. Tipping my hips forward, I pull her closer and meet her movements.

When we break our kiss, I trail my lips over her collarbone while unbuttoning her pajama shirt. The two sides part, revealing her beautiful breasts. My girl isn't a fan of wearing bras to bed.

Licking my lips, I stare at her breasts.

They're perfect with quarter-sized dark pink circles and perky nipples. She moans and shoves her chest forward when I palm her breast and rub my thumb over her nipple. A shudder leaves her as I repeat the action before lowering my head and taking the little bud into my mouth.

I love how responsive Neomi is.

I always wait in excitement after touching her. I crave to see her reactions. She moans again, louder, and smacks a hand over her mouth.

I kiss the hand covering her mouth.

"My sisters," she says as she slowly removes it.

I raise a brow and loosen my hold on her waist to run a hand down her back. "They know we've …"

She nods. "Of course. They've asked me fifteen hundred questions about it."

I chuckle. "Do you want me to put something in your mouth?"

"Like …" She stops as her gaze drops to my lap. "Like that?"

I smirk. "That wasn't what I was referring to, but I won't refuse it."

Neomi is learning what she likes in bed. We've spent our nights discovering how she likes to be touched and where she's sensitive. I've made it my mission to become acquainted with her G-spot. I want her to enjoy sex and love everything we do together.

She hasn't sucked my dick yet, but it's not something I've worried about. I'd rather end my nights inside her tight pussy than her mouth anyway. But that doesn't mean my entire body doesn't buzz at the thought of her mouth deep-throating my cock.

It seems she's ready.

And, fuck, from the way my dick jerks, so is it.

A shy smile is on Neomi's face as she slips down my lap to her knees, like I'm her king. My eyes darken while I stare at her unbuckling my belt. She licks her lips while unzipping me and shoving my pants down. When my dick springs free, she stares at it, all innocent and doe-eyed. I can't stop myself from jerking my hips forward. She studies my length and runs her finger down it before pressing the pad of her thumb along the tip, smearing the pre-cum.

I suck in the urge to tell her to suck it and put me out of my misery.

She strokes me once, twice, three times, and my body thrusts off the bed when she takes my entire length in her mouth.

"Holy fuck," I groan, straightening my back.

My girl wants to devour and pleasure me immediately.

She pulls back at my reaction, and my cock drops from her lips. "Good or bad?"

"Good, girl." I smooth her hair away from her face to give myself the perfect view of her kneeling at my feet. I want to see my dick sliding down her throat, cheeks hollowed when she takes every inch of me, filling her mouth the same way I have with her pussy so many times.

She nods, her body relaxing, and strokes me a few more times before taking me back into her mouth. Her movements are hesitant and unskilled as she focuses on sucking me.

I can't look away from her as she sucks me, like an angel sent down to pleasure me.

"Stroke me while you lick me, baby." My voice is raspy, and the words sound scratchy as they release from my throat. "And look at me when my cock is in your mouth."

Her eyes water as she peers up and slowly strokes me.

This is the most beautiful sight I'll ever bear witness to.

I want her to be so familiar with my cock that she'll have muscle memory of it—knowing how to take it into her mouth and never forgetting how I taste.

"That's my good girl," I praise, when she sucks the head between her cheeks.

This might be the most patient I've been in my entire life.

God, how I want to furiously fuck her face, ram my dick down her throat, and choke her while she moans my name.

She's not ready for that yet. But it'll come.

I have so many things to teach my new little wife.

My thighs tense, my knees lock up, and I know I'm close.

Too soon, though.

It's too soon to end this with her tonight.

I grab a fistful of her hair to stop her. Saliva trickles down her mouth when I keep her at a distance to where she can't even lick my cock even if she tried.

Rule number one: never get off without pleasuring your wife.

They should make motherfuckers say that during their vows.

To love, to cherish, to make sure you come before I do.

I'm not shooting my cum down Neomi's throat yet.

I have better plans for us.

I reach down, grab her underneath her elbows, and bring her to her feet. I tear the pajama top off her body and push down her pants and panties. When I cup her mound, she moans and falls forward, resting her palms on my shoulders to hold herself up.

She's already so wet for me.

I thrust a finger inside her. Then another. Then another.

Stretching my wife.

She jerks forward, her tits bouncing in my face, and I suck on one.

Her stomach rubs against the tip of my length.

"Step out of those pants and sit on my face, baby," I tell her while taking off my shirt.

Our heavy breathing, mixed with lust, fills the room.

She kicks off her pants and panties but stares at me for more direction, like she isn't sure *how* to sit on my face.

I scoot down the bed, laying myself flat, and give her a *come-hither* gesture. "Crawl up here and sit on my face. I'm a starved husband who wants his wife to feed him."

Uncertainty is clear on her face, and she straddles me as she climbs up the bed.

"Turn, slide the wet pussy up my chest, and rest it on my face."

She shifts, her ass now facing me, and squirms down my body until her pussy hovers over my face. I smack one ass cheek, then the other, before pushing her ass so she's nearly suffocating me with her dripping pussy. I hold her knees in place with my arms to give myself a good angle and suck on her clit.

She wiggles above me as I devour her.

Savoring my favorite meal.

"Now," I say, stopping for a breath, "suck my cock."

It takes her a moment to process what I said. She straightens her body, elongating her back, and her slit is in the perfect position for me to run my tongue along it.

I groan, rubbing her pussy juices all over my face, when she takes my cock in her mouth.

She sucks me while riding my face.

When she gets close to coming, she abandons me, all her focus on her orgasm. I'm okay with that—for now. As she falls apart above me, I lick up her release, soothing her with my words to give me more. Her limbs give out when she crashes from her high and collapses flat onto my body.

She's too exhausted to suck me.

Understandable.

Our bodies are sweaty as I slide her off me and position her onto my lap, so she's facing me.

"Ride me, baby," I tell her.

She sinks onto my cock as if it's a part of her she's missing and grinds into me.

Within five minutes, she's coming on my dick again.

Then, I allow myself to come.

Inside my wife.

We're out of breath when we finish. I shove back her damp hair and tuck it behind her ears.

She stares down at me, gasping, and says, "Well ... that was ..."

I raise a brow.

"A bit harder than it looks in porn."

I chuckle and run a thumb over her cheek. "We'll just need to practice more."

She brushes her nose against mine and says, "Practice makes perfect," against my lips.

CHAPTER TWENTY-SEVEN

NEOMI

Rain pours down on us like a new enemy during Tommaso's funeral.

A sob leaves my throat when they lower his casket into the ground.

"Goodbye, brother," I whisper as my soaked hair sticks to my face.

My ears ring as my mother cries out his name beside me.

She's done this since we arrived at the cemetery.

I squeeze her hand, wishing it'd give her some sense of peace.

We knew today would be soul-crushing for her, like she was also dying.

The funeral had a large turnout, but not everyone traveled to the cemetery after the service. They paid their respects to my father, but didn't care enough about Tommaso to withstand the rain.

As people drop roses into the hole where my brother's soul will rest, my mother's screams turn into anger toward my father. She jerks away from me suddenly and pushes him.

She yells and thrusts her fingers in his face, "Our son's blood is on your hands. I am leaving you when I get home. You rotten son of a bitch."

My mother has lost all hope and become uncaring.

The loss of Tommaso has suffocated her, and she's unable to find the strength to keep going and breathing.

It doesn't help that my father hasn't played the role of a supportive husband.

Their grieving love languages are different.

And it's destroying them.

I peer at Benny next to me. He hasn't left my side once today. Not even when a man asked him to speak in private regarding business. He's blown everyone off who isn't his wife.

I didn't get to choose my husband, but he's working on being the man I'd have selected if awarded that luxury.

My father spoke at the funeral. It wasn't for long, and he didn't say much, but it brought a weak smile to my face. Tommaso deserved to hear kind words from a father who expected so much from him.

People watch, stunned at my mother's behavior as she spits on my father's shoes. His eyes are tight and bloodshot as he attempts to console her, but she only fights harder.

The Cavallaros are falling apart.

Bria and Isabella stare at me in expectation, as if I were our mother's handler.

"I need to stop this," I say with slumped shoulders. "Stay here. I think I have to handle her on my own."

Cristian walks to Benny while I retreat to play referee with my parents, who are speed-walking through the cemetery.

They're steps away from me now as my mother pushes my father farther and farther from their son.

My heels splash into mud puddles, dropping into the mud and slowing my pace.

"Screw it," I say, stopping to remove them.

That's when I notice it.

A roll of thunder and a bolt of lightning crash through the sky as a black car with tinted windows as dark as night slowly rolls toward us. I stare at it, telling myself this day has given me morbid thoughts, but I can't seem to take my eyes off it.

As bad as I want to fight off this feeling, I can't seem to ignore it.

The car passes my parents.

Drives by the line of cars parked on the side of the street.

My gut tells me I'm right when the window slowly rolls down.

I drop my shoes at the sight of the top of a man's head … and a gun.

But it's too late.

I briefly glance at Benny.

Cristian claps him on the back, and Benny nods before strolling in my direction.

My gaze returns to the car.

Their aim is on my husband.

I scream and sprint in his direction, racing the car.

"Benny!" I yell, my voice hoarse and throat sore.

I'm close to reaching him while keeping myself in line with the shooter, so they can't hit Benny.

But it's too late.

Something smacks into my body.

At first, it feels like a pebble thrown at me, and I stand there in shock.

Pain explodes throughout my body.

I crumple to the ground, and my insides burn like fire.

My ears ring harder than they did from my mother's wails.

As I lie there on the ground, I faintly hear my name.

Yelling.

Gunshots.

I shut my eyes, no longer strong enough to keep them open.

My body is picked up, and I lie limply in strong arms.

A crack of thunder bursts from the sky as I hear Benny's voice telling me to stay alive for him.

I open my mouth to tell him I can't.

To say goodbye, but the words don't come.

One simple whimper leaves me.

A whimper of devastation that this is the end.

I can't stay alive long enough to tell my husband I'm in love with him.

CHAPTER TWENTY-EIGHT

BENNY

I don't wait for an ambulance.

In my experience, gunshot victims have a higher survival rate if you drive them rather than take an ambulance. Every minute is crucial. The ten minutes it could take for an ambulance to arrive could make a difference between life or death for Neomi. I won't take that chance.

We're in the back of the Escalade as my father speeds to the hospital.

That bullet was meant for me.

But my wife took it.

The decision will be the biggest mistake of the shooter's life.

There will be hell to pay.

"Please wake up, baby," I beg, searching for the wound.

I'm kneeling on the floorboard with Neomi flat on the back seat. I pick up her arm draped over her stomach to find the bullet entry. Heavy blood seeps from the wound and gushes through my fingers when I apply pressure to it with my hand.

I awkwardly slip my blazer off one arm and then replace my hand on Neomi's stomach with my free one to shrug out of my blazer completely. Water drips from every inch of my face as I press the jacket to her wound. When I realize that's not enough pressure, I rise, keeping one knee on the floorboard and leaning the other into her injury.

She coughs a few times and whimpers.

Her soaking wet body shivers.

My stomach knots in agony, as I know she's in pain.

"Move, motherfuckers," my father yells, blaring his horn while weaving through traffic.

"Come on, baby," I plead, shaking as I run my free hand over her cold cheek.

Stay alive for me.

Please don't leave me.

My eyes water.

A heart I never knew existed crumbles in my chest.

I stare up and beg God to take me instead.

I deserve it. Not her.

I'm the villain in this story.

The darkness. The bad guy.

Let the good stay and take the evil.

I promised Neomi I wouldn't leave her alone in this world, but I should've made her promise me the same.

My father swerves into the front of the emergency room, and I swing the door open. He circles the car and assists me in taking her out. I'm covered in blood, grass, and mud as I race into the hospital with Neomi in my arms.

"I'm sorry, son," my father says, stopping beside me.

I don't look at him.

I can't seem to peel my gaze away from the door while waiting for a doctor to update me on Neomi. A rush of torment pierces through me as I imagine my life without her. I didn't even realize she'd become such a vital part of my life.

I've never been a praying man, but I haven't stopped begging the man above to save her.

I swore I'd burst into flames if God ever heard me mutter a word to him after all my sins. But here I am, a sinner, not asking for forgiveness for my wrongdoings, but asking for a favor.

That sounds even more ridiculous.

But it's a grace I'd give up anything for.

A favor to save someone I love.

Love.

My heart twists.

Once my mother died, she took any source of my love with her. I saw what losing my mother did to my father, and I promised myself I'd never fall in love. Because having it and losing it is the worst pain ever. One that can bring even the most powerful man to his knees.

But then came Neomi, stepping into my life like an uninvited virus, but she did the opposite of what I'd thought. She healed that pain and fear of love.

And that love will grow each day we're together until it fills my soul.

I can't lose her.

We're in a private waiting room. Concetta sobs while Severino sits, stone-faced, with perfect posture. Isabella and Bria are slouched in their chairs, and their eyes are swollen. Gigi and Natalia sit quietly in the corner.

"I've never wanted to die before," I tell him with a gulp. My voice is low, only loud enough for him to hear. "But seeing Neomi unresponsive on the ground, I felt that. When the nurses took her away from me, I realized if she didn't make it out of this, I wouldn't want to be here either."

Wherever she goes, I go.

If she doesn't make it, I don't want to either.

My father exhales a long breath. "You can't do that. Who'd kill the man who shot her?"

"You."

"Son, you have too much of a thirst for vengeance, especially in a situation like this."

"I don't think she'll make it."

"She will."

"Mom didn't."

He jerks back, his head hitting the wall.

"It's a Marchetti curse."

"Don't you dare fucking say that," he hisses.

A drive-by shooting claimed my mother's life. She bled out in my father's arms before they made it to the hospital. My father has come a long way since her death, but he's never been the same. He's become crueler and more of a menace.

My blood runs hot when there's a soft knock on the door before it opens. Dr. Jansky walks into the room, and I already want to lose it. He's the doctor who broke the news of my mother's death. He'd tried to save her, even when the nurses declared her DOA, but it was too late.

He shakes my clammy hand and then does the same with Severino, Concetta, and my father.

"Neomi is stable," Dr. Jansky says before pausing, like he knows any further word said will be interrupted by our reactions.

"Oh, thank God," Concetta yelps.

I briefly shut my eyes and place my fisted hand to my mouth.

My father draws in a breath through his nose.

Severino's bulky shoulders loosen.

"She got lucky," he finally continues, his voice soothing. "Thankfully, the bullet didn't cause any internal damage. She lost a significant amount of blood, so we had to perform a transfusion." He straightens his glasses. "I want to keep her here for a few days to watch her recovery." His eyes are comforting when they meet mine. "They are transferring her to the second floor. A nurse will come and let you know when she's able to have visitors."

I end Luca's call and look at my father. "It was a Lombardi. One of Cavallaro's men took a picture of the license plate and ran it through the system."

"Stupid fuckers didn't even use an unmarked car." He works his jaw. "It's like they wanted us to know it was them."

"Word is, it was Lombardi's last wish to kill me. A son for a son."

"Last wish?" He furrows his brow. "What does that mean?"

"I have no idea, but I'll ask him that question right before I kill him." I blow out a breath. "But first, I need to make sure my wife is okay."

My father grips my shoulder. "I'm proud of you, Benny. I don't know if I say that enough, but I'm honored to be your father."

It's as if I needed those words to help deal with the guilt of today.

"What happened to Neomi wasn't your fault," he tells me. "It was Vincent's. Don't let your mind go there."

"Is that how you felt when Vinny took Natalia?"

"At first, no. I almost let it eat me alive. But then I realized it was more important to help my wife deal with the trauma of what happened than feel sorry for myself."

"I'm going to kill them for creating that trauma."

"Take care of your wife. Then, we'll kill them."

Neomi is in stable condition, but that doesn't mean she's okay.

I stay by her bedside. My hand has been in hers so long that I'm surprised they haven't bonded like scar tissue. The beeping monitors and fluorescent lighting in the room give me a headache. I'll give Concetta another hour with the lights on since she's in the corner, working on a crossword. But they will be turned off soon.

It's been eight hours since they admitted Neomi into the hospital, but there's already a row of flowers and *get well* cards. Natalia, Gigi, and Neomi's sisters raided the gift shop.

Everyone went home, except for Concetta and me. Concetta offered to stay the night with Neomi so I could go home and rest, but I told her it wasn't an option. I added that the couch and TV were all hers, and I'd sleep on the recliner.

The recliner is uncomfortable.

Worn.

Too many stressed people have sat in it by their loved ones.

Neomi has slept the entire time. As much as I want to wake her, to ask how she's feeling and tell her I'm here, I hold back. She needs her rest.

For the past five minutes, Concetta has been weirdly staring at me, as if she has a secret she wants to share but isn't sure how to reveal it.

I know she's figured it out when she slams the crossword book closed.

"You know, when we arrived at the hospital, I wanted to yell at you," she starts. "It was unfair to you, but I was angry. I still am angry. Neomi was almost kidnapped because of my son's actions and shot for yours. No matter what, we women are always the victims of a man's war."

I make eye contact with her. "I'm sorry, Concetta. If it had been up to me, I'd have taken the bullet for her."

"The thing is, she didn't get caught in the crossfire. She ran straight into it to protect you." She turns quiet for a moment, the only sound the beeping of machines, before raising a single finger. "I wondered if I'd have done the same for Severino. Honestly, I don't know. Don't get me wrong; I love my husband. But, like you, we had an arranged marriage that left me with two choices—love him or hate him. Sometimes, I hate him—especially recently." She sighs. "Neomi might not know you well, but a woman doesn't take a bullet for a man she doesn't love. You'd better give her the love she deserves back."

My throat is dry, tightening around my words. "Concetta, I don't hand out promises, nor do I ask for them because they're the easiest thing to break. But I will promise you one thing. Of the many worries you have, me hurting your daughter should never be on your list. *I promise you.*"

I didn't get a minute of sleep.

Concetta snores like she's sawing logs, wrapped in a cheap hospital blanket so thin that I wouldn't even consider it a sheet.

Neomi hasn't woken up yet, but she's released a snore or two.

And a weird-ass, random snort while sleep-talking gibberish.

I yawn and check my watch—seven a.m.

Stretching, I stand from the recliner, use the connected restroom, and leave Neomi's room in search of caffeine.

"Can you believe we have a Marchetti *and* a Lombardi? It's like mob day here."

I halt, backtrack to inch closer to the nurses' station, and peek around the corner to eavesdrop on their conversation.

A male nurse grins. "Maybe I'll find myself a Mafia boyfriend."

"Are they here because they, like, shot each other?" a pink-haired nurse asks, spinning her chair.

"How despicable can you be to shoot a woman?" the first girl who spoke asks, holding a cup of Jell-O. She points at the guy with her spoon. "I don't care who you are, Mafia man or not. That's just wrong on so many levels."

"Keep your voices down," Kimberly, Neomi's nurse, says, charging toward them while snapping her fingers. "They aren't related. The Marchetti woman was shot. Vincent Lombardi had a stroke."

Every inch of my body perks up at Vincent's name.

His being here sends me a shot of adrenaline stronger than any cup of coffee could provide. It's as if God thought I was worthy of two favors—the first being my wife didn't die, and the second, handing Vincent over to me on a hospital-bed platter.

The nurses stop. One types something on the computer, and the others grab their phones. I pour myself a complimentary coffee and wait for Kimberly outside Neomi's room. When I take a sip, I spit it back into the cup. Gas-station glob tastes better than this shit.

I catch Kimberly's attention by whistling when she leaves the nurses' station.

"What room is Vincent Lombardi in?" I ask her.

Her blue eyes widen, as if I'm insane for even asking. "You know I can't share confidential information about another patient with you."

I drag my wallet from my pants and hold a hundred between two fingers.

She scoffs. "That's nowhere near enough to convince me to break HIPAA."

"How much is then?"

"Ten thousand." Her answer is sarcastic, but mine isn't.

"Done. I can have the cash to you within the hour, but for that price, I want more than a room number."

She nods before jerking her head down the hall, and I walk alongside her.

"Vincent came in yesterday evening after suffering a stroke. This morning, they transferred him to the third floor. I'll let you know when they input it into the computer." She stops and looks from left to right. "You can't kill him. If that's your plan, wait until you leave the hospital to go through with it. They thoroughly investigate every death here."

"Just get me the room number, Kimberly. I'll worry about the rest." I raise the coffee cup in my hand. "And one more thing: tell the hospital to invest in decent coffee."

She nods and walks away, and I call my father on his burner.

I tell him to come to the hospital and bring ten thousand dollars.

"Give me thirty minutes," he says before ending the call.

Everyone is still asleep when I return to Neomi's room. I lean back in the recliner and smile.

Vincent Lombardi.

You are mine.

Kimberly steps into the room, pretending to check Neomi's fluid bags, and slips me a piece of paper with *302* written on it.

"Meet my father downstairs—Cristian Marchetti. He'll be in a black suit, waiting by a black Escalade. He'll have your money."

I'll wait until Kimberly returns before speaking to my father. I don't need cameras catching me walking out of the hospital with my wife's nurse.

My phone beeps with a text ten minutes later.

Dad: Meet me outside.

I shove the phone into my pocket, kiss Neomi's forehead, and leave the hospital to find my father waiting for me at the entrance. We take a walk, and I repeat what Kimberly told me.

My father is quiet for a moment, kicking the toe of his shoe against the pavement. "What's your plan?"

"Undecided," I reply, cracking my knuckles. "I could smother him in his sleep or administer something in his veins through an IV bag. Whatever it is, he will die by my hands."

"Not here, he won't."

My pulse rises, and I stop. "What?"

"Killing someone in a hospital is stupid."

"People die at hospitals all the time."

"I know you're hungry for revenge, but you can't get sloppy. The last thing we need is for you to get arrested or killed."

It's infrequent I rebuff my father's orders, but I can't stop myself. "You made sure Vinny died at your hands."

"Vinny was on top of Natalia with a knife. I had no choice but to kill him." He rubs the back of his neck. "We're not certain

Vincent called the hit. It's not adding up. Vincent calls a hit on you and then has a stroke?"

"Could've been the stress of failing."

My phone rings, interrupting our conversation.

Concetta's name flashes on the screen.

"Neomi is awake," she says when I answer.

CHAPTER TWENTY-NINE

NEOMI

My eyes are heavy, and it takes me a few blinks to get them to open.

My surroundings are blurry at first.

I blink a few more times to clear my vision. It helps some, but your girl is not in a position to drive or handle heavy machinery.

My arm aches as I raise it and rub at the attached IVs. Bruising around the area has already started.

It doesn't take me long to realize where I am.

The room is about as bland as Benny's *saltine cracker* house.

My head pounds as I try to remember the details from yesterday.

Tommaso's funeral.

The black sedan.

A gunshot.

My insides scorching after being hurt by a bullet.

Being shot freaking sucks.

My thoughts wander to Tommaso, wondering if he felt the same pain. I hope not. I hope the bullet's impact immediately killed him, and he didn't feel a pinch of pain. It burned when it seared my stomach. I can't imagine the pain of it tearing through your brain.

Although I'm not currently experiencing any pain.

I'm sure that's thanks to whatever pain medicine they have dripping into my veins.

"You're awake!" My mother tosses the blanket off her lap and lunges off the couch toward me. "My baby girl. You're awake!" She captures my hand in hers, and tears fall down her cheeks.

It's not hard crying, like she did at Tommaso's funeral.

It's lullaby soft.

"I'm here, Mom." I squeeze her hand. "I'm okay."

And I am.

I could've been killed. I'm grateful I'm alive.

She releases my hand and snags her phone from the couch. "Let me tell everyone you're awake."

I groan. "Please, keep it small. Immediate family only."

She nods, as if she's listening.

A few minutes later, the door swings open. Benny steps into the room with Cristian following him.

My husband's clothes—the same from the funeral, minus the blazer—are wrinkled. I stare at him as he walks around the bed to my side, and his tired eyes meet mine when he reaches me. Cristian and my mother keep their distance, giving us a moment.

A flutter swoops through my belly—not wound-related—when he brushes his thumb along my cheek.

"How do you feel, baby?" he asks.

"Like I've been shot." I smile with cracked lips.

"Pretty much sums it up."

He cradles my face in his hand, not caring he's showing this affection in front of others. "You took a bullet for me."

I suddenly turn shy. "I took a bullet for my husband."

His face turns guilt-stricken. "I'm sorry I didn't protect you better."

"You didn't shoot me, Benny." I wrap my hand around the

wrist of the hand holding my face. "You have nothing to apologize for."

"Yes, I do." His hand shakes in my hold. "I'm supposed to protect you."

"And that's what you did." I shut my eyes, remembering how he carried me through the rain and begged me to hold on to him on the drive to the hospital. "You brought me here and saved my life."

"Knock, knock!"

Our gaze swings to the doorway as a nurse walks in.

She grins from ear to ear. "I heard you woke up. Let's get you comfortable, and I'll let the doctor know."

The nurse takes my blood pressure and temperature and tells me to hit my call button if I need anything.

As the day passes, I feel like a zoo animal.

The doctor visits, asks a million questions, tells me I'm lucky, and gives me directions on how to nurse my wound when I get home. Benny pays more attention than I do and asks the doc a few questions.

My mother is up and down, kissing my cheek and then calling a family member to report my well-being status. When my father arrives, he hands my mother her favorite Starbucks drink and kisses my cheek.

My sisters visit.

So do Gigi and Natalia.

No one talks about who shot me or what will come of it, and I don't ask questions. I want to give my brain a chance to heal, to digest all that's happened, before I hear of who has to die at my husband's hands for shooting me.

By the end of the day, I'm exhausted. I smile at everyone and thank them for coming, and when the last person leaves—other than Benny, of course—I almost let out a celebratory whoop that I can get a moment of silence.

I can't wait to get out of here.

To go home, watch *Buffy*, and snuggle in bed with my husband.

"Just so you know, this TV hardly gets any channels," I tell Benny as he arranges my food onto the rolling table over my bed.

After seeing the hospital menu, I requested a juicy cheeseburger, fries, and a chocolate shake. Benny okayed it with the doctor first, and surprisingly, thirty minutes later, Monster Marchetti arrived with a takeout bag.

Cristian freaking Marchetti delivered my food.

Benny snags one of my fries. "I'm not here for the TV channels."

"You're here for the fries then?"

He winks at me. "That and this." He steals my cheeseburger, and just as I try confiscating it, he holds it out for me to bite. "And to keep my wife company."

My wife.

He once said those words with such disdain.

Now, he says them like they're magical.

I chew my bite while Benny holds the cheeseburger for when I'm ready for another.

"What would've happened if we had married years ago?" I ask when I finish chewing. "If we had to say *I do* when they signed the contract?"

"We probably would've given each other just as much of a hard time." He smiles. "But you'd have succumbed to the charming man I am fairly quickly."

I snort and dip a fry in ketchup. "Charming, huh?"

He nods, my playful Benny coming out. "I'm your Prince Charming."

"You are *so* not my Prince Charming." I wave my fry at him, ketchup sliding off it and onto the table. "Nor do I want a Prince Charming. How boring."

I drop the fry into my mouth and savor the delicious taste.

"What would you like then, dear wife?"

"A husband who's a villain to everyone but me."

He chuckles. "It appears I don't have to change anything about me in this marriage then."

CHAPTER THIRTY

BENNY

"Vincent hasn't had many visitors," Charlie, one of the hospital security guards I paid off, informs me. "The lights have pretty much stayed off all day. The nurse said the family asked for quiet and limited check-ins."

I slap a hundred in Charlie's palm. "Thanks."

I waited until Neomi was asleep before sneaking out of her room. I didn't want to leave her, but I need to pay Vincent Lombardi a visit. It's not going against my father's orders since I don't plan to kill Vincent here. My father was right. It's too risky.

Even going to his room is suspect. But I can't share a hospital with the bastard who attempted to kill me, instead shooting my wife, and not see him.

The hall is quiet, not a nurse in sight, when I stop at room 302. The door makes a quiet *click* as I open it. I tiptoe inside. The TV is playing a black-and-white movie on low volume.

Vincent Lombardi is in bed with IVs connected to his arm, like Neomi, but there are more. Machines beep around him. His wrinkled skin is pale. A breathing machine rests over his mouth. He wheezes and gurgles like he's gasping for air.

God, I wish he'd choke to death.

I step to his bedside, wanting nothing more than to wrap my hand around his neck and strangle the life out of him.

"I figured you'd come roaming in here like the vermin you are."

My back stiffens, and I shift to find a figure sitting in the dark corner. He flips on the light to put himself on display.

Antonio Lombardi.

Vincent's middle son.

My father has referred to him as the rational one on many occasions.

He spreads his legs and rests his elbows on his knees. "My guess is, you're not here for a welfare check. What was your plan? Come in here and kill him?" He scoffs, shaking his head. "Did you not consider they'd check the cameras and see you?"

I keep my voice low. "My men are good at erasing camera footage."

He scoffs again.

"But since I don't like witnesses, I'll have to also kill you. What was it I heard he said?" I tap my chin. "*A son for a son*? Me for Vinny."

"My father is dying, Benny." He rubs his shaved cheek. "Do me a favor and allow him to pass in peace."

"No." I want to say more, like his father didn't consider I wouldn't have passed in peace if his hit had been successful. But I'm a man who doesn't like to speak much to his enemies. "Men who call hits on other men don't deserve favors."

"I didn't know about the hit." He stands. "Had I known about it, I'd have advised him against it, as I've done several times since your father killed Vinny. Whenever he wanted to strike, I talked sense into him."

"What happened this time, then?"

Even though I can't see much of him, when he looks at his father, I can sense the pain.

"My father has struggled with health issues the past two months, and his decision-making has been limited," he explains.

"Yesterday wasn't his first stroke, but it'll be his last. We will place him in hospice until he goes."

"Good." I smirk. "It's time he rots."

Antonio winces. "I don't believe my father would've okayed the hit if he had been in the right state of mind."

"But he did. Right frame of mind or not, he needs to pay for his mistake. Unless you'd like to?" I raise a brow. "Make the prince pay for the king's wrongs?"

He lifts his chin. "I don't want you dead or to go to war with your family."

"Bullshit. My father killed your brother."

"Because my brother was stupid enough to kidnap your father's fiancée." He slips his fingers together and rests them on his forehead. "My uncle Sonny has called my legitimacy to become boss into question within the family. He and Vinny were close. He's made it clear to the family that I am a traitor for not wanting to ruthlessly murder your family." He lowers his hands to jerk a finger toward his father while staring at me with confliction. "As soon as he dies, everything will change. Whether that's good or bad depends on who takes over. Sonny wants to be king and wants you dead. He's the one who sent men to follow you at the club the night your car was shot up."

I smile. "Let him try."

Antonio tenses when I reach forward and grab Vincent's breathing mask.

"Rot in hell," I say, pulling the mask back and spitting in his mouth while Vincent gasps for air. The mask smacks back into his face when I release it.

Antonio punches me in the side of my jaw on my way out of the room.

I laugh while rubbing where he made contact. "If your dad makes it out of the hospital alive, my wrath will be ten times worse than that."

CHAPTER THIRTY-ONE

NEOMI

Getting shot sucks.

But being taken care of by Benny Marchetti is heaven.

A bit overbearing at times, yes.

He's been at the hospital every day.

He helps me bathe and either orders or picks up every food I crave.

He also created a *coming home* questionnaire for me to fill out before leaving the hospital. I stifled a laugh when I read the note, written in his harsh, thick-stroked handwriting.

Do you want me to move the bed into the office downstairs in case walking up and down the stairs is painful?

List of foods and snacks from the store.

List of medicines needed.

Any additional requests.

I spend five days in the hospital before the doctor discharges me. I'm grateful to be alive. They referred to me as a *good-outcome gunshot victim.* I might be sore, but the injuries could've been worse or even fatal.

A bullet lodged itself into my great-uncle Piero's spine and paralyzed him.

My grandfather was shot in the intestines and now lives with a colostomy bag.

I got lucky.

Clouds block all the sunlight on the drive. When we pull up to the house, I spot my mother's Mercedes parked in front. I sip my Starbucks cold brew as Benny whips his Escalade into the garage. He jumps out of the SUV and rushes to my side.

He's gentle while he takes my elbow and helps me out. I loop my arm around his waist and give him my weight. The house smells like a bakery, and opera music plays when we walk in.

"She's home!" Bria yells, skipping into the foyer. She wraps me in her arms.

My mom wipes her hands on her white apron and hugs me next.

I wince when she pulls away.

"Come on. Let's get you comfortable," Benny says, guiding me into the living room.

The music lowers as he helps me onto the couch.

"Be right back," he says before handing me the TV remote.

A faint bark echoes through the house.

What?

Moments later, Isabella appears in the doorway with a puppy in her arms. He's tiny with black-and-brown fur, and he can't be any bigger than her fist.

"Stop it right now," I shout. "You got a puppy?"

Bria and my mother stand on each side of Isabella.

"Unfortunately, this little guy isn't mine." Isabella pats his head and glances at Benny. "I'm only his aunt."

"Benny ..." I can't stop myself from squealing, which is

strange because I'm not a squealer or someone who gets overly excited. "Did you get me a puppy?"

He nods. "I figured he could keep you company while you're stuck at home. Your sisters said they'd come over and help when I'm not here." He rests on the arm of the couch, tips his head down, and lowers his voice. "You can make your own puppy videos now."

A tear slides down my cheek. "Thank you, Benny." I smack a quick kiss to his lips before holding out my arms toward Isabella. "Bring him here!"

"On the couch?" Benny asks.

I shoot him a look. "Uh, yeah."

This little man will be allowed on the couch, the bed, and the kitchen table. Wherever he wants.

Isabella nuzzles her nose into his fur before handing him over.

Heat radiates through my chest, and I smile. I've never felt so special, so loved, in my life. Benny listened. Even when we were hostile to each other and arguing, he remembered why I'd told him I shared puppy videos. I was never allowed to have one, so he fulfilled that wish for me.

As soon as I clutch the dog to my chest, he attacks my face with slobbery kisses.

"He's a Yorkie," Isabella explains, sitting cross-legged on the floor. "Do you have a name in mind?"

"Bruiser," I quickly reply. "We couldn't keep the last Bruiser, but this one will have a great life."

Bruiser licks my face, loving the idea, and I fall in love with his stinky puppy breath and wet nose.

I give him love, introduce myself as his dog mom, and then turn him to face Benny. "And this is your new daddy!"

Benny recoils at the sentiment and stares at the puppy like he's a sewer rat.

I push his arm. "Show him some love, Benito."

His *love* is a single tap on top of Bruiser's head.

I frown but know I'll fix this.

I warmed Benny's heart up to me.

My next goal will be to make Bruiser and Benny the best of pals.

Benny did all this for me.

The husband I thought was from hell turned into the one I took a bullet for.

The doctor instructed me to walk daily to speed up my recovery and help prevent blood clots.

Benny offered to rent out a gym so I could use their indoor track and not walk outside in the cold. I told him it was ridiculous. I prefer the fresh air.

So, we drive to the mansion and walk the estate. Even with chilly weather, the scenery surrounding the mansion is breathtaking. Birds chirp in the mature trees, and the fall flowers are in bloom. We stroll past the beautiful stone fountains throughout the property. It's protected and safer than walking in our neighborhood.

Bruiser walks on his leash in front of us, his paws pitter-pattering along the stone walkway. A leaf blows in the wind, and Bruiser chases after it.

Benny has yet to become his bestie, but I'm working on it. It took persuasion and a promised blow job—when I'm fully healed, of course—to share the bed with Bruiser.

"We never talked about the Lombardis," I say. Just the mention of their name makes my stomach curl.

We haven't spoken much about them, but I do know they called the hit on Benny. Cristian killed Vincent's son, so they wanted him to endure the same pain of losing his. But I have no idea if Vincent pulled the trigger or if he sent someone else to. The tinted windows made it too hard to see who held the gun.

It's been calm with no other attempted murders, but if Vincent is a threat to Benny and our families, he needs to go.

Benny drapes his arm over my shoulders, pulls me to his side, and snuggles me into him as we walk. "We're trying to figure out the Lombardi situation. Vincent suffered a stroke while you were in the hospital. He's dying." His jaw tenses. "He's in a facility, and I can't get my hands on him yet."

"Poison isn't an option?" I hate myself for suggesting a possible solution for murder.

"He's on a ventilator and not eating, and someone stays with him all night. They know what we'd do. I'm careful with every move I make." He scrubs a hand over his forehead. "They want him to die peacefully and are doing everything in their power to make sure that happens."

"What will happen when he goes? Will Antonio become boss?"

"Antonio said his uncle is disputing his legitimacy to do so."

"Why doesn't Vincent verbally tell them or write something down?"

He lowers his tone. "Vincent is incapacitated."

I stall our walking when we reach a wooden bench, and we sit. "When did you speak with Antonio?"

"When I visited his father's hospital room."

Sighing, I cross my legs. "Of course, you went to the dying man's hospital room." I'd be more surprised if he didn't.

Benny scrubs his hands together. "Antonio seems willing to forget about the Vinny situation and let bygones be bygones if he becomes boss. But his uncle wants us dead."

"It sounds like the Lombardi family is going to have a civil war." I shudder. That makes my heart hurt.

There will be bloodshed among brothers, cousins, friends.

For what? So one particular person can hold all the power.

Benny drops his arm along the back of the bench and kicks out his legs. "It appears so."

"If Vincent is about to die, let him die peacefully."

He flinches. "He *shot* you."

"But if the man is already knocking on heaven's door—"

"Hell's door," he corrects before I continue.

"If Vincent can't speak, he can't cause trouble. When he dies, more trouble will come. As much as I hate to say it, right now, we need Vincent alive."

"All right," I say, dragging out the last word as I snatch my phone from the nightstand and collapse onto the bed. "Your dinner options are Chinese, pizza, or Italian." I frown while unlocking my phone. "Man, I wish L'ultima Cena was on DoorDash."

I declared we were having a *dinner in bed* evening since Benny has the night off from the club. He adjusted his schedule to work every other day. That doesn't mean other Marchetti family jobs don't arise, but he always updates me on his whereabouts.

Benny drops his phone onto the dresser and empties his jeans pockets. It wasn't until recently that I realized my husband owns more than just expensive suits. It doesn't happen frequently, but sometimes, he dresses casually. Like now, he's wearing black jeans that fit him as well as his suits and a black sweater with three buttons at the neck.

He opens his nightstand drawer and drops his gun inside. "Baby, if you want L'ultima Cena delivered, I'll get you L'ultima Cena delivered."

"You always let me get my way, don't you?" I scoop up Bruiser from the floor and hold him in the air. "That's why we love Daddy, isn't it?"

I freeze as soon as the words leave my mouth.

Benny stops dead in his tracks, and his head turns so quickly that I'm shocked he doesn't catch whiplash.

Bruiser wiggles out of my arms and runs across the bed.

I settle my hand on my chest and inhale a deep breath. Shock ripples through my body as I run what I said back through my mind.

Benny's eyes bore into mine—deep and edged with an unreadable emotion.

That's Benny.

Unreadable.

He tells you what he wants you to know.

And I guess I tell him that I love him.

How can I love someone I haven't been with long?

That I don't have yearslong history with?

I've always scoffed at insta-love.

Even in a short time, we've gone through so much together.

We had a rocky start, but maybe those rocks built the foundation to our friendship ... to our love.

I'm stricken with fear when I think about it though. I don't know if Benny loves me back—or if he ever will. I don't want to be the girl in love with a man who doesn't love her back.

I slam my eyes shut at the silence.

"I meant—" I shake my head.

"Don't take it back." Benny's voice rumbles over mine. "Don't take those words back just because you're scared."

"I am scared," I whisper.

"Look at me."

When I open my eyes, he's standing at the edge of the bed.

His stare is as intense as it was that day in the billiards room. "Don't be scared of me, Neomi."

I blink away tears.

Just like I said I'd never love him.

Never beg him.

Over and over, I've ripped apart each barrier I used to protect my heart from this man.

"I'm not scared *of you*," I cry out. "I'm scared of a broken heart." I drag my knees to my chest. "You made it clear from the very start that we'd never have a normal marriage. That love would never come from you. Before I walked down the aisle, we'd done nothing but try to make the other suffer for a contract *our parents* had created, one we had no control over."

Bruiser curls up against a pillow as Benny joins us on the bed.

Benny's eye contact is unwavering, and I can't look away from him even if I tried. He drags me across the bed and pulls me into his arms. I rest my head on his shoulder.

He cups my knee and looks down at me. "I'll admit, I made poor choices then. But since we married, I haven't touched another woman. Nor will I ever. You're all I need. Before we got married, I told you love would never be in the cards for us."

I nod, unable to speak.

He tugs at my arm, silently requesting help while dragging me onto his lap. Our faces are only inches apart.

"But I didn't even have to look for love. It came to me in the form of *you*. Someone who steamrolled over all the aversions I had of love." His touch is tender as he cradles my face in his palms, as if I'm something he's terrified of breaking. "I didn't go looking for love. You brought it to me, baby."

My hand shakes as I place it over his. "Benny."

"I love you, Neomi." Each word is clear and concise, and he inches his face closer to mine as each one drops from his lips. "I love you so fucking much."

"Do …" I attempt to lower my gaze, but he lifts my chin, not allowing it. "Do you think it's too early?"

"No." His lips brush mine. "We can say and do whatever the fuck we want, whenever we want. I love you, and I want to tell you. I don't care about timing because, sometimes, timing doesn't mean shit."

I coil my arms around his neck. "I love you, Benny Marchetti, and I am trusting you with my heart."

He releases my face, interlaces our fingers, and places them over his heart. "I'd tear mine out before I broke yours."

CHAPTER THIRTY-TWO

BENNY

One Month Later

"Mob boss Vincent Lombardi died in his sleep last night," the TV reporter says, not looking one bit sympathetic. "He was seventy years old."

I smirk.

The man who called a hit on me, resulting in my wife being shot, is no longer alive.

I hate that it wasn't by my hands though.

Vincent didn't deserve the peaceful death he received.

He deserved a barbaric one.

During the time he withered away to nothing, I've been on a mission to figure out what happened the day of the funeral. From what I've learned after bribing, beating up, and killing people, Vincent called the hit.

Most of them claimed he hadn't been in the right frame of mind. No one believed him at first. He'd been eating a Big Mac while watching *The Price Is Right* when he looked at one of his men and told him to kill Benny Marchetti *that instant*.

He wasn't the one who pulled the trigger. He'd lost most of his motor impairment during his last stroke, so he forced an inexperienced soldier to attempt the hit while keeping others in the dark. Two hours after Neomi was shot, Vincent had suffered another stroke, which put him on the ventilator.

I hunted down the man who had shot Neomi. I killed him and fed his body to a local farmer's hogs. They devoured him in thirty minutes. Bones and all.

That's why I don't eat pork.

"Antonio Lombardi." I say his name as an announcement when he appears in the doorway of my office at the club. "Shouldn't you be out somewhere, mourning your father's admission into the gates of hell?"

Antonio shuts the door and steps toward me.

He called an hour ago and asked to speak with me privately.

Antonio stops in front of my desk and rolls back his shoulders. The man is typically clean-shaven and put together, but tonight, he has days-old scruff and bags under his eyes. I know a stressed man when I see one, and Antonio is at the top of the list of the most stressed-out motherfuckers I've ever seen.

I kick up my feet and lean back in my chair with a glass of bourbon in my hand. "To what do I owe the pleasure of this unwanted visit?"

Antonio is all business when he speaks. "I told you there'd be problems with my uncle upon my father's death."

"You did, but I don't understand what that has to do with me. I'm not in your family—thank God." I point my glass toward him. "Sucks for you though. Good luck in your fighting."

No family has ever survived a civil war.

When people are separated and forced to take sides, loyalty becomes meaningless. People flip-flop to whatever side is winning at that time.

"I need your connections." Antonio pinches the bridge of his nose, his face consumed with worry. "Out of respect for your father, Severino has cut off all relations with my family. That includes selling us firearms. I need you to convince Severino to change his mind and help me out."

I drop my feet, lean forward, and plant my elbows on the desk. "Even if they didn't cut you off then, do you think they'd sell anything to a Lombardi after one shot their daughter, you fucking morons?"

Antonio grits his teeth.

He doesn't accept disrespect, but he needs me.

He straightens his stance. "I'm here to make a deal. We have great connections overseas. I have multiple reps with banks the United States hasn't even heard of. Any connection I have is all yours. Talk to your father and Severino. Help me out here."

"But will those connections overseas be on your side or your uncle's?" I furrow a brow and take a long swig of my bourbon. It's smooth as it rolls down my throat.

Antonio clasps his hands together, and sweat builds along his hairline. "My uncle wants your family to pay for Vinny's death. He will go after Natalia, Gigi, and Neomi if he has to. You will also go to war with my family if my uncle takes charge."

"I'd better keep all those weapons connections for myself then, huh?"

"I have a daughter, Benny," he says, his voice stressed. "She's six, and she already doesn't have a mother. I can't leave her alone in this world."

"I have no heartstrings for you to tug, Antonio. If that's your plan B, it won't work." I shake my head and rest my glass on the coaster. "I suggest finding her somewhere to go because you'll die if you don't win."

My statement is harsh, but I'm not one to sugarcoat shit.

Antonio probably already knows the truth of my words. He's played this game long enough. It's why he's attempting to broker a deal with the Cavallaros and Marchettis. Antonio has always been the smartest of the three Lombardi sons. Vinny was dumb and reckless. Dante, the youngest and a rumored bastard, has yet to be seen publicly. He could be a tree stump for all I know.

Antonio is lucky I semi-like him.

Well, not *like* him.

I respect his smarts.

He's always been logical and the easiest to work with.

And even though I want Lombardi blood, I don't want it from him.

But I also won't side with him.

Antonio tenses his jaw. "I guess we'll all get ready for a game of bloodshed."

"Can't wait. Save me a seat."

I peer down at my phone when it vibrates on my desk.

Neomi's name and picture flash across the screen.

"I have another meeting to attend." I straighten the collar of my shirt. "You can see yourself out."

"Don't say I didn't warn you," Antonio says, shaking his head while walking out.

I answer the FaceTime call when he shuts the door behind him.

Neomi appears on the screen. Her face is makeup-free, and her hair is thick and wild. She's lying flat on her stomach in bed, giving me a mouthwatering view of her cleavage.

This is what my sneaky wife does when she wants me to return home.

She wears something sexy and calls me. She'll flash her tits or a peek of her pussy, and I always come running.

She lowers her top and palms her breast.

"Neomi," I groan. "I have a shit ton of paperwork—" I stop speaking when she collapses onto her back and lowers the phone between her legs.

Her pussy is bare and glistening with wetness.

I shut off the computer and stand. "I'll be there in ten minutes. I want you ready and waiting for me in our bed with nothing on."

CHAPTER THIRTY-THREE

NEOMI

One Month Later

We're attending a gala tonight.

I laugh, thinking about the last gala we attended, while clasping on my hoop earrings.

I stare at my reflection in the mirror. Benny said the gala was outdoors, so I chose an ankle-length black dress with long sleeves and a square neckline. A sparkling clip holds my hair on one side of my face.

"You look amazing, baby," Benny says, coming up from behind and wrapping his arms around my waist. "I love this on you."

I stare at him through the mirror's reflection. "I literally want to rip that tuxedo off you."

He chuckles and presses a tender kiss to my exposed neck.

Not only did I hit the husband jackpot with how caring and protective he is but he's also gorgeous. Before we leave, I tell Bruiser we'll be back and give him some kisses.

When I open the door into the garage, Benny takes my hand and guides me out the front door instead.

A black Escalade is running in the driveway, and Francis, Cristian's driver, circles the SUV.

I peer back at Benny. "You got us a driver tonight?"

He nods and tips his head. "I trust Francis."

Me too. He's our driver when I go out with Natalia.

"You look beautiful, Mrs. Marchetti," Francis greets before opening the Escalade's back door.

I smile. "Thank you."

Francis steps to the side and allows Benny to assist me into the seat.

Benny holds my hand during the ride. I don't think anything when Francis turns onto the road leading to the Marchetti mansion. Gigi's attending the gala with us. We went shopping for our gowns last week. But confusion rises through me when we arrive. Cars are parked around the circular drive as bright lights shine from every direction of the mansion. Guests dressed in similar attire walk inside.

"Wait." I drape my arm over Benny's. "Is your dad hosting?"

Benny skates his fingers over my arm. "We're not exactly attending a gala."

"Then, what *exactly* are we attending?"

"It's a surprise." He kisses my cheek before opening the door and helping me out of the Escalade.

I hold up my dress as we walk toward the front doors. Two servers stand in the entryway, holding up glasses of bubbly champagne. I take one of the flutes. Benny knows exactly where he's going as he leads me through the foyer and straight into the backyard.

I stop dead in my tracks as I take in the scene of the party. The backyard looks whimsical with fairy lights draped everywhere. Standing letters—*B & N*—in LED marquee lights are on the concrete, surrounded by candles. There's a table with finger food and another hanging LED sign that says, *Will you marry me?* Outdoor heaters are scattered along the yard to provide warmth.

All eyes are on us as Benny takes me toward the long white table. It's set with expensive china, and the napkin rings are shaped like wedding rings. More fairy lights, candles, purple roses in vases, and rose petals make up the centerpiece.

Tears prick my eyes. "Did you do all this, Benny?"

When I turn to him, goose bumps slide along my back. Benny is down on one knee, and our guests close in on us. I cover my mouth with my hand while inching closer to him.

"I couldn't give you the engagement party you deserved last time, so this is me making up for it," he starts.

People are watching, but just like at our wedding, in my world, it's only Benny and me.

When we're together like this, we're all I see.

He stares up at me with compassion in his eyes. "I always told you love wasn't in the cards for me and not to expect it from me as your husband. But there isn't one doubt in my being that you are my heart—my *everything*. You are the peace to the chaotic life I live.

"You deserve more than a proposal on paper in the form of a contract. You deserve a man to drop to his knee and beg you to be his wife." He takes my hand in his. "So, this is me, a man crazy in love with a woman he doesn't deserve, asking her to be his wife. To give him a chance to make each day of hers happier than the last. Be my wife by choice. Choose me as yours because I'd choose you every day of my life."

He dives his hand into his pocket and pulls out a black ring box.

There's no stopping the grin from taking over my entire face. If he wasn't on his knee, I'd jump into his arms.

My lungs burn—I'm breathing so hard.

He slowly opens the box, revealing a diamond-encrusted band.

I nod repeatedly and brightly grin. "Yes, yes! A hundred times, yes!"

My heart is on fire when he grabs my trembling hand in his

and slides the band onto my ring finger, next to my wedding ring. They look perfect together.

As soon as he stands, I clasp his face in my hands, press my lips to his, and say, "I love you," on repeat.

I hear, "Aw," and gasps and, "So cute," from our guests.

When I break our kiss, I allow my mouth to linger against his. "For so long, I was terrified I'd end up hating my marriage and I'd be forever void of love. But I was so wrong." My voice cracks, and I hold in a breath to stop myself from crying. "Love is my only option with you, Benny. There'll never be a day you won't have my entire heart. I will always choose you."

"Thank you for believing someone like me is worthy of love," he whispers against my mouth. "I love you, my wife."

I collapse onto my back on our bed. "That was the most amazing night of my life. Thank you, Benny."

My body is relaxed.

I feel like I'm in heaven.

Benny grabs my foot and removes one heel.

Then the other.

While I'm still in bed, he then helps me out of my dress and dresses me in my pajamas. This is all to prevent me from face-planting because I drank a little too much wine while enjoying our four-course dinner.

I make myself comfortable under the sheets and play with my new ring before sliding it off my finger.

Neomi and Benito, until death do us part, is engraved on the inside.

"This is beautiful," I tell him as I admire it.

Benny holds up his hand. "I had them engrave mine the same."

I grin, loving that our rings match. That grin grows as he takes off his shirt and slips it off his arms. He's started his new story on the arm void of art before. He has my name tattooed down his arm along with a tree. The tree represents what my grandmother told me about them.

Trees aren't much different from us, Neomi. Sometimes, we must accept parts of us will shed and change. But in time, something more beautiful will bloom. That's why you should never fear change, for what's to come could be better than you could ever imagine.

One night, I shared that conversation with him.

He opens his bedside drawer. "I also have one more thing for you."

"Another surprise?" I sound like a child on Christmas.

He hands me a small piece of paper.

"Bali!" I squeal as I read the flight ticket. "We're going to Bali?"

He nods. "We never took a honeymoon."

And just like with everything else, Benny remembered.

I told him Bali was my dream vacation. I grabbed my computer and showed him everywhere I wanted to visit in Bali. The first being the Ubud Monkey Forest.

I crawl across the bed, grab his arm, and pull him down on the bed with me. "I know I keep saying this, but thank you."

He holds himself up with one elbow, hovering over me, and runs his thumb over my cheek. "You never have to thank me for anything, Neomi. All I want to do is make you happy."

I cup the back of his neck. "I want that for you too."

He lowers his mouth to mine. "You have no idea how truly happy I am."

"Who knew the Mafia prince would live happily ever after?" I say against his lips before kissing him.

EPILOGUE

NEOMI

Four Months Later

We have officially moved into our new home.

Benny gave me complete creative control and an unlimited budget, but I wanted it to be *ours*. I always asked for his opinion and dragged him to different stores to make selections. We both needed our special touches in our dream house.

We decided on a French provincial style. The white brick home complements the mansion and reminds me of romance with its French countryside elements. One side has a rounded corner, giving it the appeal of a castle tower.

Benny put his *saltine cracker* house on the market, and it sold four days later.

To a twenty-three-year-old bachelor who had won the lottery.

"I still can't believe we have a room designated for the dog," Benny comments while passing the room with a moving box in his hand.

"Hey," I scold, following him while holding Bruiser in my arms. "He's our child."

"Why does he need a whole-ass room?" He drops the box in

our bedroom. "Somehow, he manages to sleep in *our* bed every night." He retrieves the box cutter from his pocket and opens it. "Even though I sent you research on why pets sleeping in your bed is bad for your sleep health."

I cover Bruiser's ears at the insult. "A.) You hardly sleep. B.) Don't act like I don't see you tap-tap"—I pause to tap on the bed —"for the Bruise Monster to lie next to you."

His mouth twitches but doesn't fully form a smile. "You're dreaming, baby."

Just as I'm about to display my evidence in the form of secretly snapped photos I took while they were sleeping, my phone vibrates with a text.

Natalia: Enzo is now accepting visitors.

The next message is a photo of baby Enzo, wrapped in a blanket like a burrito.

Poor Natalia was in labor for fourteen hours before Enzo Fredrick Marchetti decided it was his time to shine. Instead of us rushing to the hospital, I told the new mama to inform us when she was ready for visitors.

"Invites to the Enzo show now available," I sing out, holding the phone out to show him the picture.

Benny's mouth twitches again, forming *closer* to a smile than before. "Let's go meet him then."

"I was born here," I tell Benny when we step into the hospital elevator. "Room 503."

"No shit?" He hits the 5 button on the panel. "Me too."

I playfully shove his shoulder as the elevator doors close. "You just made that up."

He holds my gaze and shakes his head. "My father has Gigi's and my delivery room numbers tatted on him. I was 503. Hers was 507."

I smile, loving that we share yet another connection. As if

from the very beginning, the world knew we belonged in the same place.

The elevator dings, and we step into the quiet lobby. Light classical music plays from the overhead speakers. The doors leading into the maternity wing are locked. A nurse buzzes us in after we provide a pin number and give her our names.

When we reach their room, I softly knock on the door. Cristian answers and steps to the side, allowing us to come in. The lights are dimmed, and Natalia's lying in the hospital bed with Enzo snuggled in her arms. She lazily smiles at us.

She looks exhausted, but she's also glowing.

Benny and I wash our hands before we head toward Natalia. Enzo doesn't make a sound. My husband pays his new brother a quick glance before strolling toward the couch and sitting. Cristian returns to Natalia's side. He stands next to her like he's their bodyguard.

"Do you want to hold him?" Natalia asks, her voice subdued.

Cristian frowns, as if he doesn't want anyone else touching his son.

"Oh, stop." Natalia rolls her eyes at him. "Cristian is just on the protective side today."

I shoot Cristian a nervous glance, and he replies with a curt nod.

"All right, my new brother-in-law," I coo. "Come here."

"How about you have a seat, and I'll bring him to you?" Cristian suggests, like I'm a child holding a baby for the first time.

I sit next to Benny and make myself comfortable on the couch. Cristian cradles Enzo against his chest and pays extra attention to supporting his head.

If Cristian had his way, I don't think anyone but Natalia and he would be allowed to hold Enzo. I don't take it personally. It's a Marchetti thing. I know if he didn't fully trust me, he'd flat-out tell me no. Just like with everything, Cristian Marchetti has his reservations.

He delicately places Enzo in my arms and waits to make sure I'm holding him properly before walking back to Natalia.

Enzo is a Marchetti through and through.

I carefully lift Enzo's hat to see his hair. He skipped the peach-fuzz phase and has nearly a full head of dark hair.

"Hi, baby Enzo," I say, running a finger over his button nose. "I'm your sister-in-law, Neomi." I tip my head toward Benny. "And he's your big brother."

When I glance at Benny, he's focused on me.

Almost as if in a trance.

His body is still, and on his face is the softest expression I've ever seen from him.

He doesn't introduce himself back to his brother or say a simple *hi*. He stays quiet, watching me intensely, as I speak baby talk, run a finger over Enzo's chubby arms, and repeatedly tell Cristian and Natalia how adorable he is.

"Do you want to hold him?" I finally ask Benny.

His gaze darts from me to Enzo. When it returns to me, he chews on the inside of his lip. There's vulnerability on his face I've never witnessed on him.

"I've never held a baby before," he explains.

I smile. "Every single person who's held a baby had a time when they didn't before."

The room is quiet, and all eyes are on Benny.

It takes him a moment to answer. "Unlike those people, I don't think baby-holding is for me."

"If you don't hold your baby brother and practice with him, then I'm not having yours."

Swear to God, if I wasn't holding Enzo, I'd smack a hand over my mouth.

Enzo decides it's the perfect time to have a little hiccup.

"All right," Benny says. "Hand him over then."

Cristian stalks toward us, stopping me. He takes Enzo from me, runs a thumb across his son's cheek, and places him in Benny's arms. He adjusts his arms to cradle Enzo in them perfectly. Cristian spends more time standing over Benny than he did with me.

It takes Benny a minute to relax, and when he does, Cristian returns to Natalia. Benny is silent while staring down at his brother, needing that time to warm up to him.

My heart leaps in my chest, and I bow my head to hide my grin when Benny smiles at Enzo.

"Look at you, little man," he whispers. "Here I thought, holding you would be scarier."

My ovaries scream at me to make Benny my baby daddy. As we make conversation, I sneak peeks at the two of them.

He rocks back and forth and says, "Oh shoot," when Enzo burps.

It's the sexiest thing I've ever seen in my life.

Benny Marchetti.

Ruthless Mafia prince.

Man rocking a baby to sleep.

Out of nowhere and in the middle of Natalia rambling off a list of items to bring from the mansion to the hospital, Benny brushes his shoulder against mine.

His voice is low as he says, "I can't wait for you to have our babies, so I can do this with ours."

Chills crash through my body.

I hold a hand over my smile to hide the overwhelming giddiness running through me. My heart skips a beat at the thought of having a family with him.

We've talked about children a few times. I want them, but I'm not ready. I discussed freezing my eggs with my doctor since I'm not getting any younger.

I want our time to be right.

We didn't get the chance to create a friendship before our marriage.

I want us to know each other deeper before becoming parents.

"Has anyone heard from Gigi?" Natalia asks, breaking me away from my thoughts. She drops her phone onto her lap and frowns. "She said she'd be here hours ago, but she still hasn't shown."

"That's weird," Benny says. "I figured the runt would try to sneak into the delivery room with you."

"Oh, she tried," Cristian comments. "But Natalia said no."

Natalia's face reddens. "The less people watching a baby come out of my vagina, the better."

"When's the last time you talked to Gigi?" Cristian asks Natalia.

"A few hours ago. She said she was heading this way." She holds up her phone. "I've texted a few times, but she isn't replying."

Cristian digs his phone from his pocket, unlocks it, and places it against his ear. He kicks his feet out and leans against the wall as he waits for an answer.

His brows scrunch together when he pulls it away from his face. "No answer." His next call goes to their housekeeper, who tells him Gigi left an hour ago to come to the hospital, and she hasn't been back.

Cristian thanks the housekeeper and checks Gigi's car's GPS location. His face turns pale. He drops his phone but manages to catch it before it falls to the ground.

"It's showing she's here." He stares at the screen in confusion. "Her car is parked here."

"I'll check on it," Benny says.

Cristian's shoulders tense when he takes Enzo from Benny's arms. We tell Enzo goodbye and rush out of the hospital room.

Something is wrong. I can feel it in my gut.

Gigi is the queen of having her phone.

Snow crunches beneath our feet in the parking lot as we search for Gigi's white BMW. When we finally locate it, Benny uses his hand to wipe snow off the windshield and windows. It's empty. The doors are unlocked. Benny opens the door to find her purse and phone in the driver's seat.

"Motherfucker," Benny yells, slamming her door shut. He takes his phone from his pocket and furiously smacks his fingers onto the screen before holding it against his ear. "Raul, hack into the hospital's security cameras immediately. Gigi's car is parked here—lot A—but she's missing."

Benny turns the car on and cranks up the heat while we sit inside, waiting. He calls his father and tells him what we found. Since he has the call on speaker, I can hear the fear in Cristian's voice.

Natalia was kidnapped.

I was shot.

Who has Gigi, and what do they have in store for her?

Benny ends the call with Cristian when Raul beeps through.

"I'm sending you the footage now," Raul tells him. "You're not going to like this."

"I'll watch and call you back," Benny says, ending the call.

I lean in, resting my elbow on the center console, and he opens the message from Raul. Benny plays the video, and I gasp at what I see.

Gigi gets out of her car at the same time a black car pulls behind her. With a truck in the spot in front of hers and the black car, she's blocked in. Antonio Lombardi steps out of the driver's seat and approaches her.

"I am going to kill this asshole," Benny says while we watch.

Gigi and Antonio argue for five minutes, but there's no audio for us to know what they're saying. He points at his car. She shakes her head. They argue some more.

I release a loud gasp when he holds a gun to her head.

Right in the parking lot.

The balls on this man.

He walks her to the car, opens the passenger door, and motions for her to get in.

And once she does, he drives off.

Benny has called the contact number he has for Antonio nonstop since watching the footage of him taking Gigi.

From his cell, mine, and burners.

But no answer.

We drove straight from the hospital to Antonio's house. It was empty and didn't appear to have been lived in for days.

"We'll find her, Benny," I assure him for what seems like the hundredth time while he paces the mansion's foyer.

His shoes squeaking against the marble floor reverberate through the room.

We freeze when Benny's phone rings.

"Unknown number," he says, hurriedly answering it on speaker.

"Hello, Benny," the voice on the other end says. "It's Antonio."

"Where the fuck is my sister?" Benny screams, clenching his hand around the phone. "Every minute you fail to tell me is another minute I'll spend torturing you."

I walk to Benny and settle my arms around his waist.

"I'm not letting her go," Antonio tells him.

"What do you want? Guns from Severino? Done." Spit flies from Benny's mouth. "Now, let her go."

"I didn't take Gigi to blackmail you," Antonio explains. "I took her to protect her."

Benny scoffs. "We protect her just fine."

"Natalia was kidnapped. Neomi shot. Both of those done by the hands of Lombardis—"

"Thank you for reminding me," Benny says, speaking over him. "I'll make sure you suffer extra now."

A sudden cramp forms in my side at Antonio's reminder of

my being shot. I inhale a breath to stop myself from doubling over, not wanting to stress Benny further.

"My uncle wants to kill Gigi to get to me. I can't let that happen," Antonio continues.

"Why would he kill my sister to get back at you?" Benny snaps.

"Because I love her."

There's a moment of dead silence after Antonio's words.

Benny is frozen in the spot.

I'm trying my hardest not to be dramatic about what Antonio said. Theatrics are the last thing my husband needs right now.

"She will stay with me until I kill my uncle," Antonio continues. "No one will know where she is. Including you."

Antonio ends the call.

Benny immediately attempts to call him back.

No answer.

Benny's body shakes as he pulls me into his arms. "What am I going to do, Neomi?"

I gulp.

My husband is always so strong for me. Now, it's my turn.

I run a thumb along his jawline before caressing it with my hand. "I don't think Antonio will hurt her."

"I don't care. He's holding her hostage." He shuts his eyes. "We have to find her."

I nod and stroke his arm. "We will, and I will be at your side every minute until we do."

His body continues to shake, but the trembling subsides.

"I love you, Benny," I whisper, placing tender kisses on his cheek. "Everything will be okay."

"You promise?"

I think about all the times Benny has said he won't make promises he can't keep, but something deep down tells me I'm able to make this one to him. "I promise."

ALSO BY CHARITY FERRELL

MARCHETTI MAFIA SERIES

(each book can be read as a standalone)

Gorgeous Monster

Gorgeous Prince

ONLY YOU SERIES

(each book can be read as a standalone)

Only Rivals

BLUE BEECH SERIES

(each book can be read as a standalone)

Just A Fling

Just One Night

Just Exes

Just Neighbors

Just Roommates

Just Friends

TWISTED FOX SERIES

(each book can be read as a standalone)

Stirred

Shaken

Straight Up

Chaser

Last Round

ABOUT THE AUTHOR

Charity Ferrell is a USA Today and Wall Street Journal best-selling author of the Twisted Fox and Blue Beech series. She resides in Indianapolis, Indiana. She loves writing about broken people finding love while adding humor and heartbreak along with it. Angst is her happy place.

When she's not writing, she's making a Starbucks run, shopping online, or spending time with her family.

Made in the USA
Monee, IL
08 June 2023

35472749R00185